Her Sheltered Cove

DARCI BALOGH

For my hippies :)
My daughters Taylor and Jodi
And my sister Terri
Here's to all of the adventures to come!

Chapter One

Angie admired her shiny new 1967 Volkswagen bus, or *hippie van* as she liked to think of it. Its rounded edges shone bright in the summer sunset, giving her a tiny thrill. Freshly painted pink and white with gleaming chrome bumpers, her little hippie van was officially ready for take off.

She screwed her face up in faint confusion. Was it possible for a 1967 vehicle to be called new? Purchased nearly four weeks before with the severance pay she received from the metaphysical book store, the van was new to her at least. With a full engine overhaul, fresh paint job, and completely remodeled interior it certainly didn't look over 50 years old. She decided to allow Eckhart, the name she had christened her van, to be considered new.

"We all deserve a fresh start, right Eckhart?"

The van didn't answer, but she felt its energy and decided if Eckhart could agree with her, he would.

Something vibrated deep in her tote and Angie jammed her hand into the large bag to feel for her phone.

"Where are you?" Sofia demanded to know as soon as Angie answered. "We don't see your car."

"Look for the pink and white Volkswagen Bus," Angie said, a bubble of excitement rising in her chest. She had managed to keep her new van, and her new plans, a secret from everyone except Thomas up until this point. Now it was time to let the cat out of the bag.

"A pink and white Volkswagen bus?" Sofia's confusion was tinged with annoyance. She wasn't a huge fan of surprises.

"I'm in the parking lot on the west side." Angie glanced at the empty spots around Eckhart. "You can't miss it."

A confused conversation between Sofia and their other two friends who were with her, Luna and Bridget, followed, along with Sofia instructing the driver to go to the west parking lot. Angie listened to all of it with amusement and a giddy anticipation. She was finally going to let her friends in on her big life plans.

When the stretch SUV finally pulled up next to Eckhart and parked, Sofia, Luna and Bridget spilled out and greeted her.

"You got a new car?" Luna asked, her eyes only dimly reflecting concern about Angie overspending when she didn't have a job.

"It's more than just a car," Angie reassured her, moving to the back side door to show them.

"It's adorable! I love the pink!" Bridget exclaimed.

"Did you trade in your old car?" Luna asked.

Angie nodded excitedly. "I sold it and got a deal on this little gem." She glanced into the stretch SUV for more passengers. "Aren't Tawnyetta and Michael with you?"

Sofia gave a brief head shake. "They had to come a little later. They were longer at her parent's house than expected."

Tawnyetta was in the final stretch of her pregnancy, which had turned even more exciting when they discovered they were having twins. She and her husband had flown to Denver to spend some time with her family before returning to Scotland to settle in and deliver the babies.

Angie frowned. Her hand hovered over the handle of the side door, uncertain if she should proceed without everyone there.

"And Ian can't break away?" she asked Sofia, disappointed.

"They're still rehearsing," Sofia answered. "He said he would be done soon and come find us."

Angie nodded. Suddenly nervous as her friends stood expectantly in front of Eckhart, her excitement fizzed into anxiety. Compared to the big concert Ian was playing in Denver in just a few hours and Tawnyetta's impending motherhood, her own news might come across as silly.

"Is the inside cute?" Bridget asked, undeterred by Angie's hesitation and always interested in decor.

Angie nodded. "It is. Thomas helped me build it out."

"Thomas?" Bridget huffed. "He knew about this before us?"

"Well, are you going to show us?" Sofia asked, glancing at Angie's fingers resting on the door handle.

"I am. I was just expecting everyone to be here."

"I don't think they'll mind if we take a peek," Luna reassured her.

"Besides, Thomas has already seen it," Bridget pouted.

Thomas had, in fact, done a lot more than just see the inside of the vintage van. A carpenter and builder by trade, he had basically remodeled the entire inside to create a completely mobile living space for Angie.

"I can't thank you enough for doing this," she had told him when they finished a few days before Ian's big concert.

Thomas, their long-time dear friend who was like a brother, had grinned happily at her, running his hand along the smooth butcher block countertop he had just finished putting in. "Anything for you, Ang." His eyes had lifted to the cleverly designed storage space he had installed along both sides of the van's ceiling. "You sure this is enough room for you?"

Angie had nodded assuredly. "For me and for Fidget."

Thomas had chuckled. "Right. How could I forget Fidget. Yours is the first custom built cat litter box I've ever made." He had smiled warmly at her. "I think you and Fidget will be real cozy in here."

Angie wished Thomas had arrived in time to show off his handiwork to the others. She could use his calm support.

"Oh for goodness sake, Angie, let us see the inside!" Bridget was running out of patience.

Angie couldn't think of another reason to delay. The longer she waited the more anti-climactic it might be.

"All right, stand back." She turned the handle and pulled on the door. It opened with ease and clicked satisfyingly into place.

"Ooooh," Bridget pushed her head in and climbed into the back of Eckhart. "This is darling!"

One-by-one all of them crawled into Angie's new living space, but only she knew the biggest surprise at all.

Sofia and Luna settled in on the cushioned bench seat that would also fold out into Angie's bed. Angie hopped up to sit on the butcher block counter while Bridget investigated all of the tiny drawers and special hidey holes that Thomas had built in for storage.

The handcrafted interior was mostly constructed of repurposed wood with a few charming exceptions like the copper kitchen sink and the strings of shining white fairy lights draped across the ceiling. Angie had chosen Boho designs for the rug and the curtain that acted as a door to her tiny bathroom as well as the fabric covering her cushions and pillows. More pink, but also a lot of lavender and pale green.

"Angie this is really cute! Did you decorate it yourself?" Luna asked.

"I did. Thomas helped me a lot with the design and, obviously, the cabinet building. Basically anything made of wood or metal was mostly Thomas."

Bridget sniffed, always a little annoyed at Thomas no matter what he did. "I wonder where he found the time these days, what with that new girl he's dating."

"What new girl who is dating?" Tawnyetta poked her head into Eckhart's open door. She was immediately distracted by the interior. "Wow, Angie! When did you buy this?"

Angie hopped down from her perch and ushered the very pregnant Tawnyetta into the ever tightening interior of the van.

"Right after I was laid off. I used my severance pay."

Luna and Sofia moved so Tawnyetta would have a comfortable seat in the center of the cushion and positioned themselves a little awkwardly, teetering on either end.

"Some girl named Zero or something like that," Bridget said, still stuck on who Thomas was dating.

"Her name's Zara," Luna corrected.

"Hey, Luv, are you in there?" Ian's red head popped into the van doors and he broke into a huge smile when he saw Sofia.

"How was rehearsal?" Sofia asked as he climbed inside and made his way to her side.

"It went great, we're ready for tonight!"

"How exciting, Ian," Luna said. "Sofia said it's sold out!"

"Yep, it's going to be a packed house." He took in the tight quarters of the camper van and laughed. "Though not as packed as this!"

Lord Michael, Tawnyetta's ever attentive husband, poked his head inside the van doors next. "I'll have a look from out here, if that's all right." He turned his head from side-to-side in a brief inspection. "Are you planning on taking this camping Angie?"

Angie's nerves fluttered and her hands felt sweaty. Now that everyone had arrived there was no reason not to make her announcement. She took a deep breath and looked at her friends with excitement.

"Actually, a little more than camping," she said.

Nobody responded. They only sat silently looking at her, waiting for further explanation.

"You are sitting in my new place," Angie said. Then, as an afterthought, she raised her hands up in a 'ta-da' gesture, which resulted in her bumping Bridget's nose with one hand and Ian's shoulder with the other.

As the news sank in with her friends, Angie could tell it wasn't being met with the rousing support she had hoped for.

"Wait, you're going to live in *this van*?" Sofia asked, pointing her well manicured fingernail toward the pink and purple rag rug at her feet.

Angie's resolve to join the nomadic van camping life she had been watching online for months didn't feel quite as strong as she wished it did. She nodded, red curls bobbing as if to emphasize that they were behind her even if her friends were not.

Switching her attention from Sofia to Tawnyetta, Angie smiled hopefully. Tawnyetta was the one person she could always count on to approve of a new adventure.

"I'm going to live in Eckhart," she said firmly.

Tawnyetta's face, a little puffy with later term pregnancy, looked confused. "In Eckhart? Is that a place?"

"No, no," Angie laughed and swept her hand around in a circle indicating the van. Ian shrank back to avoid being hit, but Bridget's nose got grazed once more and she let out a little yelp. Angie ignored her. "I named the van Eckhart...after Eckhart Tolle."

Only Luna nodded in complete understanding.

"What about your apartment?" Sofia asked, ever the pragmatist.

"My lease is up this month. And since I lost my job I thought this would be the perfect time to make a change."

"Well, this is quite a change," Michael chimed in, still leaning in the open door and craning his neck to look at Thomas' workmanship. "It looks like it has everything you need."

"It does." Angie jumped at the chance to show off some of the features. "There are locks on the cabinets and drawers so they won't open when I'm driving and that seat you're on pulls out into a bed." She pointed at Tawnyetta who looked down as if half expecting to see the bed pop out underneath her.

"Brilliant," Ian interjected as he opened and closed the small, square refrigerator door. "It's a bit like a doll house, isn't it?"

"What about Fidget?" Bridget asked. Angie's dainty calico cat was almost her namesake and she got a little worried if Fidget was ever not living in the lap of luxury.

"Fidget will fit," Angie reassured her, but she hesitated to show them the built in cat box. Squished so tightly together in the van's interior didn't seem like the right time to discuss Fidget's bathroom habits.

Luna, who was prone to sit silently through the group conversations and offer her thoughts once everyone else was done talking, gave Angie a warm smile and began, "Well, I think if this is something you really want to do–"

Various buzzing and ring tones erupted from each of their phones. A usual sign that whoever wasn't with them had texted.

"Thomas," Angie knew without checking that it was him. "He was going to bring champagne to christen Eckhart."

Sure enough, Thomas' text to all of them read, *Time to celebrate! Where's the party?*

Angie quickly texted him back the van's location in the parking lot outside the venue where Ian's concert would be later in the night. Just minutes away, Thomas arrived with two bottles of champagne, one to break and one to drink, and a bottle of sparkling apple juice for Tawnyetta.

"So how do you guys like it?" Thomas asked. He had manage to get himself and his three bottles inside Eckhart and over the copper sink where he popped the top off of the first bottle of champagne.

"It's really cute," Luna offered.

"It's kind of small," Sofia complained while trying not to sound complaining.

"I don't think she'll be hosting a lot of inside parties, Sofia," Tawnyetta said.

"Oh, I don't know," Ian joked as he pressed closer to Sofia. "Being close isn't all that bad."

"She's got everything she needs in this little space," Thomas said proudly. He handed out plastic cocktail glasses with champagne to each of them. "I made sure of that."

"I can't believe you knew about all of this and didn't tell us, Mister," Bridget said, taking her glass of champagne.

Thomas acted hurt. "I can't believe you think I can't keep a secret."

Bridget took a sip of champagne and turned away from him, pushing past everyone else to stand at the farthest end near the driver's seat.

"You could have hinted that something big was happening, that's all," Bridget continued. "And why don't you ever make any of this custom cabinetry for me?" She pouted.

Thomas poured Tawnyetta her sparkling juice and handed it to her with a crooked grin then spoke over his shoulder to

Bridget, "I didn't know you wanted a pimped out camper van to move to California."

There was a collective gasp.

"California!?" Luna and Tawnyetta said in unison as the rest of them gawked at Angie in surprise.

Red shot up Angie's neck and into her cheeks. It felt as if every freckle on her nose was blazing hot.

Thomas turned to her apologetically. "They didn't know?"

"I hadn't told them that part yet," she said quietly, even though the whole gang could hear every word she uttered.

"You're moving to California in a camper van," Sofia said, not so much as a question, but more of a clarification that she understood.

Angie stood up tall and straightened her shoulders. She had decided on this epic change weeks ago, but had not told the rest of her friends because she knew they often found her a little flaky. She wanted to get everything ready and planned out before telling them so they couldn't say she was dreaming an impossible dream – and so they couldn't talk her out of it.

Champagne in hand, her best friends staring at her in disbelief, Angie spoke with certainty, "Yes, it's true. I've decided that Fidget and I are moving into Eckhart full time and driving to California to live by the ocean."

Chapter Two

To say that Angie's announcement came as a surprise didn't quite capture the stunned silence that followed.

The heat in her cheeks permeated the rest of her body and sweat broke out under her arms and down her sides. Champagne still raised in the air waiting for her friends to toast her decision, her arm trembled in rebellion at being extended for so long.

In a show of solidarity and an attempt to break the tension, Thomas lifted his glass to hers and tapped it gently. "Hip-hip-hooray," he said in his regular speaking voice. Shouting it out seemed too much for the moment.

Angie's bottom lip quivered.

"No, no, Angie." Tawnyetta reached her hand toward Angie as if she could pat her on the shoulder from where she sat. "Don't cry, we're just surprised, that's all."

"You don't think it's a good idea, do you?" Angie asked, tears welling up in her eyes.

Sofia winced, obviously thinking it was a terrible idea, but not wanting to contribute to Angie's tears.

Ian ignored Sofia and leaned toward Angie, his spiky red hair and sequined scarves covering his rock T-shirt added drama to his words. "I think it's a great idea. California is full of exciting things to do. Lots of people. You'll have a great time."

Sofia scowled softly, then with a bit of hope, asked, "Do you have a job lined up?"

Angie shook her head 'no'. She had made her decision to move to California during a chakra cleansing meditation and everything with buying the van and Thomas helping her had fallen right into place, almost like magic. She hadn't given a lot of thought to what she would do after she arrived.

"I figure all of that will become clear when I get there," she said, adding a note of confidence so Sofia wouldn't be worried.

"We'll be out there a lot, too," Ian reminded Sofia with a nudge.

"That's true," Sofia agreed.

"But you're leaving Colorado." Luna's big brown eyes gave Angie the sad puppy dog treatment.

A twinge of regret plucked at her heart. Leaving all of the people she loved in her home town of Denver was the hardest part of this life change.

"Tawny and FiFi already moved away, and now you?" Bridget whined.

"Hey," Thomas interrupted, putting his palm up towards the others in an attempt to defend Angie from their criticism. "This is a big deal and it takes a brave person to make this kind of decision. We should do whatever we can to help."

There was a pause as his word's sank in. Angie focused all of her energy on clearing the negativity that swirled around her and letting strong, clear, cosmic energy flow from the sky and into her crown chakra.

With great effort and a little help from Sofia and Luna, Tawnyetta stood up and squeezed herself and her pregnant stomach directly in front of Angie. Tawnyetta's amber eyes gazed kindly into Angie's, warming her heart.

"This is an amazing adventure you're about to take. I'm so excited for you...and proud!" Tawnyetta said.

"Hip, hip, hooray and Bon Voyage!" Thomas called out.

Finally coming to terms with her big move, they all started calling out, "Bon Voyage, Angie!" The sound of their happy congratulations rang loud and clear through her new van home.

Only a few days later, Angie hit the road.

After Ian's concert, which was a huge success and a lot of fun, everyone else had to get back to their daily lives. All Angie had to do was gather up the last few, very few, items from her apartment that she hadn't moved into Eckhart yet, grab Fidget, fill up with gas and be on her merry way.

Within two days she was driving up I-70 into the Rocky Mountains, bringing her home and her cat with her. Headed to the Pacific Ocean and the land of her dreams...California.

She would take her time traversing the great Rocky Mountains and the beautiful desert lands on the other side as she traveled.

No need to rush.

As Sofia had pointed out, she didn't have a job waiting for her, nor did she have an apartment she had to move into. She was free to go north or south, east or west, as fast or as slow as she wanted. Invigorating.

Angie shifted from third to second gear as Eckhart strained to pull up the steep grade of the four lane highway that routinely welcomed trucks, skiers, tourists, and even every day commuters into the snowy peaks and mountain passes. The 1967 engine protested a little, but the lower gear would keep her moving at a semi-reasonable speed alongside all of the mountain traffic. Definitely sticking to the slow lane, but not at a standstill.

She didn't mind the fact that Eckhart's engine wasn't the most powerful. Nor did she mind the manual gear shift or the retro dashboard. Angie had been raised in an earthy hippie culture that embraced the Reduce-Reuse-Recycle mantra. The fact that she was repurposing this old van as her new home and becoming a nomad fell well under the umbrella of her parent's dream for her life.

Fidget, her timid calico kitty, sat sweetly in the passenger seat staring out the window. A rescue, she was also 100% approved by her parents and Angie was glad to have her as a companion. The little cat's chin barely reached the bottom of the window so she could watch the mountains pass by on their right.

Occasionally a tiny shiver would move through Fidget's whole body and end with a flick at the tip of her tail. Angie had asked the vet about it, but apparently there was nothing wrong. It was just the way she was.

"Want some music?" Angie asked, shuffling through a basket on the floor between them that was full of cassette tapes. Another cool thing about Eckhart, he was so vintage she could actually play cassettes. Between her parents donating some of their favorites and what she had scrounged up at thrift stores, Angie had quite a selection. "We've got Fleetwood Mac, Jimmy Hendrix, Tom Waits...and..." Angie pulled another tape out of the basket. "Earth, Wind, and Fire! How does that sound?"

Fidget blinked her green eyes at Angie, her body and tail trembling.

"I'll take that as a yes."

Angie fumbled with the cassette as she steered and managed to push it into place just as her cell phone rang. It was Luna. She punched the button to eject the tape and answered her cell on speaker.

"How's it going?" Luna asked.

"Fine so far, we're chugging into the mountains!"

"That's good. We miss you already."

Angie laughed, "I've been gone, like, two hours."

"I know, but you're never coming back."

"Not never! I can come back whenever I like. I just need to scrounge enough money for the gas."

"I know, I know." Luna sounded sad.

"Don't worry, I'll be back to visit before you know it. And you can come visit me, too," Angie reassured her.

"I know. I'll make a plan to do that soon." Luna sounded perkier at the idea of a trip to California.

"See? Don't you feel better already?"

"I do, thanks."

"You're welcome."

"And Angie?"

"Yes?"

"If you ever need gas money to get home, you let me know, okay?"

Angie blinked back tears. "I will. Don't worry, okay?"

"Okay."

Torn between the excitement of driving into her new future and the depressing reality that she was leaving her friends behind, Angie said goodbye to Luna, tossed her cell phone into her tote bag on the passenger side floor, and pushed the cassette tape back into the player. The familiar upbeat horn intro to Earth, Wind and Fire's song, September, pumped through Eckhart's surprisingly good speakers.

"Ooooh, Fidget, I love this song!"

As Fidget watched her nervously, Angie raised one hand in the air and pumped her fist up and down with the beat, singing out loud, "Do you remember..."

She bumped her palm against the steering wheel and snapped the fingers in her free hand to the rhythm, all while shifting her torso back and forth, a neat little move she had learned in belly dancing class. Nothing lifted her mood quite like dancing.

By the time she made it to her campsite for the night, Angie was pooped. Driving over mountain passes, stopping for gas and to stock up on supplies, and making sure Fidget was using her facilities properly, all added up to a long day.

She was tickled to pull into the spot she had reserved weeks before at a KOA campsite near Grand Junction and try out her new van kitchen. Angie wasn't a huge fan of gas station snack food and was ready for something home made.

An hour later, she was decidedly less than tickled. The process of cooking in a camper van was a little more tedious than she had expected.

First, she ran of water. She had neglected to fill up her five gallon water container that Thomas had built to gravity feed into her kitchen sink. So she had to take the large plastic container over to the community water tap at the campground. Unfortunately, she did not take into account how heavy it would be once filled.

As she strained to pull her water back to Eckhart she met a few of the other patrons of the campsite. An elderly couple in a streamlined camper trailer who fussed over her dilemma, but didn't have the strength to give her a hand. A couple of scout leaders who had their hands full with a rowdy group of 5th graders. And a large family who had a huge RV and a gangly, pale teenage son who was keenly interested in helping her with her water jug.

With his help, she managed to lug the full container back to Eckhart. Not comfortable inviting him inside of her van, she had to hoist the container back into place. By then she was completely out of breath and she still had a full meal to cook.

"Next time I need to make sure to fill up before I go to my space," she noted out loud as she busied herself gathering ingredients for dinner.

To her dismay she realized that she hadn't closed the tiny refrigerator properly and the shelf sized freezer that was holding her two small trays of ice cubes had melted, flooding the bottom of the fridge with cold water. The bread and cheese she had popped into the fridge was soggy and ruined, but the raw vegetables were still edible.

Angie rummaged through them to find some she could chop up to make soup. A few carrots, an onion, and a few pieces of celery would do the trick.

"At least they're pre-washed, right?" she asked Fidget, who was perched on the back of the cushioned bench, watching her with curiosity. None of this concerned Fidget, of course. Her dinner came pre-made out of a can.

Angie turned her attention to chopping the vegetables and realized she hadn't practiced unfolding and bracing her tiny foldable table that Thomas had built. It was a great design, but not exactly intuitive, and it took her what felt like forever to figure out how to set it up so she could chop safely. By the time she was done she had lost all motivation to cook soup. That would entail using her propane stove for the first time and washing dishes afterward.

With a sigh, she tossed the onion into her copper sink to use later and grabbed a box of crackers out of her dry goods box. Sitting down on the bench seat she munched miserably on a carrot and surveyed her tiny living space.

"I guess I should have tried some of this out a few times before hitting the road," she said to Fidget. Fidget mewed and stretched out her front paws to knead the cushion in agreement. "You're right, it's late...and I'm tired, too..." Angie yawned.

She glanced out Eckhart's window at the other RV's in their spots. Suddenly, she felt a little uneasy about changing into her pajamas. It didn't feel natural to her to change inside the van. She decided to sleep in her jeans and T-shirt, maybe add her hoodie for warmth. Once she got used to this nomadic lifestyle she would put on pajamas like normal.

Nighttime in the Rocky Mountains was cold, which was not a surprise to Angie. She had been camping countless times since she was a child. But something about sleeping inside of a vehicle instead of a tent put more of a chill in the air. She went to bed in her hoodie and jeans, but had to pull on a sweater, a jacket, two pairs of sweat pants, an extra pair of wool socks, and her ski parka, just to stop shivering long enough to fall asleep.

Finally, dawn glowed gold and pink through Eckhart's windshield, waking Angie out of a deep, mummified sleep. She moved to sit up, but the bondage of her layers of clothing wouldn't allow it. That turned out to be a good thing because Fidget was curled into a tight ball and snuggled right up next to her hip. Moving too quickly might have pinched the little cat.

Angie turned slowly to her side and pushed herself into a sitting position, taking care not to fall off of the narrow pull out bed. Wrapped in what felt like her entire wardrobe, stomach growling from not getting a good dinner, tired and sore from lack of sleep on a rather uncomfortable new bed, Angie couldn't keep from laughing out loud with joy.

"I did it!" she said with delight. Fidget warily opened one eye and looked at her. "*We* did it, Fidget!" Angie laughed again and stroked the little cat's soft back. "We made it through the first night of our new life...success!"

Chapter Three

Tempted as Angie was by the countless adventures available to her along her route to California, she couldn't get the call of the ocean out of her mind. Always interested in spending time in the outdoors, she had already experienced the rustic beauty of western Colorado and Utah many times during her life. Those destinations would have to wait.

Three Deer River Campsite in the Mendocino Forest was her target and getting Fidget and herself there while keeping Eckhart in one piece was all she could focus on.

Under normal circumstances, in a regular car with a friend or two to share the driving, the trip from Denver to her reserved RV camp spot at Three Deer River would have taken one long day of driving, definitely no more than two if they stopped to sleep.

However, with Eckhart being on the older side and carrying the extra weight of her rebuilt living quarters, Angie didn't feel comfortable pushing it. She had figured it would take four driving days and three nights on the road to get them safely to the Mendocino Forest. In reality it took even longer.

She hadn't taken into account the amount of time needed to cook and clean up every day. Then there was the desert driving. After several discussions with more seasoned travelers along the way, she decided to reschedule so she was driving across the hottest parts of her route in the dark to avoid the possibility of overheating Eckhart's engine. This split her drive time up to the wee hours of the morning or late at night and added two more days total to her trip.

When she finally steered Eckhart into her Three Deer River camping spot, she was overdue for some rest and relaxation.

"Who knew the nomad's life would be so exhausting," she said to Fidget, who was curled up in the passenger seat on a little pillow she had bought for her in Reno that read 'The Biggest Little City in the World'.

The cat only twitched the orange and white side of her face. The black side remained totally still. She was sleeping soundly and had grown so used to Angie babbling at her that the sound of her voice didn't even wake her anymore. Angie smiled and shook her head as she parked Eckhart securely then climbed out of the driver's side door.

The first thing that hit her was the cool, salty breeze coming off of the unseen ocean. It was like an elixir.

Angie breathed in deeply and let the fresh air fill her lungs. The scent of the forest at her back and the ocean somewhere ahead of her combined and enveloped her senses in an almost magical way. All of the uncertainty of her decision to move and the challenges of her trip dissipated into nothing.

Making sure the windows were lowered to allow for proper air flow, Angie closed the van door quietly so as not to disturb Fidget and looked for the pathway to the beach.

She had chosen Three Deer because of its proximity to the ocean. It didn't take her long to locate the wooden walkway leading over an embankment. With each step on the worn wooden surface Angie felt a surge of renewal in her soul. The soft scratching of sand on the walkway beneath her shoes told her she was going in the right direction. Her heart swelled and she found it impossible to take normal breaths. Instead, she breathed in deeply as she walked, creating a spiritual experience.

Whether an ancient memory, a heartfelt desire, or a figment of her imagination, Angie believed without question that the ocean called to her.

Before she topped the embankment she could see the water. Stretching out to the horizon. Deep royal blue. Undulating waves that raced up to greet her on the sand.

"Hello," Angie said to the ocean, not considering for a moment that it might be an odd thing to speak to the water. "It's been a long time, hasn't it?"

The ocean sent another wave in response and Angie hurried to the shore to greet it, stepping right into the water and soaking her slip on tennis shoes as the wave rushed over her feet and up her legs, just reaching the bottom of her sundress. The breeze washed across her arms and chest and face, lifting her curly red hair off of her shoulders and playfully sending the long tendrils in several different directions.

She took off her shoes and tossed them onto the sand. If she was certain nobody else might come across her, Angie would have stripped off her sundress and dove in. She longed to feel the water on her skin and float in the ocean's arms.

She glanced around. Surprisingly there was nobody else on the short beach where she stood. Large rocks guarded both ends on either side, shielding her from anyone's view on nearby stretches of beach.

Another wave wrapped around her calves, inviting her in, daring her to do it. Angie laughed and lifted her skirt higher, stepping further into the water. Enticed by its refreshing cold.

Angie eyed the blue horizon with a smile. "You're a naughty one," she said with amusement.

Another wave splashed against her, soaking the front of her sundress all the way up to her waist. She had to make a decision quickly or the ocean would make it for her. With one more careful scan of her surroundings coming up empty of any other human being, Angie made up her mind.

She pulled her sundress off over her head and threw it behind her. The breeze touched her stomach and breasts. Cool and invigorating. There was no going back, not that she wanted to stop. The next wave came and Angie sank down into it, letting the water she had longed for engulf every inch of her body.

With a shallow dive she was swimming under water, her hair moving with the current, her body feeling light and fluid. She came up for air, not daring to stand completely in case anyone had arrived at the beach while she was under. The coast was clear and she dove again, relishing the feeling of flying that swimming always allowed.

Several feet from the shore she put her feet on the sand and stayed in a sitting position, her face and head in the sunshine, her curly hair straightened with the weight of the water and floating around her in all directions. She knew she could never have her childhood dream of being a mermaid come true, but this was awful darn close. She giggled at the thought.

The waves came and went, alternately pressing and tugging at her body where she rested. She paid close attention to the water's pull on her feet and noted its strength. Riptides were a very real danger and nothing to mess around with. As much as she was enjoying herself, she decided it would be best to end her swim and return after she had checked local safety warnings.

"Don't worry," she said out loud. "I'll be back."

She wasn't kidding either. She had already decided that her new life would include a nice dip in the ocean every day. Though it probably shouldn't be a skinny dip every day, she thought with a smile. That would be all right, she would just have to live in her bathing suit.

A voice came to her over the breeze. A man's voice. Several men's voices, in fact.

Angie's stomach jumped and she quickly scanned the beach and rock outcroppings. Luckily she couldn't see anyone, which hopefully meant nobody could see her either. Their voices must be carrying on the wind. Still, it was time to get dressed and avoid any unnecessary embarrassment.

She hurried out of the water and slipped her sundress over her head without waiting to dry off. One side of it fell heavy against her thigh and she remembered she had put her cell phone in her pocket to take a selfie when she got to the beach.

"Lucky I didn't wear this into the water," she said to herself.

Refreshed and happier than she had been in a long time, Angie took a selfie in front of the water, wet hair and all. She sent it to their friend group text so everyone could see she had arrived safely.

She added a note to the picture, *Made it to the beach! Wish you were here!*

Within moments her phone buzzed. It was Sofia.

"You're in Mendocino?"

"Yes, at the Three Deer Campsite."

"We're at Fort Bragg!"

"You are?" Angie wasn't sure exactly how far away Fort Bragg was, but it wasn't as far as Los Angeles, she knew that much.

"We're finalizing some details for Ian's movie. We'd love to come see you if you're ready for visitors!"

Angie thought of Fidget's kitty litter box that needed

cleaning and the fact that she hadn't folded up her fold out bed from the night before. Then she remembered that Eckhart's small space took a very short time to clean. Besides, she and Fidget had been on their own for several days. It would be nice to see a familiar face.

"Of course! I'm always ready to see you and Ian," she answered.

"Perfect, we have a couple of people with us. Do you mind?"

Angie couldn't think of any reason she would mind anything at the moment. She was still riding high after her swim.

"No problem. All are welcome!"

Chapter Four

Angie's hair was not quite dry when Sofia, Ian, and their friends arrived. She had pulled it into a messy pony tail as she quickly straightened up Eckhart, cleaned out Fidget's litter box, filled up the kitty water and food bowls, then put a kettle on her propane stove to boil for tea.

"How was your trip?" Sofia asked as they hugged in greeting.

"Really great," Angie told her. No need to fill everyone in on the gory details of her van life challenges. "I'm getting the hang of it."

"This is really cool." Ian sat down in one of the folding lawn chairs Angie had placed next to the open side doors of Eckhart, creating a kind of patio at her campsite.

Pleased at his praise, Angie smiled. "Thank you. It's not the Ritz."

"Maybe not," Ian continued in his adorable British accent as he stretched out his arms to encompass the towering trees, blankets of grass and wildflowers, and clear blue sky above. "But you can't beat the location, can you?"

"That's for sure," a short, dark haired woman with black rimmed glasses stepped forward and stuck her hand out to Angie. Dressed in worn jeans and a black T-shirt, she gave off a no nonsense air as did the short, dark haired man standing next to her who looked almost like her twin.

Angie took her hand and shook it. "Hello, I'm Angie."

"Where are my manners?" Ian stood quickly, towering over the short dark couple. "This is Tillie and Brandon Pollard. They're the directors of the movie I'm working on." He gestured a long arm dramatically toward Angie. "This is Angie Levine. Sofia's childhood friend."

"Nice to meet you." Tillie peered over the top of her glasses at Angie as she shook her hand. "You've got a great look. Have you ever acted before?"

Angie chuckled and waved the question away. "No, no, I'm not an actress."

"Too bad," Brandon said. "We could use a look like yours."

"Really?" Angie was surprised. She didn't know she had a particular look.

Tillie nodded in all seriousness, quietly assessing Angie from the messy curls on top of her head to her bare feet. She nudged Brandon and nodded again, speaking to him as if nobody else could hear them. "Wouldn't she be great? It wouldn't take much work and she would fit perfectly."

"Work for what?" Angie asked, not sure how to take this curious couple, if they were a couple. Angie wondered if they might be brother and sister. They looked so much alike.

"Don't mind them," Ian said. "They've been hunting for extras all over this area."

Tillie nodded again. Or maybe she had never stopped. "We don't have a huge budget to pay a lot for extras. So we thought we would try to find more locals instead. That way they wouldn't have travel time from L.A."

"That's the plan," Brandon spoke up, chuckling a little to himself and punctuating the chuckle with a snort.

"Would you want to be an extra?" Sofia asked. Angie could see her excitement at the prospect of a paying job of any kind. Sofia liked life to be planned out and employment to be steady.

Angie didn't know what to say. Her new life was not terribly expensive and she had planned ahead enough to not have to worry about money for several months. She had figured that there were plenty of metaphysical bookstores in California and she could pick up some part time work with them. She had never considered doing any acting.

The tea kettle started to whine and she took the opportunity to ignore the question and fix everyone a cup of tea. With her back to them all she said, "I hope you like green tea. I don't have any other kind."

They all agreed green tea would work, no problem. But when she turned back around to hand them their cups it was obvious that Sofia and the Pollards had not moved on from the subject of her employment.

"Do you have any other work lined up?" Sofia asked.

Ian frowned at Sofia and said softly, "Maybe she doesn't want to be on camera."

"It's not that," Sofia said with assurance before looking back to Angie. "Is it?"

"No, I don't mind being in front of a camera. I haven't ever really thought about it. I mean, I'm not an actress or anything," Angie said.

"You don't have to be, not really," Tillie said. "Extras don't have lines. You're basically in the background. We'll tell you how to move and everything. It's not difficult."

"I'll be there, too," Ian offered with a laugh. "I'm writing the score and they roped me into being an extra, too!"

"Indie filmmakers can't be picky," Brandon teased with

another chuckle and another snort. Then, lest she misunderstand what he meant, "But you're exactly what we're looking for."

"You really would be perfect," Tillie added. "We pay fifty dollars a day and feed you while you're one set."

"Their location is only about thirty minutes up the coast from here," Sofia added. "I was there. It's very pretty. Right on the beach."

That did it. Get paid to hang out at the beach all day? What could be better than that? Angie looked at their expectant faces and made up her mind. "Why not? If I'm going to live in California, I may as well be in a movie, right?"

"Right!" Tillie said excitedly. "And I know exactly the scenes that we're going to put you in!"

Later, as Angie sat on the beach and watched the sun setting on the horizon, all gold and pink and amazing, she sifted thoughtfully through the sand at her fingertips. Fidget's harness bell tingled as she lightly pounced on imaginary prey. Angie was glad the little cat had been easy to leash train.

She made kissy sounds at Fidget who immediately whipped around and hopped comically toward her as if she was also prey. Angie lifted her hand, palm facing the cat. Fidget hesitated for a microsecond then fake attacked her hand, batting it quickly with both of her front paws before leaping backward.

"You're feeling feisty, aren't you?" Angie laughed. "It's nice to stay in one place for a whole day, isn't it?"

Fidget was no longer listening. She had turned her attention to an especially shiny stone in the sand, staring at it to see if it was going to move.

Angie sighed contently. It was nice staying in one place, at least for a little while. Most campsites didn't allow anyone to stay more than 14 days so she would have to move Eckhart and Fidget someplace new in less than two weeks.

"I guess I'll find a site closer to the movie location," she said out loud, turning her mind to her earlier decision to work as an extra. She hadn't had much time to think about it before she agreed. Now that she was on the quiet beach watching the sun go down she felt a twinge of regret at being so hasty.

What business did she have on a movie set? What kind of movie was it? She hadn't even taken the time to find that out. What if it was one of those slasher films? She frowned. She was not interested in being part of putting that kind of violent vibe out into the world.

"Ian wouldn't work on a slasher film, would he?" she wondered.

Fidget didn't answer. Angie's concern deepened. Maybe she should have gotten used to her new nomadic life and left finding a job off the table for a little while longer. Maybe it was a mistake.

She pulled her cell phone out of her pocket and texted Sofia, *Ian's movie isn't a slasher film, is it?*

A few minutes later Sofia texted back, *No, it's a pirate movie...and maybe a musical I think? It's a lot of things. Why?*

A little relieved, Angie replied, *I didn't want to be part of any negativity? You know?*

Angie could almost see Sofia's head nodding reassuringly as she texted back, *Right. You don't have to worry about that. It's not bloody or a horror film. Ian says it's more of a love story between a pirate and a mermaid.*

There are mermaids?!!!

Lol - Yes, there are mermaids.

Well, that makes it all good!

AND Peter Pineapple is the pirate! The lead pirate I should say.

Angie's stomach flip-flopped. The memory of meeting Peter Pineapple, otherwise known as Xavier Patel, on her last trip to California zinged through her body, leaving her nervous and flustered and excited all at once.

Her thumbs hesitated over her cell phone. She wasn't sure how this news made her feel. How he made her feel.

A new text from Sofia, *Remember? I thought I told you he was the star when we met him with Ian.*

I remember, Angie answered, but she hadn't remembered. She had gotten so caught up with getting laid off, remodeling Eckhart and moving to the ocean that that little piece of knowledge had completely slipped her mind.

"Does it really matter?" she asked Fidget, who turned and gave her a funny little wink before zeroing back in on the shiny rock.

The sun had sunk even lower on the horizon. The waves lapped at the shore. A steady cool breeze lifted off of the ocean and rippled through her hair. She took a deep breath in through her nose and concentrated on grounding her chakras into the sand when she exhaled.

A buzz interrupted her meditation.

Sofia again.

Can you imagine? You're going to be in a movie with Xavier Patel? Peter Pineapple LOL He's gorgeous, tho. You'll have so much fun :)

Again, a flutter of nerves moved through her body. Xavier Patel was gorgeous. And sleek and wealthy and famous. And intimidating.

"Nonsense," Angie shook her curls to knock the thoughts out of her mind. "He's an earthbound soul like anybody else. No reason to be nervous about seeing him again."

Then, to satisfy Sofia, Angie texted back, *It will be fun :)*

But deep down, she wasn't so sure.

Chapter Five

Unbeknownst to Angie, extras on movie sets, even low budget indie sets, don't run in the same circles as the stars of the film. It was with much relief that Angie figured that fact out on her first day.

Upon arriving she was greeted warmly by Tillie then ushered into hair and makeup with two other extras, Marissa and Kristina, without any contact with anyone else.

"You three are in a separate group than the townspeople and pirate extras," Tillie explained. "In fact, if you're interested, we would like to have all three of you be in the background for the mermaid scenes."

"Ooh," Kristina, a short blonde who had ignored the instructions to not wear any makeup to set in a big way, clapped her hands together like little girl.

"We'll be behind Elizabeth?" asked Marissa, a dark beauty with rich brown hair.

Tillie nodded.

"Who's Elizabeth?" Angie asked. Having just been introduced to a flurry of extras and film crew, she wasn't sure who was who anymore.

Kristina looked at her with thinly veiled annoyance. "The star, of course."

"Elizabeth Carlton, she's the love interest for the pirate. The mermaid he falls in love with," Tillie answered.

"Oh," Angie was a little behind the curveball, because she didn't know the story. She'd never even seen the script. "Is there a script around that I could see? Just so I know what's going on?"

Kristina and Marissa looked aghast at her nerve. Tillie merely nodded distractedly. "Of course, we should have some extras laying around. In the meantime, are you all good with getting made up as mermaids?"

All thoughts of the script and running into Xavier Patel again disappeared.

"*We're* going to be mermaids?" Angie asked, delighted at the prospect.

Tillie nodded. "Yep. If you're good with it?"

"Oh, yes!" Angie said. She looked to her fellow mermaid extras to share her joy with them. Kristina was scowling.

"Have you ever worked on a movie set before?" Marissa asked.

Angie shook her head 'no'. Kristina scoffed and pushed past Angie toward the empty makeup chair. Tillie was talking quietly to the hair stylist, seemingly unaware of the mermaid extras' conversation.

"Have you?" Angie asked.

Marissa nodded knowingly and gave Angie a cool smile. "We've been acting for a while. I've been in a few commercials and Kristina," Marissa tilted her head toward her friend who had climbed into the makeup chair and was staring at her reflection in the wide mirror. "Kristina's been on a TV show."

Angie could tell by the weighty look Marissa gave her that she was expected to be impressed. Wanting to make nice with her fellow mermaids, she asked, "Oh? What show?" She was immediately sorry for asking, because she never watched television. She doubted she would recognize the name of the show, which would probably put Kristina in an even more sour mood.

"Big Dates, Little Women," Kristina said loudly from the makeup chair.

Angie had never heard of it, she tried to look fascinated. "Really?"

Marissa nodded soberly, pleased that Angie was sufficiently awed by this fact.

"I made it all the way to the fourth episode before I didn't get on the Big Man's Short List," Kristina said.

Angie couldn't help herself. "The Big Man's Short List?"

Kristina rolled her eyes. "The list that the guy makes of his date choices."

Angie was at a loss. She didn't understand anything that Kristina was talking about.

Marissa leaned in to speak in a low tone, "It was a reality dating show. She wasn't chosen to continue dating the guy on the fourth episode."

"Oh!" Angie finally got it, but the look on Kristina's face was pure annoyance again.

"He was a total jerk anyway," Kristina said.

Angie couldn't think of a way to respond that might make Kristina less irritated. Luckily, they were interrupted by the makeup artist holding a huge jar of cold cream.

"Next time don't wear any makeup to set, please. We just have to take it all off to get you done up right anyway."

Before Kristina could respond, the makeup lady smeared a big glob of cream over her eyes and Angie was saved from having to make small talk about the girl's reality television experience. Television wasn't Angie's thing. Especially reality television.

She volunteered to be last in the makeup chair after

Kristina and Marissa. With them being actual actresses and her merely passing by, it seemed like the right thing to do.

Waiting outside for her turn, she checked her phone and saw two missed calls from Luna. She hit the call button.

"Hi, hi, hi!" Luna answered.

"Hi yourself," Angie replied.

"How's everything going out there? How's the movie star life?"

Angie glanced at the construction trailer that had been turned into a makeup trailer and its location in the middle of a gravel parking lot. There were several more construction trailers and two RV's parked in a circle in the middle of the lot. Film crew, mostly guys, mostly teenagers, wore slouching cargo shorts and dull grey and black T-shirts as they carried equipment from several parked trucks across the wooden walkway that she assumed led to the beach.

She had no idea what the shiny metal stands with long metal arms they carried were. Nor did she know what was stuffed into the backpacks and duffle bags draped over their shoulders. The huge black containers some of them rolled behind them looked like speakers at a rock concert, but she couldn't know for sure. All she did know was they were working hard, kicking up a lot of dust, and it was a decidedly unglamorous scene.

"Not like anything I've ever seen about Hollywood, that's for sure," Angie said.

"You don't like it?"

"No, it's not that. In fact, Luna, they're making me into one of the mermaids!"

"Oh my gosh," Luna laughed out loud. "That's perfect! Do you get a fin costume and everything?"

"I think so. I don't know exactly how it will work yet. I'm waiting to go into makeup."

"That sounds so exciting. I hope it's fun! How's Fidget handling van life?"

They had all been instructed to park on the far side of the lot and walk in to the trailers and Angie could just see Eckhart's pink roof sticking above the other vehicles. It was a mild 70 degrees with a nice breeze and she had left all of the windows down to keep air movement for Fidget inside.

"She's fine. She doesn't seem to mind the traveling. I need to make sure I can go check on her when we have a break though."

She was just about to tell Luna about the other mermaid extras and ask her if she had ever heard of a show called *Big Dates, Little Women* when the makeup lady opened the door and called her name.

"'I've got to go. I'll call you later," Angie said.

"Okay, break a leg," Luna said happily.

Angie wasn't sure if that sentiment was considered lucky when shooting a movie. Not like in the theatre. She didn't have time to ask. The makeup lady, Shivaun, plopped her down in the seat and got straight to work washing Angie's face with with a mild cleanser.

"Thank goodness you're not wearing makeup like those other two," Shivaun confided. "It adds so much time to take all of that nonsense off first."

Angie smiled politely. She didn't want to say anything unkind about her co-mermaids.

Like a woman on a mission Shivaun found the perfect foundation match for Angie's fair freckled skin and rubbed it in carefully. "You have beautiful skin, girl. Has anyone ever told you that you're naturally photogenic?"

"No, that's never come up."

"I've been doing this for a while and I've noticed the camera really takes to skin like yours. Kind of gives it a certain glow, you know?"

"Does it?" Angie had never heard such a thing. She watched with interest as Shivaun used a blue sparkling powder on her eyelids and cheekbones. It was like blush, but mermaid style. Angie smiled.

"Try not to smile, if you can."

"Sure," Angie straightened her mouth and tried to keep her face as still as possible for Shivaun's sake. As she watched the blue, green and pink glittering tones being layered onto her reflection, she was mesmerized by the transformation. Shivaun didn't only apply makeup to her face, but to her throat, chest, shoulders and arms.

"Mm, mm, mm," Shivaun mumbled, as if she had just taken a bite of something delicious. "You are lookin' aquatic."

"It's too bad my eyes aren't blue," Angie said. Her dark brown eyes normally looked almost black in comparison to her pale skin. With her sparkling blue and green mermaid skin, she worried that they didn't match.

"Oh, no," Shivaun reassured her. "I think it gives your look an edge, you know? It's unexpected. But don't worry, if they want you to have blue eyes we can always do contacts."

After makeup was hair. The hair stylist, Anthony, was just as thrilled with Angie's mass of red curls as Shivaun had been with her skin. When she sat down in his chair he gasped with delight and twirled her around to face the mirror then used both hands to grab fists full of her hair, lift it above her head and drop it dramatically.

"Your hair is gorgeous!"

Now that her makeup was set she was allowed to smile, so she did. "Thank you, I got it from my Mom."

"Well send Mom some flowers, because you owe her a big thank you."

Angie laughed. For someone that spent very little time in front of a mirror doing her hair or putting on makeup, this special attention was turning out to be fun. It was like

Halloween amped up a hundred times over. She had never gone to such trouble for a costume.

Her actual costume for the film, she found out when she was reunited with her fully made up co-mermaids in the costume trailer, was a bikini top encrusted with sequins and small decorative shells. Tillie and Brandon stood with the woman in charge of costumes, Lacy, and had picked out their favorites for each of the mermaids.

"Let's go with pink for you." Tillie pointed at Kristina. "Yellow for you." she pointed at Marissa. "And for you," she turned to Angie and looked her over, admiring her mane of shimmering red hair. "Oh, you would look great in blue, but that's for the lead actress." She thought for a moment and looked at Lacy. "Do you think green would be good?"

"Oh, yes, I have a sea green," Lacy answered, producing the bikini top from a nearby box. "It's got starfish."

"Perfect, let's go with that."

"What about the bottoms?" Angie asked.

"For the first scene you're going to be sitting in the water up to your waist," Tillie explained. "We have some swimsuit bottoms for that. You can wear your shorts over them until we're ready to shoot."

"Oh, okay."

Tillie paused, then asked all three of the mermaid extras, "You're not afraid of the ocean or anything like that?"

"No," Kristina and Marissa answered in unison then looked at Angie.

"Not at all," Angie said, mildly amused at the question.

"Good, we're almost ready. The A.D. will come and get you when it's time."

There were camp chairs set outside under some trees where they could wait...and wait...and wait. The other mermaids were glued to their cell phones, not that Angie minded. She was enjoying being dressed up in her mermaid garb with the breeze blowing softly through her mermaid hair.

Her eyes wandered across the busy parking lot, falling on Eckhart's roof. "Oh, Fidget!" Angie popped out of her chair.

Both Kristina and Marissa gave her odd looks.

"I need to go check on my cat," Angie said. "I'm just going over there." She motioned to the far edge of the parking lot. "If they come to get us can you tell them I'll be right back?"

Kristina and Marissa looked at each other then back at Angie. "Sure, no problem," Marissa said.

Without another thought, Angie hurried away.

When she peeked into Eckhart's partly open driver's side window she saw Fidget curled up in the middle of the passenger seat, sleeping soundly.

"Hi kitty," Angie said as she pulled open the door to let in more fresh air. Eckhart wasn't hot on the inside, but she still thought Fidget could use a quick walk outside. She glanced back and could just make out Kristina's bright blonde hair and pink mermaid top still lounging under the trees.

Quickly opening all of Eckhart's doors and windows, Angie grabbed Fidget's chain from the pocket on the back of the passenger seat. Still half asleep, the little cat rolled onto her back for a tummy rub as Angie tried adjusted her harness. As Angie bent over her to click it together, Fidget seemed to see her blue-green skin and wild mermaid hairdo for the first time.

Shocked, Fidget spit at her and twisted out of her grip, bounding out of the nearest open window. Her leash, which Angie was not holding tightly, followed the cat out the window, whipping back and forth before sliding completely out of sight.

"Fidget!"

Fidget did not come bounding back.

Angie rushed to the other side of Eckhart. Fidget was nowhere to be seen. There were only cars and more cars. So many people had arrived after she parked, the whole edge of the parking lot was packed. She dropped down on her knees and looked underneath the car directly next to hers.

"Fidget?"

No Fidget.

She moved to the next car, checking along the sides and quickly underneath. Nothing.

Conscious that she may run out of time before finding her cat, Angie moved along the row of parked cars hurriedly, calling Fidget's name.

Finally, she spied the handle of Fidget's leash disappearing under the front of a black sports car. Angie dropped to her knees in front of the car and peered underneath. Huddled against the inside of a back tire, Fidget stared at her suspiciously, her leash just out of Angie's reach.

"Come on, Fidget, I don't have a lot of time to do this," she said, laying down on her belly in the gravel. Maybe she could scoot under the car and get to the leash.

To her astonishment, Angie heard movement in the car. Then came the sound of the driver's door opening. Finally, feet clad in black leather boots came out of the car and onto the gravel.

"Excuse me?" A man's voice came from above the hood.

Unable to reach the leash, she was afraid the man would spook Fidget into flight again.

"Please, can you be quiet for a minute?" she asked the voice, firmly.

There was a pause before the man answered, "You want me to be quiet?"

"Yes," Angie hissed up at him. "You're scaring my cat." She turned her attention back to Fidget, a bit frantic to reach her before she escaped into the deep woods behind them. "Come here, Fidget. Come here, honey. It's just me."

There was a soft click of the door closing. A knee clad in

thick wide pants that were tucked into the top of knee high boots so they billowed out over the edge, lowered slowly onto the gravel.

"Can I help?" The man asked.

"Yes, please, can you go to the back in case she runs out that way?

Without a word the man moved to the back of the car and knelt down, peering underneath. Angie could see more of him in this position. He had long black hair and a long black beard, some of it braided with glass beads dangling from the end. A white billowing shirt, a wide leather belt, she realized he was wearing a pirate costume.

"Now what?" he asked.

"Can you reach her leash?"

"Maybe...watch for her, she may run to you when I put my hand underneath." He laid down on his back and slowly moved his shoulder and arm under the car.

"Come here, Fidget. Come here," Angie called gently, hoping he was right and Fidget would be so scared of him that she forgot to be scared of her.

Fidget mewed a few times as she watched his hand get closer and closer. Her whole body was shaking.

"Come here, honey, come to me," Angie said again. She, too, reached her hand toward the cat.

With a frightened meow and a sudden spurt of energy, Fidget scurried away from Angie's hand and ran up the man's arm onto his chest.

"I got her, I got her," he said, Fidget mewed miserably from where he held her against his chest.

Angie hurried to her feet, all thoughts of keeping her hair and makeup pristine were gone. Washed away by the worry of losing Fidget.

The man stood up on the opposite side of the sports car.

Gently shushing Fidget who he held carefully in capable hands.

Angie could see that she had been correct. The man was dressed as a pirate. And she could see one more thing that hadn't been clear during their interaction under the car.

This pirate was none other than Xavier Patel – the star of the movie.

Chapter Six

Peter Pineapple himself was holding Fidget on the other side of the sports car.

He stared at her for a long moment.

She stared back. Gawked was more like it.

Xavier Patel was an absolutely gorgeous man. Tall, lean, dark skin, deep brown eyes, it was obvious why he was a star.

But dressed as a pirate he was too much for Angie to process. She had never really thought she had a thing for the pirate look, but in the moments that passed between them she came to understand her deep attraction to a man in an unbuttoned white shirt with billowing sleeves, dark brown pants cinched with a wide leather belt and tucked into boots that hit just above his knees.

Fidget mewed, bringing her out of the daze he had put her under.

"Oh my gosh, thank you," she said, hurrying to his side of the car to retrieve her cat. "I thought I might lose her."

"You're welcome," he answered, watching her with an expression that was difficult to read under his long beard.

Fidget mewed again, drawing his attention, almost as if he had forgotten he was holding a cat. "Who is this little one?"

Angie reached for her. "Her name is Fidget." Fidget pulled away from Angie and into Xavier Patel's chest. Angie was surprised, though she couldn't blame Fidget for wanting to be closer to him. At their new proximity she could smell his cologne, musk and spices. Magnificent.

"Hello Miss Fidget," Xavier Patel spoke sweetly. "What's the matter?"

"I think she might be afraid of my makeup," Angie offered.

Xavier Patel took a moment to let his gaze wander from her hair down to her starfish encrusted sea green bikini top. Lifting his eyes back to meet hers, he said, "Surely not. You look beautiful."

Angie's cheeks flushed pink. Certain he could see her reaction even through her blue and green makeup, she tried to think of a response.

"I'm a mermaid," was all she could come up with, like she was a five year old at a kindergarten Halloween party.

Xavier Patel's eyes smiled, drawing her in. Her heart was warm and open, but her mind was fuzzy. She drew a blank on what to do next.

"Hey, hey!" A shout sounded somewhere nearby. Angie couldn't tear her gaze away from Xavier Patel's shining brown eyes. "Hey, you! They're looking for you," the voice came again.

Xavier Patel glanced over his shoulder at the shouting that was coming from behind him. Angie followed his look to see Kristina strutting toward them, thrusting her hand back and forth in the air in an annoyed wave. She was fixated on Angie, barely paying attention to the guy in the pirate suit.

She reached them, her blue eyes scolding Angie before she

even spoke. "They're ready for us on set. You can't just wander away like that. You're wasting everybody's time."

Snapping out of the trance Xavier Patel seemed to have over her, Angie realized she had completely lost track of time. "I'm so sorry. I was looking for my cat..." she gestured meekly to Fidget, still in Xavier Patel's arms.

"Your cat?" Kristina scoffed, indignant and out of breath. "Why would you bring your cat to–" she stopped mid-sentence as the pirate she had only seen from behind turned around and she realized his true identity.

Kristina's eyes practically bulged out of her head in surprise. She opened and closed her mouth like a fish out of water that was gasping for breath. Angie hoped she hadn't looked quite so bizarre when she had been shocked at the sight of him.

Feeling a little sorry for her, Angie wanted to try and save Kristina from further odd behavior. She moved to take Fidget again. "I'm sorry, I'll just put her back on her bed and be right there." Fidget batted her hand away with a tiny growl. "Fidget, stop, it's me." Fidget swiped her paw once more against Angie's hand, this time drawing blood with a small, but efficient scratch. "Ouch!"

There were more shouts and more agitated waving in their direction by Marissa and other crew members. Kristina remained mute, staring limply up into Xavier Patel's pirate beauty.

"It looks like they need you now. I can watch her for you, if you don't mind," he said, his eyes still smiling at Angie while simultaneously avoiding eye contact with Kristina.

"Oh, I don't know," Angie replied, already feeling like she had made an awful mistake bringing Fidget along, or even accepting this job in the first place. She hadn't thought much about how she would manage taking care of her cat while she was working.

"It's no trouble," he said, then leaned closer to her as if they were about to share a secret. "And I think she might like me."

She couldn't think of any more reasons to object, so she shrugged weakly and nodded her agreement. With that, Xavier Patel escorted her and, to a lesser extent, the star struck Kristina, to the set where Tillie and Brandon were waiting with the camera crew.

"Look what I caught while I was out fishing." He presented Angie and Kristina to the directors.

"I'm sorry we're late, it's my fault," Angie confessed. "I got..." she glanced at the pirate Xavier cuddling Fidget, "...distracted."

"It's all right, let's get you on your mark," Tillie said kindly. She spied the ball of calico fur in Xavier's arms, moving closer to pet Fidget's ears. "And who is this?"

"This is Fidget," Xavier answered, giving Angie a questioning look to make sure he had her name right. She nodded and he continued, "I'm watching her for someone, if that's all right?" He lifted her up so Tillie could see she was on a leash and harness. "She won't be any trouble." Angie wasn't so sure about that statement, but she didn't say anything to contradict him.

"No trouble, maybe we'll have her make a few cameos," Tillie responded with a grin. Turning her attention to the scene set up she said, "All right, let's get everyone in place."

Still flustered from everything that had just taken place, Angie found herself taking off her shorts so she could get into the water with just her mermaid top and swimsuit bottoms. Never one to have a problem with body image or nudity, Angie was surprised to feel a bit vulnerable. She glanced nervously at Xavier who was seated in a tall director's chair petting Fidget and watching her being led into the water.

The image of an attractive pirate stroking Fidget's head

and holding her pink leash with the bell attached to the end was a little bizarre. She tried to think of how they would possibly be able to put Fidget in the movie at all. As a pirate cat? Certainly not as a mermaid cat. That wasn't even a thing.

"All right, you ladies are going to sit here and you'll be sunning yourselves," The assistant director, an older round bellied man who reminded Angie of one of the guys who made deliveries to the metaphysical book store, ushered them each onto a section of a large flat rock whose surface was beneath the water. When sitting on it, the water came up to Angie and Marissa's belly button. "Use these to pretend to brush your hair, but don't really brush your hair. We don't want to have to send you back to hair and makeup." He handed them each an oversized long handled hair brush.

"This isn't going to work," Kristina complained. She was so much shorter than the other two that the water reached the bottom of her mermaid top when she sat down.

"Can we get a booster over here?" The assistant director shouted. Kristina looked embarrassed. One of the crew walked into the shallow waves holding what did look a lot like a child's booster seat from a restaurant. After positioning Kristina on the seat so she didn't look like she was sinking, the assistant director continued his instructions. "All right, the two biggest things to remember is don't talk and don't look at the camera, the main action, or any of the crew. It won't hurt if you look at each other, but nobody else. You're just minding your business brushing your hair on this rock. Got it?"

Angie and her co-mermaids nodded.

Negativity swelled in her solar plexus, jumbling up into a tight ball of nerves. If she'd had time before they started she could have meditated and cleared her chakras. She only had time to concentrate on grounding herself onto the rock, allowing the gentle soothing ocean water to steady her nerves.

She studied the cove where they sat. It was bordered on

almost four sides by rock outcroppings, with only a small opening on the far west side that would allow any boat to enter from the wider waters. It was a beautiful spot. Even without the help of the filmmakers she could imagine a real mermaid or two sunning themselves here.

Angie's attention turned to the odd shaped brush in her hand. White, like the others, its shape was organic, almost like the curve in a sea shell.

"Do you think these are supposed to look like bones?" she asked her co-mermaids.

"Shh!" Kristina looked at her sternly and hissed through clenched teeth, "We're not supposed to talk."

Again, nerves swirled in her chakras. Angie began miming brushing her hair and dared a sideways glance at the main actress who was dressed not as a mermaid, but as a normal woman in a glamorous evening gown, and was standing on the shoreline chatting with Tillie.

Angie stopped miming. "I don't think they're filming yet," she said helpfully.

"I don't care," hissed Kristina again. "Just be quiet!"

Surprised at the care Kristina was taking in the assistant director's instructions when she had so blatantly disregarded the instructions about not wearing makeup to the set, she looked to Marissa for her reaction. Marissa gave her a shrug that Angie took to mean there was nothing to be done and they should all do as Kristina said.

Angie sighed and went back to watching the main actress. What had they said her name was? Elizabeth something? Angie didn't recognize her, but that wasn't surprising. She wasn't totally up to date on current celebrities.

From what she could see Elizabeth was quite pretty. Blonde, extremely thin, with long skinny legs and arms. Angie wondered what she would look like as a mermaid.

"All right, is everyone set? We're ready to roll," the

assistant director called out. Angie wished she had asked his name, she didn't like thinking of him only as his title.

Despite sitting in her assigned spot, holding her prop brush, and understanding the instructions, Angie had a feeling she was going to do something wrong.

"All right, ladies, start brushing," the assistant director instructed them. "And remember, don't look at Elizabeth or the camera."

Right. No problem. Angie lifted her brush and ran it in the air along her hair line. Some of the wilder parts of her hairdo caught on the bristles of the brush and her eyes widened in dismay. It was going to be difficult to keep the brush from catching on her curls so she decided to fake brush the underside of her hair, that way she could use her other hand to cover the bristles and nobody would be any wiser.

"Roll camera," the assistant director said.

"Speed," someone else answered.

A few moments went by and she heard Tillie say, "Action."

Gazing out over the water and pretending to under brush her hair, Angie concentrated on feeling like a mermaid, assuming this would project the appropriate look of what Tillie and Brandon were after.

Out of the corner of her eye she saw Elizabeth stumble onto the beach. Not having read the script, Angie had no idea if that was part of the story, but nobody yelled 'cut' so she assumed it was. Elizabeth moved along the shoreline in her gown, apparently in distress, looking back from where she had come every now and then as if someone was following her.

Angie kept her eyes lowered to the water but tilted her head in the other direction so she could see if anyone did follow Elizabeth onto the beach. Secretly, she knew she was watching for Xavier in his pirate outfit. If he did enter the scene then who was watching Fidget?

As if she conjured him up by thinking of him, Xavier Patel did appear, but not in the scene with Elizabeth. He stood in his full glorious pirate costume with the crew, watching Elizabeth as she struggled through whatever imaginary problem she was having in the scene, calmly stroking Fidget who he still held in his arms.

As unbelievably attractive as he had been when she first saw him dressed as a pirate, seeing him taking such care of Fidget sent his attraction level into the stratosphere. Angie murmured a barely audible coo of appreciation.

Kristina snapped her eyes to Angie's, warning her to be quiet with a flare of her nostrils. Angie clamped her mouth shut and went back to staring at the water. But something kept pulling her attention away from the beautiful blue water. Something electrifying.

Unable to ignore the magnetic pull coming from the shoreline, Angie allowed her eyes to shift ever so slightly to see what she could see with her peripheral vision.

It was him. The pirate.

Past Elizabeth acting next to the water. Past the directors and cameras. Past the crew. Xavier Patel was watching her on the rock, and her alone.

She could feel his gaze on her from that far away. Sense his deep brown eyes wandering lazily across her skin. A shiver went across her shoulders and down her arms. Her hands felt suddenly chilled even though her cheeks were hot.

It was all she could do to keep from lifting her eyes to his. His stare was so powerful that she wasn't sure if she hadn't already responded to him with a flick of her eyes and broken the rule of not looking directly at anyone but her fellow co-mermaids.

Just as she was wondering how long this scene was and if she could keep control of herself for as long as it took, there was a loud ringing sound from somewhere on the beach. A cell phone that jolted everyone out of the moment. Elizabeth stood up straight, breaking character, and asked, "Who's phone is that?"

"Cut," Tillie called out, a twinge of annoyance in her voice. The entire crew looked back and forth to each other, but nobody moved. The ring sounded again. "Find it," Tillie instructed. Several crew members moved into action, searching the beach for the sound.

The ring tone was painfully familiar and Angie knew even before a crew member held up her shorts from where she'd dropped them before coming into the water that the offending phone was hers.

"Got it," the crew member called out.

Angie dropped her head in shame, but not before she caught a fiery sideways glance from Kristina.

Great. She was off to a stellar start with her co-mermaids, that was for sure.

"Sorry," she called out weakly. "That's mine."

"Phones need to be turned off," the assistant director, whatever his name was, reiterated to everyone, but he meant it as a direct instruction to her. Driving the point home, he turned to her and held her phone high in the air so she could see. "Can I turn this off?"

"Sure, yes, of course...sorry," she said again.

Mortified, she looked away from him and the directors and everyone else, but she caught Xavier's gaze again. He was still waiting casually on the sidelines, still petting Fidget, and still watching her, seemingly unfazed by her film set faux pas.

Chapter Seven

Angie's first day as a mermaid only got worse.

For someone who loved the water and had uprooted her life to live near it and swim in it, her body didn't hold up as well as she would have expected when actually sitting in water all morning.

Take after take, as she ran the brush near her hair, she noticed her fingertips starting to shrivel. She was getting water-logged. Also, her bottom was chafed from sitting on the rough rock in the saltwater. And she was afraid her skin, fast to freckle, might be burning in the sun.

She wondered when they would be done, or at least have a chance to step out of the water for a while. Watching Elizabeth repeat the same scene where she stumbled onto the beach in her evening gown and looked fearfully behind her over and over again grew tiresome. How many takes would they need before they got it right?

Scowling into the water at her waterlogged toes she heard the assistant director call out 'Take 16'. That seemed like too many takes. Maybe this Elizabeth person was an incompetent actress.

Thoughts of wrapping the scene so she could get out of the water overrode every other distraction, even the distraction of Xavier the pirate gazing lazily at her from the shore. It took all of her will power to remain seated on her chafing behind until suddenly, it happened. Angie and her co-mermaids were released from their perch. Time for a break and a makeup check.

"Oh, girl, I think you need more sunscreen," Shivaun told Angie. She was inspecting all of the mermaid extras' makeup to see if they needed any quick fixes. "It looks like you're getting some pink spots where the makeup's thin."

"I didn't think about putting sunscreen on this morning," Angie confessed.

"I always suggest using sunscreen before you come to set, but for you I think it's an absolute necessity. I've got some here," Shivaun pulled a bottle out of one of her many drawers and dabbed the cream onto Angie's arms and chest.

"I always apply sunscreen in the morning before any makeup touches my face," Kristina chimed in, happy to point out Angie's mistake. "It's a no brainer in this industry. You have to be ready for anything on set if you want to make it as an actress."

Marissa nodded in agreement.

"No harm done, we'll get this on and you'll be ready for the rest of the day," Shivaun said, ignoring Kristina's little speech.

"Do you know how much longer we'll be in the water?" Angie held out her hands and showed Shivaun her water-logged fingertips.

Alarmed, Shivaun said, "Oh my goodness, you're shriveling up!"

Kristina and Marissa quickly checked their fingers, which didn't seem to be suffering in the saltwater as badly as Angie's.

"Here's some lotion," Shivaun handed her a sample sized

container. "Put some on now and then every morning and night that you're in the water for very long. It helps to stay moisturized."

"Thank you," Angie said gratefully. As she unscrewed the lid from the container, thoughts of Fidget came to her mind. "I wonder if I could step out and check on my cat? Before we go back in the water?"

Shivaun paused uncertainly. "I don't know how much time there is. I'll ask Adam."

"Who's Adam?" Angie asked.

Kristina could not contain an eye roll before informing her, "He's the assistant director."

"Oh, yes, I was wondering what his name was," Angie said, happy to know, but wishing she would have asked Shivaun that question out of Kristina's hearing.

"Knock, knock, can I come in?" A man asked as the door pushed in a few inches.

"That's probably Adam coming to get us. If I were you I wouldn't ask for special favors and slow down production any more than you already have," Kristina warned, her brow pinched into a rather ugly glower.

Before Angie could respond, the door opened further revealing that the man in question was not Adam at all. It was Xavier, still in his pirate attire and still holding Fidget.

"Fidget!" Angie rushed to her cat. Overcome, she failed to think about how close retrieving Fidget would bring her to Xavier's chest.

"She's been doing fine, mostly sleeping, but I thought maybe she wants water or food?" His thoughtful concern was nothing short of adorable, especially coming from someone so fiercely dressed.

Angie took Fidget carefully. The cat didn't resist, thank goodness. Instead of hissing and pulling away like before, she allowed Angie to pull her to her own chest. The little cat was still warm and purring from sleeping on Xavier. He must have a calming affect on cats.

Angie could not say the same for his affect on women.

The mere act of taking Fidget from him caused their hands and arms to touch, sparking tiny pulses of electric attraction through Angie's body. Having spent all morning snuggling on his chest, Fidget carried the scent of his cologne on her fur. The combination of spices and musk once again caused Angie's brain to go fuzzy, just like it had earlier.

"Xave, I heard you were cat-sitting for someone," Shivaun teased.

Xavier smiled, blasting the tight quarters of the makeup trailer with charm. "It was my pleasure." He nodded politely toward Angie, "Though we were never properly introduced."

"Oh, I can do that," Shivaun volunteered. "Ladies, this is Xavier Patel. And these are the background mermaids, Angie, Kristina, and Marissa."

Xavier had not taken his eyes off of Angie while Shivaun made the introductions. When she was done, he bowed his head quickly at her and said, "Please, call me Xave." Then, remembering his manners, he nodded at Kristina and Marissa in turn.

"Thank you, Xave," Angie tried to say his name casually, coolly, as if it was a name like any other. She wasn't sure she was successful. "For taking care of Fidget all morning." She glanced at Kristina and Marissa who both beamed at Xavier, their faces frozen in a kind of hyper glee.

Embarrassed for them, she looked back up at Xavier, but found he wasn't paying any attention to either of her co-mermaids. His eyes were trained on her, a queer confusion on his face.

Squeezing Fidget lightly in her arms she said, "I should probably take her back to her bed..." her voice trailed off, realizing she may be about to cause yet another problem.

"I was going ask Adam if they could give her a few extra minutes?" Shivaun said to Xavier, looking at Angie to see if that would be enough time. Angie nodded.

Xavier...no, *Xave*...dismissed the question with a wave of his hand. "I'll tell Adam. I'm sure it's fine." He looked back to Angie with a warm smile. "Take your time."

Angie had forgotten she left all of Eckhart's doors and windows open when she chased after Fidget. She quickly shut the van doors and made sure the windows were down, but not far enough that Fidget could climb out. Although she was pretty sure that would not be a problem for the rest of the day. The instant they had reached Eckhart, Fidget ran straight to her food and water bowls to eat and drink her fill, then curled up on the cushion seat in the back of the van.

"Have a good nap," Angie told her softly as she closed the door and hurried back to the set. The day was still mild, and she had made sure to park on the shady end of the parking lot. She would check back again to make sure Fidget was okay.

"I didn't know you were friends with one of the stars," Kristina said sweetly when they had settled once more into their watery seats.

"I'm not," Angie assured her. "Well, I did meet him, barely meet him, once before, but I'm sure he doesn't remember. Today we just kind of ran into each other."

Kristina sniffed and Angie wasn't sure if she believed her or not.

"God, he's gorgeous," Marissa gushed. "And as a pirate? Sheesh!" She mimed fanning herself as if she was about to faint.

Angie chuckled and nodded in agreement.

Kristina let out a loud, awkward giggle and switched her gaze to Xave who was on the shore preparing for his upcoming scene.

"It's not about what he looks like, Marissa," Kristina

corrected. "It's about the fact that he's a leading man. A real leading man. I mean, can you imagine what might happen if he took a liking to one of us? A man like that could make or break a girl's career."

Angie was pretty sure Kristina wasn't including her under the umbrella of 'us', which was fine. She wasn't an actress after all.

Kristina turned to her, all smiles and camaraderie. "Don't forget about us, Angie."

"Okay…" Angie wasn't sure what she meant.

"If you run into Xave again with your cat or whatever. Don't forget your fellow mermaid friends." Kristina made sure to finger quote the words 'run into', as if Angie wasn't telling them the whole story.

"Oh, right, okay," Angie smiled, but she didn't think there was any reason to believe Xave would ever speak to her, or babysit her cat, in the future. He obviously had no memory of them being introduced by Ian several months before, she didn't see that changing as he got busier and busier acting in the movie.

Angie took her lunch to Eckhart to eat with Fidget and relax a little bit. Her whole day had been thrown off and she needed to re-center. After she ate and played with Fidget for a few minutes, she did a quick 10 minute meditation to realign her chakras.

Feeling pretty good, she turned on her phone to see who had called and was met with several missed calls from Sofia and even more texts from everyone else. She hit the button to call Sofia back and got a warning that her phone was low on battery.

"How is that possible when you were off all morning?" she asked the phone, plugging it into the adapter that made Eckhart's cigarette lighter into a USB charger.

"How's everything going?" Sofia asked.

"Well, to start with I forgot to turn off my cell phone and then you called right in the middle of a take," Angie informed her.

"Oh no! I'm sorry, how embarrassing," Sofia said, her tone more amused than apologetic.

"It's all right. It is kind of funny," Angie giggled. "It's just been one flub up after another for me this morning."

"What else happened?"

Angie filled her in on the whole incident with Fidget and Xave, finding the story more and more amusing as she spoke.

"Wait, back up," Sofia said. "Fidget didn't know you because you're dressed up as a mermaid?"

"Right."

"You get to *play* a mermaid in the movie?!"

"Yes!"

Sofia laughed out loud. "That's amazing, Angie!"

Angie admired her shimmering blue and green arms. "It is kind of exciting, but harder than it sounds."

"Oh, right, it's probably not easy walking in the fins."

Angie laughed. "No, we don't even have fins yet. That will be hard, won't it? I'm already having problems without any fins. My hands and feet are all waterlogged from this morning. If I have to be in the water all day long I'm going to shrivel into a giant pale prune."

"That wouldn't be good," Sofia agreed, still laughing.

"I'm not sure I'm cut out for any of this. I'm glad I'm just an extra. Honestly, though, I am a little worried about how I'm going to take care of Fidget this whole time."

"I'm coming up with Ian the day after tomorrow. He's scheduled to be a background pirate. I can help with Fidget while we're there."

Relieved to know her friends would be joining her on this filmmaking adventure, Angie returned from her lunch break.

"We're going to have you three fitted for your fins this

afternoon," Adam told them. "We'll keep your makeup on for that process so they can get a better idea of the whole look."

Angie was relieved. Hopefully they wouldn't schedule another half day sitting on that rock for a while, if ever again.

Angie and her co-mermaids spent the afternoon in the seamstress room inside the costume trailer, which was filled to bursting with magical costumes. Billowing white shirts, black pants, red and purple sashes, and wide brimmed pirate hats festooned with ostrich feathers took up almost all of the space on the racks. It was a vast wonderland of pirate clothes and paraphernalia.

The other racks held a small section of evening gowns and dresses as well as men's suits and working men's shirts and pants. There were so many boots of so many different sizes and styles on the floor underneath all of the racks that Angie wondered how in the world the costume people kept track of them.

The other section of racks didn't take up as much space, because the costumes were for the mermaids and mermaids wore much fewer clothes. At the very end of the mermaid rack, however, Angie spied several elaborate mermaid bikini tops with shimmering cloth streaming in thin strips off of the sides and back. Each of those mermaid tops also had crowns encrusted with costume jewels pinned to their hanger.

Angie stopped to admire them. There were five sets altogether ranging from the palest blue to a deep blue, almost black. The details were astonishing. Every inch of the material and the matching crown had some sort of embellishment, whether it be a glittering jewel, small sparkling shells, shimmering sequins or silver thread stitching in the shape of waves on the surface of the ocean.

She reached out and touched her favorite, the ice blue version, and was disappointed to find that the sparkling shells were plastic.

"I wouldn't touch those if I were you," Kristina warned. Angie pulled her hand away, growing weary of her co-mermaid's constant stream of instructions on film set etiquette. "Those are Elizabeth's," Kristina said haughtily.

"So she turns into a mermaid in the movie?" Angie asked, trying to sway the conversation to something other than what she should or shouldn't be doing.

"No, she plays both the human who marries the pirate and the mermaid he falls in love with, who look the same, but are, obviously, different species," Marissa answered. Angie was surprised at her lengthy explanation. Marissa had remained so quiet most of the day.

"That sounds interesting. I'd like to read the script just so I know the story."

"They don't usually hand scripts out to extras," Kristina told her. "We don't really need to know what's going on to be in the background."

"Right," Angie understood, but she didn't like it. "I've never really liked being a cog in a big machine. When I'm part of something I like to know what that something is...you know?"

Kristina blinked up at her like she was nothing but a silly cow who had learned how to speak. With a shake of her head she dismissed Angie's comment and reiterated, "Just don't touch Elizabeth's costumes."

Saved by the seamstress calling her name, Angie escaped the company of her judgmental co-mermaids and endured what felt like an eternity getting measured and pinned for her mermaid fins. The day was dragging on and on and she was sleepy. She had to fight back several yawns and was so tired during her fitting that she forgot to ask how she would walk while wearing the fins.

After her fitting she was sent back to makeup to get cleaned up, as were Kristina and Marissa. By the time they were done it was nearly dusk and the crew were packing up lights and equipment and loading them back into the trucks. Several cars had already left the parking lot when Adam pulled the three of them aside.

"You all did great today. Thanks for putting in all of the extra effort," he said. Not waiting for their response he continued, "We're switching you three to a different category than the general extras. I've got your next call sheet here for you and I emailed you a copy, too. Short story is you don't need to be here tomorrow or the next day. But you'll be back on Thursday morning."

Relieved at this news and done for the day, Angie made her way back to Eckhart. Without trying to notice she saw that Xave's black sports car was already gone. Not that he was supposed to say goodbye to her or anything. She simply noticed, that's all. Once inside Eckhart, she flopped down on the cushion, exhausted. She was happy to take a few minutes to relax before driving back to the RV park.

"There is a plus when your car is also your house," she said to Fidget, who rubbed her head against Angie's arm vigorously. "I guess you're glad I'm not blue anymore?" The little cat purred.

Angie grabbed a handful of granola and a banana out of her tiny kitchen and set about answering everybody's texts that she had ignored all day.

Sofia had spread the news that she was playing a mermaid in the movie and all of her besties had something to say about it. Angie chuckled as she read their jokes and congratulations, texting back to each one, but not calling any of them. She was too worn out to talk on the phone.

She was too worn out to stay awake, it turned out. Before she knew what was happening, Angie drifted off to sleep as the day shifted to night outside.

It was dark when she woke suddenly, not remembering

where she was. There were no lights on inside Eckhart and no lights at all in the seaside parking lot. The moon did cast some light and as her eyes adjusted she remembered where she was parked. At the film set, not the RV park.

"I must have been really sleepy," she said to Fidget, who was also waking up, yawning contagiously.

Bleary eyed, she made her way to the front of the van and climbed into the driver's seat. Pulling her tote out from a hidden compartment under the passenger seat, she reached in and searched for her keys. They weren't there.

Alarmed, she searched again and could feel no keys in the large bag. Fully awake, Angie scanned the dark parking lot. Completely empty.

"No, no, no..." she muttered. Sticking her fingers into the deep corners of her tote. Nothing.

She reached up and switched on the dome light, but the expected warm glow of the light did not appear. The light was weak, too weak to see much more than a dim yellow enhancement of everything in the front seat. That was enough for Angie to see her keys sticking out of the ignition.

"Oh, jeez, there they are," she said with a sigh of relief. "Let's get out of here, Fidget."

She put her foot on the brake and turned the key.

Nothing.

The engine didn't turn. Didn't even try.

Eckhart was dead.

Chapter Eight

Fear tickled her neck.

Angie looked around to reassure herself that nobody was lurking nearby. Or maybe she was looking for help.

Either way, there was nobody in sight. The parking lot was totally empty.

She flipped on the headlights. The same sickly yellow light pressed out from them, but only reached just in front of the van. There was no juice in the battery and without the battery Eckhart was like a sailboat becalmed on windless water. He wasn't going anywhere. And neither was she.

A growing sense of unease rose in her chest. She turned the key off and pulled it out of the ignition then flicked off the lights. The dark night engulfed her little pink van with only a half moon peeking through the treetops above to offer any relief.

Fidget mewed in the back seat.

"It's okay, it's okay," Angie said, more to herself than to the cat.

She climbed into the back and found her phone. She had unplugged it from the adapter to text. Only 42% charged.

"I should probably save that for an emergency," she told Fidget.

She eyed the front dashboard again. Maybe the adapter had drained the battery? She had left the doors wide open for half the morning as well. Perhaps that was the problem.

She frowned. At the moment, it wasn't really important how the battery had died. The big question was what to do about it.

Fidget mewed again.

"Do you want to go outside?" Angie decided to do something she would normally do in the evening to calm her nerves.

Under the looming trees, the sound of the ocean in the distance brought her back to the present. Instead of taking Fidget across the gravel parking lot, Angie took her just inside the forest's edge.

The earth was soft under her feet and the fresh air helped clear her mind. Fidget liked it too, running on silent paws under the shrubs and wrapping her leash around the tree trunks. The tinkling sound of her silver bell brought to mind stories of fae folk and other magical woodland creatures, pulling Angie's attention away from her modern day concerns.

After their walk she checked her water supply and found she had plenty for the night. She set up her camp chair and folding table outside Eckhart's open back door, just like she would at the RV park.

Feeling lighter and decidedly less nervous she talked to the cat, "We'll be fine, Fidget. We're like snails, we bring our house with us and if a park ranger comes by to give us a ticket for camping in the parking lot maybe they can help us start the engine!"

She scrounged what she could from the refrigerator before

its contents spoiled. Angie preferred vegetarian fare, so there wasn't any meat to worry about.

She filled a bowl using what remained of her plain yogurt and the green grapes from the fridge then added a handful of peanuts and honey. A yogurt sundae, just like her mom used to make.

Munching on her meal under the night sky while Fidget had fun jumping in and out of Eckhart, Angie thought about her parents. If she had a fully charged phone she could call them and check in, but what would she say? That she was stranded in an abandoned parking lot somewhere on the Pacific coast in Northern California? She didn't want to worry them. They were hippies, but they were also parents. Her mom, especially, was always reminding her to do things like go to the dentist, get her yearly physical, keep up on her insurance payments.

Angie stopped chewing. Insurance!

She put her bowl down and flipped through the screens on her phone to her car insurance app. The welcome screen popped up and there, lo and behold, was the button for emergency roadside assistance.

"Thanks, Mom," she said, her thumb hovering over the button. She paused, glancing at her half-eaten yogurt sundae and the cozy pillows stacked up inside of Eckhart waiting to be made into a bed for the night.

Weary from her long day of being a movie mermaid, all Angie really wanted to do was curl up under her warm blankets and sleep. The thought of waiting for a tow truck to come find her in the dark and tow Eckhart to some unknown mechanic's shop that wouldn't be open until morning sounded exhausting. She wouldn't be able to sleep in Eckhart. She would have to find a hotel, and one that allowed cats to boot.

No, she wouldn't be calling for emergency roadside service. Not right now, anyway.

She would wait until morning. Early morning, so she could be gone before any of the crew arrived. A sudden thought of Xave discovering her sleeping in her van caused a pang of embarrassment.

Strange. Angie wasn't prone to feeling inadequate or ashamed. She meditated and did light and energy work, much of which was focused on accepting herself and others for what they were, not what they pretended to be. She brushed her thoughts about the actor aside. There wasn't any reason for her to worry about what Xavier Patel thought about her living situation.

Turning off her phone to ensure she would have enough battery to contact emergency roadside service in the wee hours of the morning, Angie shifted in her chair and went back to eating her yogurt. Pleased she was at peace in nature and not at a cruddy hotel next to a mechanic's shop, she bit down on a grape, but missed and bit her lip instead.

"Ow, ow, ow!" She covered her mouth with one hand and leaned sideways to put the bowl back on the table. Eyes squinting from the pain, Angie tried to swallow what was in her mouth without choking, but her throat muscles wouldn't cooperate. Through the pain, she envisioned a park ranger telling her mother that she had choked to death on a grape in the middle of the night in an empty parking lot.

Angie bent as far as she could away from the chair, spitting the contents of her mouth onto the ground. Three in tact grapes and a blob of yogurt lay at her feet. Collapsing dramatically back into the chair to nurse her burning lip, she accidentally knocked the support leg of her folding table and it dropped to the ground, breaking her bowl neatly into two halves.

"Augh!" she shouted, not able to use her lips to form words yet. She kicked her feet out, throwing a tantrum and sending gravel flying in all directions. "Augh-augh-augh!" The pain was excruciating, searing into her lip and wrinkling her face into a mask of agony.

Tears squeezed out of her eyes and she covered them with her hands, trying to press the misery of her situation back. Frustration overtook her and the tears kept coming, pushing relentlessly until she couldn't hold them back anymore. Her lip was throbbing and she was stuck in a parking lot with a broken van, no friends or comfort anywhere around.

Angie dropped her arms, dangling them off the sides of the chair. Then the sobs came. Ugly and wet, turning into a wail every so often that lifted into the night and was swallowed by the trees and the half moon above.

After a few minutes, or more, she couldn't be sure how long she cried to the moon, her sobs turned to sniffles. The sounds of the ocean in the distance and the rustling of the night breeze through the trees remained. Wiping her eyes with the palms of her hands, she heaved one last sigh. Her little pity party hadn't changed Mother Nature in the least.

It was time to get some sleep. She would deal with everything in the morning.

Up well before the sun, Angie called for emergency roadside assistance. When it finally arrived she and Fidget rode in the front seat with the tow truck driver as Eckhart was hauled to the nearest mechanic.

Dawn broke as they drove and Angie swore she recognized Tillie and Brandon and some of the other crew driving in the opposite direction. She almost ducked down into the seat as they passed, but realized even if they didn't see her, they would see Eckhart. It would be difficult to not see a pink van being towed down the road. At least she wasn't expected to show up and be a mermaid for a few more days.

"You're gonna need a new battery," said the skeletal mechanic wearing coveralls with the name 'Skeet' sewed onto the chest.

The garage had been highly recommended by her tow truck driver. It looked to her that it was the only mechanic's shop in the minuscule town, but she was in no position to argue. She had been a little worried they might come up with all kinds of things that needed to be fixed on Eckhart, real or imagined. She was relieved that it was only a battery. A battery shouldn't cost too much to replace.

"Is that all?" she asked.

The mechanic stared at his computer screen and tapped his long fingers on a keyboard covered with a greasy plastic protector as he spoke. "Looks like, but we don't carry what you need in this store. We'll need to send Larry to pick it up from Apito."

Angie stared at him, still groggy from her early wake up call. "Apito?"

"It'll take him a little bit to go round trip. We're already booked up today, but we can squeeze you in," he smiled at her with large yellowed teeth.

"Thank you."

"You're probably lookin' at two, three o'clock by the time we're done."

"Oh, I see." Deflated, she took in the cramped seating area that the shop provided. Four bright orange plastic chairs, an old coffee table full of Popular Mechanic's and People magazines, and a vending machine all looked like they had seen better days.

Motioning to a short row of shops across the street, the mechanic said, "There's a coffee shop over there, the Vanilla Bean, they have a good bakery, too."

"Thank you," she said uncertainly. Fidget mewed from her travel position tucked gently inside Angie's tote bag.

"Don't worry about your cat. Maggie's pretty laid back. She don't mind the occasional pet coming inside. And seein' as you're stranded, I don't think she'll mind at all."

The delicious smell of fresh baked goodies and hot coffee grew stronger as Angie walked toward the Vanilla Bean and when she opened the door and stepped inside her mouth started watering. Taking a deep breath through her nose to savor the delicious smells, she looked around the darling coffee shop and bakery.

Done up in a rustic cottage style with worn wood tables and chairs, plumped up loveseats and overstuffed chairs for more seating, it was an inviting coffee shop. The beamed ceilings, greenery from indoor plants spilling off of shelves, whitewashed brick walls and a reclaimed wood counter complete with a giant chalkboard hanging behind displaying the menu, added so much character.

Angie approached the glass display case next to the counter that was nearly bursting with a variety of scones, muffins, cookies, tarts, and cupcakes. There were even several different kinds of protein balls.

Angie's stomach growled. It seemed like ages since she had eaten. She could barely make up her mind about what she wanted, because she wanted one of everything.

"How did you get that burn, dear?" A middle aged, heavyset woman with short grey hair stood behind the counter eyeing Angie's shoulders and chest.

"Burn?" Angie pulled her chin into her chest so she could look down at her own shoulders.

It didn't take long for her to see what the woman was talking about. Long streaks of red sunburned patches starting at the middle of her chest and reaching out over her shoulders and down her arms screamed angry red. They were puffed up, inflamed, and in the pattern of tentacles as if she had tried to hug a radioactive octopus and it hugged her back. The thin areas of her movie makeup really had let through too many UV rays for her skin to handle.

"You have anything for sunburn?" the woman asked. She had a way about her that made Angie think she dealt with straggling wanderers on a daily basis. She must be Maggie.

"No, not really. I have some moisturizer."

"Well, after your coffee, you may want to check out the Apothecary. They'll have something that can help."

"I will," Angie was grateful for the suggestion. Coffee shops and apothecaries were two of her favorite places. Carefully, she tilted her tote bag toward Maggie and Fidget popped her calico head out of the bag. "Is it all right if she stays inside with me? She's on a leash."

"Isn't she precious! Of course, dear, we love kitties around here. What's her name?"

"Fidget."

"Nice to meet you, Fidget," Maggie reached over the counter and patted the cat's head. "My name's Maggie." She turned her face to Angie. "And what's your name?"

"Angie," she answered, the tension she had been feeling since the day before began to melt away. She liked Maggie and she liked this little town. "What's the name of this town? I didn't see a sign when we drove in."

"You have entered Polypody Cove, my dear. And we don't have a sign. We like to keep everybody guessing," Maggie chuckled at her own comment. "What can I get you?"

"I'll have a soy vanilla nut latte and a blueberry lemon scone, please."

Angie pulled out her wallet, but was interrupted by a man behind her.

"Allow me," he said, stepping up to her side.

Startled, Angie looked up to tell him 'no, thank you', but she was too surprised to speak. Xavier Patel stood next to her, pulling several bills out of his wallet.

Chapter Nine

Out of his pirate costume, Xave was still a distractingly handsome man. Black wavy hair, high cheekbones and a pleasant smile complete with perfect pearly whites. His large dark eyes behind prescription tortoiseshell frames were just as magnetic as when they had smiled at her over his pirate beard. The glasses, plus a pair of comfortable black shorts and an off white pullover, made Angie think of a school teacher on summer holiday. A super sexy school teacher.

Maggie paused, pleased at his interruption for Angie's sake.

"No, no, you don't need to do that," Angie managed.

"Please, I would like to. Isn't that your pink van in the mechanic's shop? You've probably had a bad morning?"

There was no denying her bad morning. "More like a bad 24 hours" she blurted out.

Concern clouded his smile. "Well, then I insist."

Angie couldn't think of another reason to refuse his kind gesture and she didn't understand her strong urge to do so, so she tried to accept gratefully.

"Won't you join me?" Xave motioned to two comfortable sitting chairs at a low table cluttered with a half empty coffee cup, several pencils and an eraser, and an open script.

"I don't want to bother you."

"It's no bother. I'm just reviewing some lines for today."

It was difficult to deny his invitation, what with his gentle prodding and her desire to have someone else take over decision making, if only for a few minutes. She was tired and everything felt a little off balance. Xave was calm and collected plus he seemed like a genuinely caring person.

"Sure, for a few minutes," she allowed.

He smiled, gallantly picking up her scone and latte and taking them to his table. She followed, barely wrapping her mind around the fact that she was going to have coffee with Xavier Patel, movie star and former voice of Peter Pineapple, the cartoon idol of her childhood.

She sank into the chair, grateful for its softness. The plush fabric was luxurious and one of her favorite colors, turquoise. Tucked away in the front corner of the coffee shop they had a view of the whole place.

"This is so inviting," she said.

He nodded in agreement. "I stumbled upon this place when I went location scouting with Tillie and Brandon. It's a great coffee shop."

"What did she say the town was called?" Angie had already forgotten.

"Polypody Cove. I looked it up. Closest translation from the latin that I can tell would be Fern Cove."

"That's a nice name," she said, taking a sip of her latte and losing herself for a moment in the hot deliciousness. "Do you come here every day?"

He nodded, mid-sip of his own coffee. "It's on the way to set and its pretty quiet." He leaned toward her, sharing a confidence, "And nobody knows who I am."

Angie glanced around the room. Besides her and Xave there was only Maggie behind the counter and two elderly gentlemen seated at separate tables.

Xave watched her scan the room and added, sheepishly, "Not that I'm a huge star or anything."

"I wouldn't say that. You're pretty famous." She turned her attention to her blueberry lemon scone. It was warm, dribbled with lemon icing, and smelled amazing. Her stomach growled again.

She broke off a corner and popped it into her mouth. The buttery, lemony, fruitiness of it was absolute heaven. Relishing the bite in her mouth, she broke off another piece to follow it as soon as she swallowed, forgetting momentarily that Xave was watching. Her mouth stuffed with the second bite, she remembered. Looking up she saw that she still had his full attention.

Xave had a curiously thoughtful look on his face as he watched her chew. Finally he said, "I'm sorry for staring, but have we ever met? I mean before meeting on set?"

Angie nodded, swallowed most of what was in her mouth then took a sip of her latte and swallowed again before she could answer without spewing scone crumbs all over the table.

"Yes, we have. I'm friends with Ian Law. His girlfriend, Sofia, is one of my best friends in the world. You both came to pick us up at the beach in L.A. several months ago. It wasn't a big deal. I'm not surprised you didn't remember."

Recognition lit up his eyes. "Of course, of course, I do remember that." He studied her more closely. " I must have been thrown off by your makeup yesterday."

Makeup. Angie suddenly remembered her conversation with Maggie and the fact that she was covered in an octopus shaped sunburn. She hadn't thought much about her hair or what she was wearing with the tow truck driver. She had been focused on getting Eckhart to a mechanic.

"Would you mind keeping an eye on Fidget while I use the restroom?" Angie asked, holding her tote open and lifting Fidget, fully outfitted in her harness and leash, onto her lap.

"Fidget, you've been hiding all this time?" Xave said, his eyes dancing merrily. He took the leash from Angie. "I'm happy to watch her. We're old friends, now, aren't we Fidget?"

"Thank you." Angie left him talking to the cat and made her way to the restroom.

When she faced her reflection in the mirror she was horrified. Half of her mop of hair had fallen out of the band she had pulled it back with in the early morning, while the other half had remained, making her look like she had just rolled out of bed. Her eyes were bloodshot from lack of sleep and she had picked up some smudges of grease from the garage on her hands and forearms, which had transferred to her cheeks and forehead when she touched her face.

The worst, however, was the octopus sunburn.

Starting just under her collar bones where her heavier mermaid face makeup had shifted to body makeup, tentacles of bright red puffy skin snaked down her chest, shoulder, and arms.

No wonder Xave had felt sorry for her and bought her coffee. She looked like a person experiencing homelessness or someone who had been in a bizarre accident.

There wasn't a lot she could do about the sunburn until she visited the apothecary shop so Angie washed up the best she could in the small bathroom. She carefully applied some of the moisturizer Shivaun had given her onto the burned patches, and used a comb to untangle her hair and pull it back into a proper pony tail.

Studying her reflection one last time she sighed and said, "That's the best it's going to get." With little hope that she would make any other impression than that of a pitiful drifter, she returned to the table.

"You look refreshed," he said, all politeness.

Angie cringed. She knew that she looked like some kind of attack victim in a sci-fi movie, but she gave him the brightest smile she could muster.

"Thank you, but this sunburn I got yesterday is pretty weird looking, don't you think?"

Ignoring her invitation to call her weird looking, Xave's handsome brow bent. He was troubled by her comment. "Are you sure it's a sunburn? Could you be allergic to the makeup?"

Angie shrugged. "I don't know. I don't wear a lot of makeup usually."

"We should check with Shivaun to be sure."

The subject being a little awkward for strangers, Angie simply agreed and let the matter be settled. She took another bite of her yummy scone.

"So, have you gotten a lot of roles since you've been here?" he asked.

"Acting roles? No, this is my first one." She took another bite. Hungry and giving up on any idea of flirting with a gorgeous man after seeing what she looked like, all of her attention diverted to enjoying her scone to the fullest.

After a pause, Xave asked, "Did you move to California to be in movies?"

She took a sip of her latte to wash the scone down, shaking her head. "No."

Xave continued to watch her, not quite computing what she was saying. "But you got a part in this movie?"

She nodded. "Yes."

"But you *don't* want to be an actress?"

"No...but I *have* always wanted to be a mermaid." She shoved the largest piece of scone yet into her mouth, her eyes sparkling with fun.

Xave grinned, amused. He looked down at his plate then

back at her, a twinkle in his eyes. "That's a rather unusual goal."

She grinned back, still chewing. She managed to swallow most of what was in her mouth and said, "I thought so too." Angie raised both of her hands, palms up in the air, as if presenting herself as a prize on a game show. "But look at me now!"

This time Xave laughed out loud. At least her freakish sunburn could be used as fodder for jokes.

"You're doing great, you know, as a mermaid," he said, still chuckling.

"Thank you," she said.

"And having a part of any kind in a film is a big deal...even if you don't actually want to be an actress."

She smiled warmly. That was kind of him to say. He seemed to be a kind man, buying her coffee and saying nice things. Fidget liked him, too.

An alarm went off on his cell phone and Xave turned it off then finished what was left of his coffee in one big gulp.

"I've got to get to set," he explained. "Can I give you a ride?"

"No, thank you. I'm waiting for the mechanic. Besides I don't come back to set until Thursday."

It might have been her imagination, but she swore he looked disappointed. She brushed the thought aside. She was sure she hadn't made that great of an impression.

As she watched him walk down the street to his expensive car, emanating wealth and success with every step, she wondered if actors could be trusted like other people. She wondered if his acting ability made him more difficult to read and if his kindness and warmth was as sincere as it seemed.

Also, she wondered what he would think if he knew she was living in her van.

Chapter Ten

Angie spent the rest of her time in Polypody Cove strolling through the small downtown area and perusing the other stores. There weren't many, but each of them were charming in their own way.

Besides the Firedancer Bar & Grill and Pie's Otta Pizza, which she didn't check out until later in the day for lunch, there was a used book store combination tea shop called Leaves and Pages that captured her attention for a while.

Leaves and Pages was stuffed with books. Shelves and shelves of them filled the shop only receding in the areas that had been set up as reading nooks throughout. She sipped on a delicious cinnamon spice tea while meandering through the book shelves. The past few months, few years if she was honest, she hadn't spent enough time reading.

That was going to change.

Part of the dream of living the van life was not only to see the world, but to have more time to spend doing things like reading. Staying out of the rat race and sinking into a simpler life. That's what she had been looking forward to.

Not that she had necessarily accomplished that goal since

she left Denver. A lot of her time had been spent getting a handle on living in Eckhart. Then she had agreed to be in the movie.

Angie had a pang of regret over that decision. The movie had interrupted what she had been hoping would be a more quiet existence. Then again, she was earning a little money and she got to dress up as a mermaid, not to mention becoming acquainted with Xave. It wasn't all bad. And it was short term. She wouldn't be involved with movie making for the rest of her life.

"Do you like sci-fi or fantasy?" The clerk, a small, slender fellow with quick eyes and perfect hair, asked her.

She had been standing in front of the sci-fi fantasy section for a while, pondering her existence.

"Oh, fantasy for sure," she said assuredly.

His eyes brightened and he reached past her to pull out a book with a deep green cover and beautiful scrolling text in silver. "Have you read this?" He held it up for her to see the title, *Sister Dragon*.

"No, I haven't."

He pushed the book into her hands. "I highly recommend this. It's the first in a series, so if you're a fast reader you'll have plenty more to quench your thirst for a good story."

Such a beautiful cover. And heavy, the book must have been at least 500 pages. It would be nice to have something new to read during the evenings.

"With such a high recommendation, how can I resist?"

Angie purchased *Sister Dragon*, the next book in the series, *Mother Dragon*, and a small book of poetry called *She is Me* by J. Iron Word. Poetry used to be something she read often. That was another habit she wanted to take up again. Imagining long serene days sitting on the beach reading or lounging in the cozy comfort of Eckhart with a good book made her smile. She was almost glad that her battery had died and given her the opportunity to discover Polypody Cove.

Despite her morning's wonderful experiences, the crowning moment of her long wait in the charming little town had to be the Blooming Bee Apothecary Shop.

The scent alone was enough to send her mood soaring.

Candles, incense, handmade soaps and lotions, live plants, dried herbs, oils, stones, crystals, and homeopathic books filled the shop with the same distinct aroma that she had always loved about the metaphysical bookstore. Angie felt right at home the moment she walked in.

There was something even more special about the Apothecary. The shop actually made teas, tinctures, ointments and other treatments for whatever ailed a person. A wall of fat glass jars with metal screw on lids full of the special ingredients for these concoctions graced the space right behind the counter, which was being manned by two identical women.

Angie did a double take when she saw them. They weren't just dressed in the same crisp white shirt tucked into blue jeans and wearing matching deep gold Blooming Bee Apothecary aprons, they matched in every way possible. They were both brunette's with short spunky hair styles, they were both short with boyish figures, they had the same hazel eyes and, she realized, the same face. They were twins.

"Hello," the twins said in unison.

"Hello," she answered, stepping further into the room, drawn in by the positive healing vibration.

"You've been facing some challenges, haven't you?" One of the twins, the one with the name Stacy embroidered onto the bib of her apron, said with a knowing smile.

Taken aback for a second, Angie remembered that most likely everyone in town had seen Eckhart towed into the mechanic's shop early in the morning. They must all know that she had car trouble.

"Well, yes, but all is well. They got the battery for my van so it should be ready soon."

The other twin, Tracy, let out a twitter of a laugh and said, "Your van may be fixed, but there are bigger challenges...yes?" She cocked her head in a move reminiscent of a small bird. Stacy cocked her head the same way. Angie couldn't decide if them moving in unison was weird quirky or funny quirky. It was definitely quirky.

Fidget, who was following Angie on her leash since most of the extra room in her tote was taken up by book purchases, paused and stared at the women. She must have taken notice of the twin's resemblance to the sparrows she liked to watch flit through the air at dusk.

"I–uh–I guess I have been facing some challenges. I just moved here from Colorado, if that counts."

"Of course that counts! Moving is one of the biggest stresses you can go through," Stacy said. She pushed a tall stool out from the counter, inviting Angie to sit down. "Are you interested in any specialized treatments?"

She was. Very interested.

Angie took a seat, a bit relieved. She had been doing a lot of work aligning her chakras, but maybe her life could use a specialized boost.

"We give all of our first time customers 25% off, too," Tracy added, lifting a felt lined tray containing a moon shaped pink stone and rows and rows of small glass vials onto the counter.

Angie studied the vials, which each contained a liquid. There were varying colors between vials. Some were clear while others held different particles of what looked like ash or leaves or tiny pebbles suspended in the liquid.

"Have you ever had muscle testing done?" Tracy asked. Angie had not. "We can narrow down what elements you may need more help with than others with this test. It's quite simple and non-intrusive and it only takes a few minutes."

"All right, I'll try it," Angie agreed.

The twins ushered her to a larger, more comfortable chair set up behind a folding bamboo screen that acted as a room divider. As she settled into the chair, which was set up to lean back, Stacy explained the process.

"We place this disk on your forehead to align your chi. Then we place each of these vials on your chest, one-by-one, and see if it disrupts the flow."

"Okay, how can you tell if it does...disrupt the flow?"

"I keep my hand here," Tracy touched Angie's palm with her two forefingers. "If that's okay with you?" Angie nodded. "That way I can feel any change in your chi, even if you don't feel anything."

"And where should Fidget be while we do this?" The twins looked confused. "My cat's name is Fidget."

"Oh, of course, Fidget can sit in your lap if you like," Stacy said with another twittering laugh.

Settled back in the chair with Fidget sitting curiously in her lap, Angie gave the go head to start muscle testing. The pink disk shaped stone was smooth and cool on her forehead and Tracy's fingers were warm in her palm. Still, Angie wasn't completely sold on the muscle testing process as Stacy methodically picked up one vial at a time, placed it on Angie's chest, looked at Tracy for her response, then removed the vial and went on to the next one.

After the first dozen vials didn't garner any kind of response that Angie could feel, she asked, "Is it working?"

"Yes, you may not feel anything when it does, but I will," Tracy said.

Stacy placed the next vial on Angie's chest and, to her surprise, her scalp started tingling.

"There's one," Tracy said before Angie could tell them what she felt.

"What is it?" Angie asked, intrigued.

"Let's get through all of them and then look at the results," Stacy suggested. "It's better to look at everything as a whole."

Encouraged that something was at least happening, Angie waited patiently while they finished the muscle test. Only three other vials illicited a physical reaction from her body, but each reaction was unique.

One made her nose and throat tickle. One sent a shiver down her arms and gave her goosebumps. And one felt heavy, almost sad, like a sinking feeling in the center of her chest. As if the tiny vial was impossibly heavy.

Back at the counter sitting on a stool, Stacy went over the findings with Angie while Tracy poured them all a cup of tea. The four vials that had caused a reaction were set up in a line in front of them.

"First of all, we need to get you something to help your sunburn heal."

Angie agreed. She had forgotten all about her sunburn as she shopped in Polypody Cove. Everyone had been so welcoming and hadn't mentioned how odd she looked.

Stacy continued, placing her finger on one vial. "This one is connected to skin health, so we need to get you something that will support your skin and help keep you from getting a sunburn in the future." She moved her finger to the next vial. "This one means you are allergic to some of the flowering plants here. And these last two indicate..." Stacy's face fell a little as she searched for the right words. "It indicates that you're not connected the way you want to be. That you may benefit from a little more romance in your life."

Angie was stunned. "They say that?"

Stacy and Tracy both nodded.

"More *romance*? What does that mean exactly?"

The twins smiled, stifling their bird laughter and Angie thought she understood. She peered at the two vials. One had clear amber liquid and one had more of a pinkish tint with little purple flakes floating around in it.

"How can you tell?" she asked.

"This one is connection, community, that kind of thing. And this one," she picked up the pink vial. "This one affects your sexual energy, which, when it's not flowing properly, and combined with this one," she picked up the amber vial, "Usually means romantic connection."

"Sex?" Angie blurted out.

The twins twittered.

"Not just sex, but a healthy sex life, which would mean romance, yes?" Stacy asked.

"I suppose so." Angie thought about the heavy sinking in her chest during the muscle test and felt a pang of sadness. It had been months since she had been on any kind of date and years since she had a significant other. She hadn't been focused on her relationship status since she got laid off and decided to move. Could these two ladies really feel evidence of loneliness in her chi?

"Don't worry, we can help you with all of this," Tracy said.

"You can make a tea that will improve my romantic life?"

"Well, not a tea, it's a tincture. And I think we should do the aromatherapy as well, don't you agree, Tracy?"

"Oh, yes," Tracy did agree. She smiled broadly at Angie. "We'll get you a combo that will work."

"Something like a love potion?" Angie asked, half serious and half joking.

"Something like that."

Wind chimes tingled as the front door to the Apothecary opened. With the sound came a warm breeze from outside, carrying the smell of musk and spices. The familiar scent drew her attention immediately and she turned to see who had opened the door.

"Excuse me," Xave said to the twins as he took off his sunglasses. Seeing her, he stopped in his tracks, his eyebrows lifted in surprise. "You're still here?"

Angie tried not to be affronted by the words he chose. Heat filled her cheeks and she could only imagine that her octopus sunburn was flaming red.

"My van should be ready any minute now," Angie explained, a little on the defense, not sure why she felt the need to explain anything.

"Good afternoon, Xave," Stacy and Tracy said in unison. He must be a regular, which may have explained the look the twins exchanged when he slightly fumbled his entrance after seeing Angie.

"Good afternoon," Xave joined them at the counter, his eyes still on Angie. "Is everything all right? I didn't realize you would be stuck here all day or I could have seen if one of the crew could have driven you home."

Flustered under his gaze and still blushing furiously over being discovered in the middle of discussing her non-existent love life, Angie didn't feel like explaining that her van was her home.

"Oh, it's not a big deal. I've been enjoying myself."

Fidget recognized Xave and wrapped around his foot, purring.

"Good afternoon, Fidget. You're an adventure cat, aren't you?" Xave said in that high pitched tone people reserve for pets and babies.

He wore the same clothes he had left in this morning, except they were slightly rumpled. Probably because they had been folded up while he donned his pirate costume and were now on their second wearing of the day. Xave looked a little disheveled, too. Not as bright eyed and refreshed as he had been over coffee at the Vanilla Bean.

"We'll get your items put together for you," Tracy said to Angie before sweeping the tiny vials up in one hand and leading Stacy to the far end of the back counter.

"Thank you," Angie said, smiling after them before turning back toward Xave and wondering what she should try to talk about while she waited.

"We'll be right back to help you, Xave," Stacy called over her shoulder.

"No problem, I'm in no hurry," Xave replied.

He looked back at Angie and smiled politely. Should she ask him what he was picking up? Maybe that would be as embarrassing as him asking her what treatment they were putting together for her.

Oh, just a little something to try to fix someone who has zero sex life and is utterly alone.

No, that wouldn't work. She needed to think of something more benign. Chatting at the Apothecary was a lot like chatting at the pharmacy. There was an ever present danger of becoming too intimate with someone's seriously personal issues.

Xave seemed as much at a loss for words as she was. He reached down and patted Fidget then straightened and smiled awkwardly at Angie, averting his eyes to the counter top to check out the display of bite sized dark chocolate bars.

"You got done early today?" Angie asked, finally landing on something neutral.

"Yes, wrapped for the day. They're getting Elizabeth's close ups...which are taking a long time." Something like annoyance creeped into his voice, but he didn't say anything further.

Jealousy pricked her as she thought about Xave wishing Elizabeth could also be wrapped for the day. Maybe they had plans. Maybe they were a couple. Lots of famous actors and actresses had romances when they made movies together, didn't they?

She shook her head to knock the outrageous envy out of her thoughts. Xavier Patel could date whoever he wanted. It was no business of hers.

An awkward silence fell over them as Angie wrestled back thoughts about Xave's love life and he fiddled with his sunglasses.

Stacy, or Tracy, Angie couldn't tell which, called out to her from the end of the counter, "Almost done with your–" Angie shot her a look and the twin rethought what she was about to say. "…your *items*."

"Thank you," Angie said sweetly and picked up her tote. As she was rummaging for her wallet wondering why she always lost her wallet in her tote whenever she was in a hurry to leave, her cell phone rang from its depths. Smiling apologetically at Xave, who was watching her with interest, she grabbed the phone and answered, "Hello?"

"Yeah, this is Skeet down at the mechanic shop," the man on the other end said. His name really was Skeet.

"Yes?" Angie held her smile, hoping she sounded poised as she listened to news on her van.

"Your van's all ready to go. Battery's in and everything's running good."

"Oh, excellent," she said, though her words didn't quite sound like her own. "I'll be right over to pick him up–I mean *it* up." She hung up and caught Xave's eye, beaming at him with what felt like too much bright energy. "Everything's fixed. I can go home now."

"Good, I'm glad it all worked out," he said, an amused smile in his eyes.

"Yes, I'll just pay for my things and be off." Angie stood and led Fidget to the cash register where the twins were packing her items into a small brown bag. She didn't know why, but she seemed to be channeling the haughtiness of a celebrity shopping on Rodeo Drive.

She blamed Xave's presence. He made her nervous, which caused her to say and do weird things.

Stacy put a jar of ointment, a small glass bottle of tincture and another of essential oils, plus a bag of herbal tea into the bag. She held up a piece of notebook paper with handwriting on it so Angie could see it before stuffing it into the bag. "We wrote down all of the instructions for you. If you have any questions you can pop back by or give us a call any time."

"Wonderful, perfect, thank you so very much," Angie said, not caring what she sounded like anymore, just wanting to leave. She paid for her items and took her bag then turned to walk past Xave. "Lovely to see you again," she said, wincing at her choice of words.

Xave, who had put his sunglasses back on while he waited, dropped them down his nose and looked at her over the top of them, accentuating his dreamy dark eyes.

"You too, see you in a few days?" he said.

Angie nodded quickly and hurried out the door with Fidget on her heels. Just as she stepped outside she swore she heard one of the twins let out a bird-like giggle.

Chapter Eleven

"And you're doing fine with only this much room?" Sofia's face was pinched with concern as she stuck her head inside of Eckhart's tiny living space.

She and Ian had come by the campground for a visit and they had all spent a pleasant time sitting underneath the shade of the awning that was fixed to the van. Ian had settled right in, enjoying the outdoors and the folding lawn chair. Sofia had not seemed as comfortable.

"I really am," Angie reassured her. "I mean, how much space does one person actually take up inside of a normal house? You know?"

"Not much," Ian agreed, taking a sip of his ice cold bottle of beer.

Sofia was reluctant to agree. She and Ian had rented a spacious beach house in Los Angeles while Ian worked on the score for the indie film and travelled around to concerts across the US. Angie could have parked Eckhart inside of the modern style kitchen with room to spare, not to mention the vast living room, four bedrooms, and on and on. The place was sleek and top end, not anything like her little VW van.

"I don't expect everyone would enjoy this lifestyle," Angie said with a wistful look at Eckhart's shining pink and chrome exterior. "But I've been having fun with it...except for the mechanical issues."

Sofia cringed at the thought. "That must have been a nightmare."

Angie shrugged. She hadn't told them about Xave buying her breakfast or the love potion Tracy and Stacy had created. "Oh, I don't know, I spent some time in the town and met some of the locals. It wasn't horrible."

"Well, you're braver than I am, Angie," Sofia admitted. "I don't think I could be this loose and free with my lodgings."

Ian pretended to be shocked. "You don't say. That is a revelation of sorts, isn't it?" He looked to Angie for her agreement as he stood up and swept his arm around Sofia's waist, breaking her focus on Angie's alternative living arrangements and making her laugh.

Angie had to laugh, too. She raised her own bottle of beer to the two of them in a toast. "To van life!" She said, knowing that Sofia would always be worried about her tendency to live outside of society's norms. That was just how Sofia was.

"To van life!" Ian responded, pulling Sofia closer to him until she repeated the toast. Satisfied, he turned his attention back to Angie. "And how are you liking the actor life?"

A flutter of butterflies lifted in her stomach and she took another swig of beer to settle them down. The thought of returning to the set the next day had been pressing at the back of her mind. She had not yet taken the herbal tincture that the twins had said would help improve her love life and she wasn't sure why.

Normally she was pretty bold about alternative medicine, but this time her heart was full of apprehension.

She knew it had something to do with Xave. Whenever she thought of the love potion she thought of him and vice versa. Then she felt silly for thinking of someone like him, a huge movie star, in a romantic way. He must have women throwing themselves at his feet all the time. She didn't know if she wanted to be part of that kind of frenzy.

"Don't you like being in the movie?" Sofia asked, her face pinching with concern again.

"Oh no, that's not it," Angie said quickly, realizing she had drifted off into her own thoughts instead of answering Ian's question. "I like it just fine. It's interesting. Not really what I expected, but then I didn't know what to expect."

"Grueling, isn't it?" Ian asked. "I've done my bit of work on music videos. Long days, lots of waiting around."

"I thought you liked it," Sofia said.

Ian nodded whole heartedly. "I do, I do, but it's like Angie says. Not what you expect. Still, it's a great feeling of accomplishment when it's done. Wouldn't you agree?" He looked to Angie again for her opinion.

"Yes, it is. I think maybe it's because when you're in the middle of it all you kind of lose yourself and become part of the whole team. All trying to get the shot."

"Do you really feel like you're a mermaid?" Sofia asked, only half teasing.

Angie grinned. "Not completely, but it is fun to pretend."

Later, after Sofia and Ian had left to spend the night at their hotel, Angie took Fidget to the beach to watch the sun go down. She stuck the small bottle of herbal tincture in her pocket and took it as well.

Strolling in the space where the waves exhausted themselves before pulling back into the ocean, she enjoyed the sensation of wet sand shifting under her bare feet. Incoming waves washed across her toes and a cool breeze fluttered the cloth of her skirts. Fidget kept her distance from the water, preferring to investigate seashells and bits of kelp in the dry sand as she walked alongside Angie.

The sun dipped lower on the horizon, brightening the blue in the sky, tinging the clouds pink and orange, and intensifying everything with color.

That's how she felt. Intensified.

Ever since she had left the apothecary her whole body seemed on high alert. She hadn't slept soundly, waking whenever Fidget switched positions or the breeze moved through her wind chimes sending mellow notes through the night air. Her visit with Sofia and Ian had been fun, but her mind kept wandering to Xave in his sunglasses watching her leave the apothecary with the love potion. The same love potion that was burning a hole in her skirt pocket.

Angie stopped walking and turned toward the setting sun, letting the ocean breeze push her long hair back from her face and taking a deep breath. She reached into her pocket and wrapped her fingers around the small glass bottle. A tingle swept up her hand, moved into her arm and shoulder and sent a shiver through her neck.

She pulled the bottle out. Not one to question the reality of the metaphysical, Angie looked down at the bottle with curiosity.

Was this tincture actually powerful enough to put her into a physical tizzy? Or did she merely *want* it to be that powerful? She thought back to meeting Xave the first time on the beach when Ian introduced them. Her feelings had been conflicted then. Just as they were now.

He seemed to be a nice man. Definitely good looking. But she wasn't sure she wanted to be involved with someone so...so wholly different than she was.

Besides, she had never tried to alter the feelings of another person with tinctures or energy shifting or anything like that. Her practices had only ever focused on turning inward for peace and harmony or bringing peace and health to people she loved.

She glanced back down at the bottle in her hand, which seemed to be growing heavier and heavier with each passing moment. The twin's instructions had said to focus on finding a love connection or focus on the person she was romantically interested in then drink the tincture. All at once.

Angie stepped away from the water and sat down in the sand facing the sunset. The undulating waves that normally soothed her soul were carrying something else today. Melancholy, centuries old, perhaps longer, pushed into her chest. For the first time she could remember, oneness with nature didn't feel like enough to make her happy.

Her throat tightened with emotion and she had to blink back tears as she suddenly understood.

She was lonely.

It was true. Tracy and Stacy had sensed something in her that she hadn't been willing to admit to herself.

She had moved to the Pacific so she could be near the ocean and live in a place that she loved. Now that she was here the fact that she didn't have a partner to share it with was coming to the surface.

Fidget mewed and put her front paws on Angie's leg, peering at her face in the pink light that reflected off of the clouds.

"Don't worry. I'm fine," Angie reassured the cat. She stroked her soft head, sniffling from her moody tears.

A particularly large wave swept onto the shore, reaching all the way to where she sat and splashing both her and Fidget with water. Fidget leaped into the air with a jolt and ran behind her back, making her laugh.

"Okay, okay," Angie said out loud to the cat and the persistent ocean. "I'll try it." She lifted the bottle up in front of her so the sunset could shine through the liquid inside. "It can't hurt, right?"

Neither Fidget nor the ocean answered, but Angie didn't

need them to, she had already decided. She would take the tincture in the general sense without focusing on Xavier Patel at all. That would invite romance into her life without trying to manipulate the feelings of another person. She felt good about that.

She took a few deep breaths and concentrated on the wide world around her, asking to find a romantic connection with the soul she was most compatible with. When she was fully centered, Angie took the lid off the bottle and raised it to her lips, closing her eyes as she did.

Just as she tipped the bottle up and poured all of its contents into her mouth an image of Xave in his pirate costume flashed through her mind. Bold and gorgeous, his impressive black beard, his deep dark eyes burning with desire.

Angie's eyes flew open, but it was too late, she had emptied the tincture into her mouth. She had no choice. She had to swallow the love potion with Xave fully on her mind.

Chapter Twelve

Nothing was exactly normal the next morning on set. The day began cool and misty, not the sunshine they had all grown used to. Too cold for the mermaid extras to sit in the water in the background as they shot Elizabeth's mermaid scenes. Angie and her co-mermaids had only gotten their hair and makeup on before the schedule was rearranged due to the weather. They were told to take a break at the craft services picnic tables.

Angie wished she had a copy of the script so she could keep up on what was happening. Most of the scenes she had been part of were meaningless because she didn't understand the story as a whole. So far her request for a script hadn't been fulfilled and it felt pushy to keep asking. Tillie and Brandon had their hands full with directing, she could see that much from afar.

"Tell us more about when you met Xavier Patel, we're dying to know the details," Kristina said.

Bundled up in a fuzzy grey and pink sweatsuit with her blonde mermaid hair and wild mermaid makeup, she sipped a hazelnut latte provided by craft services and blinked innocent blue eyes at Angie.

Angie, also bundled up against the cool wet weather in a pair of worn jeans and a dark purple hoodie, was a little surprised at the question.

"Which time do you mean?"

Kristina's eyebrows lifted in mock astonishment, gaping her mouth open at Marissa then back at Angie. "How many times have you met him? You must run in some big time circles!"

Angie ignored her sarcasm. She tried to give people the benefit of the doubt, not let their negativity get to her, but this morning Kristina was a little hard to take. Angie's nerves were already flitting back and forth in her stomach. She hadn't slept well and she was waiting to see Xave on set, concerned that she had somehow involved herself with him on an unseen level by thinking of him when she drank her love potion. She wondered if anything between them would change.

Kristina mentioning him brought all of that uneasiness to the surface.

"It hasn't been that many times," she answered. "And I don't run in any kind of big time circles."

"Angie, there you are!" Ian called out from the other side of the craft services breakfast table, which was surrounded by other cast and crew members. He held a cup of coffee in one hand and a danish in the other. He pointed the danish at Angie. "Don't move, I'm coming over!"

Kristina and Marissa both looked genuinely astonished this time.

Ian, heavily tattooed, spiked red hair, and golden eyes, was a striking sight to be sure. He sometimes illicited surprised reactions even when people didn't know about his rock star status. She couldn't be sure her co-mermaids were impressed with that or merely his unusual good looks.

"I didn't recognize you with all of your incredible make-up," Ian said as he arrived on their side of the break area and pulled a chair up next to Angie. "Then I got a look at your hair and thought it must be you." He studied her face for a few long moments. "My God, you look positively ethereal."

"Do I?"

Ian nodded sincerely then turned a scrutinizing eye at Kristina and Marissa. "And are these lovely ladies also mermaids?"

"Yes, this is Kristina and Marissa," Angie gestured to each of them. "And this is Ian Law."

Marissa's previous astonishment erupted into elation. "Ian Law, from The Tellers!?"

Ian dipped his head in a quick nod. "That would be me."

"Oh my God! I love your music!" Marissa, who up to that point had presented a fairly mild personality, was completely overcome with Ian's presence.

"Thank you, I appreciate that," Ian said.

"Are you in the movie?" Kristina asked him, just as impressed by Ian, though keeping her enthusiasm under control.

"I'm writing the score for it, mainly. But today I'm stepping in as an extra to help Tillie and Brandon out."

"Really?" Kristina seemed surprised that someone would volunteer for a lowly extra position when they were already part of the larger movie making team. Marissa didn't say anything, instead releasing an embarrassingly loud giggle.

"Where's Sofia?" Angie asked.

"She's around here somewhere. One of the assistant producers was having some problem with their laptop." He smiled with pride. "My girlfriend's a genius."

Kristina and Marissa took in the mention of a girlfriend with varying degrees of dismay. Marissa's face fell, but she remained silent. Kristina seemed less bothered, but still probed for more information.

"So you're friends with Tillie and Brandon?" Kristina asked.

Ian had taken a bite of his danish and nodded as he chewed.

"And you know his girlfriend, too?" Kristina asked Angie.

Angie couldn't help but feel like Kristina was keeping an overabundance of data on her and everyone else on set. Perhaps that was necessary when one was an aspiring actress.

"There she is," Ian half stood and waved his long arm until Sofia, who was moving carefully behind the lights set up for the next scene, saw him and waved back. Ian sat down in his seat again. "I'm glad she's done with that. I don't want her to miss the ship."

"The ship?" Angie asked.

"Oh, they haven't told you?" Ian scanned all of their faces and saw only blank stares. "You're in for a real treat today, mermaids. They're bringing the pirate ship into the cove. They're not just building out a set over the water, it's an honest to goodness ship."

The restless nerves in Angie's stomach rose up and sent new shivers through her abdomen and up into her chest.

"Pirate ship?" she asked weakly.

"Angie, you look amazing!" Sofia exclaimed as she joined Ian. "You really do look like a mermaid." She pulled her camera out of her pocket and aimed it at Angie.

"We're not supposed to do that," Kristina said.

Sofia paused. "Take pictures?"

"Share details of the movie, like makeup and costumes, on social media. They want to keep everything under wraps until it screens," Kristina continued with her instructions.

"Oh, well I won't share this. I just want to document it,"

Sofia responded, pretty much ignoring Kristina's abrupt interruption.

Angie made her best mermaid face for Sofia, taking note of how irritated Kristina was. Funny for someone who broke some rules without any thought whatsoever to suddenly be quoting rules to others. Angie was sure Kristina didn't do it to be helpful either. She was actually jockeying for position.

A murmur moved through the crew nearby and all eyes turned to activity on the shoreline.

"I bet it's here," Ian said excitedly. He hopped up, popped the rest of his danish into his mouth and took Sofia by the elbow, jerking his head in the direction of the commotion indicating they should all join him.

The arrival of the pirate ship was as epic as Ian had hoped it would be. Everyone gathered on the beach to watch while Adam spoke on his cell phone with whoever was onboard.

The cove where they were filming was not large, but still large enough to accommodate a fair sized sailing ship. The gloomy weather added suspense to its arrival by obstructing their view. Angie understood why it was exciting for everyone to watch the bow of an ancient looking pirate ship appear out of the mist and sail into the cove, but her excitement was over the top.

That she didn't understand at all.

It wasn't like she was an avid sailor. She loved the water, but growing up in Colorado meant she had never been around boats much in her life. As she waited with the others her nervous energy billowed from her core through her whole body and out her skin, giving her goosebumps. Her heart pounded with anticipation. So much so that she found it difficult to take deep breaths.

She moved slowly away from the others and took up a position on a small outcropping of rocks, away from the main group. For some reason she wanted to experience the arrival of the ship alone.

A long pole jutting sideways emerged from the heavy mist on the other side of the large black rocks on the north side of the cove. The pole grew longer and longer until she could see that it was attached to something bulkier. Then the bow of the ship appeared, dark and ominous, a large figurehead carved into its front.

Angie peered at the figurehead, trying to make out the details from her vantage point. As the ship creeped closer, the body and head became clearer and clearer, until the true form of the mythical being carved onto the bow showed itself.

Angie gasped.

It was a mermaid.

A beautiful mermaid made to look as if she was writhing in ecstasy at the front, just where the ship met the water, just underneath the boots of its captain.

Suddenly the whole ship broke out of its foggy tomb. Gliding into the cove so smoothly it seemed like a dream. White sails fluttering high above the wooden hull. Crew dressed as pirates shouting and waving at the beach.

Still not breathing, Angie's eyes were wide as they connected with the dark glittering gaze of the Captain.

Xave.

Chapter Thirteen

X ave was a sight to behold. He made a stunning pirate with his long black beard and a huge Captain's hat, his loose white shirt cinched in with a wide leather belt over black pants and high boots. She knew all of this since she had already seen him in his pirate costume.

But she had never seen him like this.

He stood powerfully on the bow of the ship, wind blowing through his luscious locks, commanding a whole crew of pirates who were busy on the deck doing whatever a pirate crew does. Angie knew the whole thing was staged for the movie, but it looked so real. He looked so real.

And more than that. He was looking directly at her.

During the scenes she had been in with Xave up to this point, his attention had always been on his co-star, Elizabeth.

Not so today.

Angie felt his eyes locked onto her, pushing into her very soul. Even as far in the distance as he was she was absolutely certain Xave's deep brown gorgeous eyes had not strayed from her since the ship entered the cove.

Indescribable pleasure shot out of her heart and filled her

chest, slipping down into her belly and below. Warm and sweet. Intoxicating.

Angie gasped for air. She had stopped breathing for a long moment. Caught up in the strange connection she felt between her and Xave, the Pirate Captain, as he approached.

Legs weak and light headed, there was nowhere to sit down and nothing to hold onto out on the rocks where she stood alone.

She felt her body sway. Somebody nearby shouted. Her vision darkened. The only part of her view remaining strong and full of light was Xave standing on the ship.

One thought crossed her mind right before she slipped into unconsciousness...*the love potion was too strong*.

Waking up with Tillie, Brandon, Adam, Sofia and Ian hovering over, Angie was too groggy to speak. She was laying on her back looking up at all of their faces with nothing but sky beyond.

"Angie, Angie can you hear me?" Adam asked.

She could hear him, but she couldn't respond.

"We need to call an ambulance," Sofia said.

Angie managed to shake her head slightly in an attempt to say 'no'.

"I think she's coming round," Ian said hopefully.

Suddenly, Xave's face popped into her view. Still in his Pirate Captain hat, his dark eyes full of concern. "Is she okay? What happened?"

The sight of him sent a zing of energy into her heart that was so fast and strong she sucked in her breath and sat straight up.

"I'm fine, I'm fine," she tried to reassure the others as they all took a step back. All except Sofia and Xave. Angie pushed on the rock beneath her, trying to stand up.

"Take it easy," Sofia said.

"What happened?" Angie asked, trying to include everyone in her question, but unable to draw her eyes away from Xave.

"You fainted," she heard Adam say.

Xave's concern deepened. "Please don't stand up, Angie. Rest here until you feel better."

His voice was so soothing and when he said her name it was like glitter exploded between them and all she could see were sparkles and light.

Xave sat down carefully next to her and took her hand in his. "I'll sit and wait with you."

"Okay," Angie said meekly. She resisted the urge to put her head on his shoulder, but only because she had on her mermaid makeup and didn't want it to rub off on his pirate costume.

"Can we get some water over here?" Adam called out to one of the production assistants.

"Angie do you have any medical conditions that would make you faint?" Tillie asked.

Angie shook her head dreamily, still intoxicated by Xave's presence. He smelled like salt and sand and leather and the scent was making her dizzy all over again.

"Angie," Sofia knelt down so she could look her directly in the eye. "Did you eat breakfast?"

Angie blinked. "I don't remember."

"How about anything from crafty?" Xave asked.

"I don't remember," was all she could say as she stared into his eyes.

Xave smiled at her, the corners of his eyes crinkling into the impossibly attractive expression someone got when they really liked who they were looking at. He must really like her.

"Would you like a sandwich?" he asked gently.

"Yes, please," she said.

"Vegetarian?" he asked.

She nodded and smiled coyly.

"Can we get a veggie sandwich over here with plenty of cheese, please?" Sofia called out. She seemed baffled at the interaction Angie was having with Xave, but glad to have a plan on how to handle the situation.

"Do you want anything to eat?" Angie asked Xave sweetly.

Xave chuckled, keeping his eyes trained on hers. "Not right now, thank you. Let's get some food into you first."

After she ate her sandwich Angie's mind cleared. Xave sat next to her the whole time, making sure she drank some water and felt better before he got up and offered her his hand to help her stand.

She felt strong enough to move from the rock at that point, but totally embarrassed that she had caused such a commotion. Once everyone knew the crisis had been averted they had pretty much gone on with their work, but Xave had stayed with her, Sofia, and Ian on the rock.

Basically she had monopolized the star's time once again. She was never going to hear the end of it from Kristina.

More than that was bothering Angie, however, as she and Sofia made their way to the costume trailer. Sofia had insisted on accompanying her, and both Ian and Xave were needed on other areas of the set.

"What was that all about?" Sofia asked when they were finally alone.

"What?"

Sofia looked at her, dumbfounded. "All of *that!*" She pointed behind them in the general direction of the rock where she had fainted and Xave had come to her rescue. "The fainting. The drama. The puppy dog eyes."

"Puppy dog eyes?"

"Yes! You being all ditzy and meek and making puppy dog eyes at Xave."

Angie was incensed. "I didn't make *puppy dog eyes* at him."

"Yes you did," Sofia insisted. "Or maybe you were making gooey mermaid eyes at him. Whatever you want to call it."

"Gooey mermaid eyes?"

"Yes! After you fainted. What was that all about?"

"Me fainting?"

"All of it," Sofia stopped walking, forcing Angie to stop in order to keep talking to her. "You've been acting really weird all day. And then you fainted. And then..." she flapped her hand in front of Angie's face. "You were all gooey eyed. You're acting really, really weird."

Angie felt all of the color drain from her face. "Oh no..."

"Oh no, what?"

Angie knew in her gut what had happened. She had felt different all day and her reaction to seeing Xave on the ship had been way over the top. Deep down she understood why, but she also knew Sofia, being the sensible logical numbers type, would poo-poo her suspicions.

Angie bit at her lip and looked back at the rock, the scene of her gooey melt down. "I'm not sure..."

"You are sure, you just don't want to tell me."

"I don't think you're going to believe me."

Hurt, Sofia argued, "Of course I'll believe you."

Torn, Angie hesitated. If what she suspected was true she was going to need some help figuring out how to handle it.

With a mounting sense that she had gotten herself in over her head, Angie decided to confide in Sofia.

She leaned in, her voice low so nobody nearby could overhear, "I think it's the love potion."

Chapter Fourteen

"What?" Sofia asked, her dark green eyes clouding darker with confusion.

Angie was worried now, afraid she had ingested something truly powerful that could interrupt the natural flow of her life. "I took a love potion last night," she tried to explain.

"A *love potion*?" Sofia stared at her, incredulous. "What in the world are you talking about?"

Angie glanced around nervously. Whenever Sofia got riled up her voice carried and the last thing Angie wanted was for everyone to find out about the love potion and think she had tried to trick Xave.

"Yes," she whispered hotly. "A love potion. I took it as kind of a general thing, but I think I accidentally attached it to Xave."

Sofia stared at her for a few long moments before responding. "There are no such things as love potions, Angie."

Angie snorted a laugh. "I beg to differ. Didn't you see me faint?"

"Anybody can faint for a thousand different reasons. That's not proof!"

"I don't faint. And how do you explain my gooey eyes, as you called them?"

"Maybe you have a crush on Xave. You wouldn't be the first, I'm sure. Maybe you haven't eaten enough protein today. Maybe you've been living alone in your van for too long. I don't know what happened. But I do know what *didn't* happen. You didn't take some kind of magical love potion, because there's no such thing as magical love potions."

Angie glared at Sofia. Sofia didn't understand. She would never understand because Sofia didn't want to understand anything beyond what she could prove with math or science.

"Well, I know what I felt," Angie said, turning back toward the costume trailer.

"Of course you felt something," Sofia said, falling in step beside her. "If you drank some concoction and you didn't know what was in it you could have felt a lot of things. That's probably why you fainted. Where did you get this...this *potion*?"

"From an apothecary," Angie answered, knowing Sofia would not be satisfied with that answer.

Sofia scoffed. "Apothecary? What was it, an herbal remedy store? They could have put anything in it! Do you have it on you?"

"Why, so you can have the bottle analyzed?" Angie was losing patience with Sofia's disbelief.

"We should look at the ingredients and see what's in it," Sofia said, a little less argumentative.

"I don't want to talk about it right now. I have to get into costume." Angie wished she hadn't brought up the love potion at all. She knew how she had felt on the rock and she knew there could be no other explanation for the way Xave had come to sit by her side and help her after she fainted. He was also under the influence of something that none of them could understand. Not even Sofia with her science brain.

Sofia walked quietly next to her until they were at the steps leading up to the door. "Angie, wait," Sofia grabbed her arm gently. "I didn't mean to make you mad. I'm just worried about you."

Angie paused, trying to think of a way she could take it all back so Sofia wouldn't know anything about the potion. She didn't want to worry her, but she also didn't want to listen to all the reasons she shouldn't believe in what she believed in either.

"Angie, can we talk to you a minute?" Tillie called out to her as she, Brandon and, to her surprise, Xave joined them at the steps of the costume trailer.

"Sure." Angie glanced at Sofia, suddenly anxious.

"We want to ask you something," Brandon added, speaking up in a manner uncustomary to him.

"Oh?" Angie focused all of her energy on not staring into Xave's eyes. Why was he with the sibling directors? Were they going to fire her because of her fainting spell?

"How would you like to be the star mermaid?" Tillie asked with an encouraging smile.

"The...star mermaid?" This was so far from what she had been thinking, Angie couldn't quite take it in.

"We want to take some of the load off of Elizabeth so she can focus on the main role," Tillie explained.

"Elizabeth?" Angie asked weakly. Even though she wasn't looking at Xave she could see his pirate form just to the right of Tillie. And she could smell his leathery salt watery scent.

"And we haven't shot any of the scenes between Xave and the mermaid he falls in love with yet, which Elizabeth was going to play," Tillie kept explaining.

"We think you two have great chemistry," Brandon added, waving his finger between Angie and Xave.

Angie's knees wobbled. She shot a panicked look at Sofia.

"If you agree, we'll do a little rewriting so it works in the story," Tillie said.

"The story…" Angie had never had a firm grasp on what the story of the film was, so she didn't know if it would make sense for her to be Xave's mermaid love interest or not. She did know the idea of it made her feel like a balloon tethered to the ground by a single thin string.

"Will she have lines?" Sofia stepped forward, instinctively understanding that Angie was having a difficult time processing their request and needed management.

"No, the mermaid doesn't ever speak. She'll have a lot more scenes, though. One-on-one scenes with Xave mostly," Tillie answered.

The thin string broke and Angie the balloon lifted upward.

"And you'll get paid more," Brandon mentioned.

As if money was Angie's motivation for anything. She almost laughed, but Sofia took naturally to her self-appointed role as Angie's talent agent.

"How much more?" Sofia asked.

"Three hundred a day," Brandon answered.

Sofia looked at Angie, impressed with the proposed increase in her pay, but Angie didn't respond. She was floating above them, all sounds of the conversation muted and far away.

"I think you'd be brilliant," Xave said.

The tone of his voice, deep and pure, penetrated her flighty thoughts and suddenly she was back on the ground looking into his shining eyes.

"You do?" she asked.

Xave moved forward and took her hand, sending electric jolts through her fingers, up her arm and into her heart.

"You're a very convincing mermaid."

She murmured something, but her lips weren't forming words properly and it came out sounding a little like 'arp'.

Xave chuckled. "What was that?"

"Nothing, that was nothing." Sofia stepped in between them and put her arm around Angie's waist, turning her back toward the steps leading into the costume trailer. "She's going to think about it, aren't you Angie?"

Angie nodded, still staring feebly into Xave's eyes. "Yes, thinking..." Her words faded away.

"She'll let you know this afternoon," Sofia said with finality.

"Great, thanks," Tillie answered and led Brandon and Xave away.

"What is the matter with you?" Sofia hissed as she helped Angie up the steps.

"I told you, it's the love potion."

"That's ridiculous," Sofia denied the obvious explanation. "We'll get you some coffee and some more to eat and then you need to decide if you want to take their offer." She paused and stared firmly at Angie. "They're offering you a lot more money, Ang. You could use more money, couldn't you?"

"Oh, yes," Angie giggled, the delightful floating feeling still overwhelming her system. "Money is fun."

Sofia sighed. "It's more than fun, it's necessary to survive. And maybe if you took this job you could find a cute apartment out here instead of living in your car."

"Eckhart is a van, not a car."

"Okay, maybe you could find a cute apartment instead of living in your *van*," Sofia answered. "But first you're going to have to figure out how to be around Xave without completely falling apart."

Chapter Fifteen

"GiGi!" Bridget's unmistakeable greeting rang through the air, piercing the early morning silence of the campground.

Angie sat straight up from a sound sleep, frightening Fidget who had been curled up against her side.

"Wha–?" she mumbled groggily. For a moment she thought she might have been dreaming.

"GiGi!" Bridget again, this time accompanied by a knocking on Eckhart's sliding side door.

No. She wasn't dreaming.

"You're waking up the whole campsite, Bridge," Thomas' voice, more hushed, but still clear enough for Angie to hear, sounded through the van's wall.

"Are you sure she's actually here? Not just parked here?" Bridget asked impatiently.

Angie stood up and unlocked the van door, sliding it aside to find Bridget and Thomas standing outside.

"Oh!" Bridget exclaimed, taking in Angie's pajamas and wild hair before looking past her at Eckhart's indoor living space. "You are in there!"

"I am," Angie answered with a sleepy smile. She stepped out of Eckhart and gave them each a big hug. "What are you guys doing here?"

"We had a long layover and thought we'd drive up and see how you're getting along," Thomas answered. "How's the van holding up?" He poked his head inside.

"Great, it's really great," Angie answered. "You can go in and poke around if you want."

Thomas did just that, but Bridget stayed outside trying to coax Fidget over to her after scaring her awake. "Come here kitty. How's my little Fidget?"

"How did you know where to find me?" Angie asked, setting up the outdoor folding chairs for them to use.

"Sofia told us how to get here," Bridget stated.

Angie suddenly remembered that Sofia and Ian had gone to L.A. for the day. Sofia had filled her in on their plans after joining her for a quick meeting to let let Tillie and Brandon know she was accepting the role of the star mermaid. She had been a little over the top protective during the conversation, but Angie knew she was just trying to look out for her best interests.

"She gave us super explicit directions," Bridget said, giving Angie a look that said everything anyone needed to know about Sofia's explicit directions.

"Yeah," Thomas poked his head out of Eckhart. "They were detailed."

"Have a seat. How long is your layover? Do you have time for coffee?" Angie asked.

"There's always time for coffee," Thomas took the seat next to Bridget under Eckhart's awning. He stretched and yawned, looking at the trees surrounding the campsite. "It's nice up here."

Angie busied herself making coffee on her small stove. "We can walk to the ocean if you have time." She had known about their plans to go to Scotland to be with Tawnyetta and Michael for the birth, but had forgotten exactly when that was happening.

"That would be nice," Bridget said. She picked Fidget up and held her in her lap. "We have time for that, don't we, Mister?"

Thomas grunted his agreement.

Angie was struck at how similar Thomas and Bridget's relationship was to Ian and Sofia's. Except Thomas and Bridget weren't a couple, just old friends.

"Sofia's worried about you." Bridget leveled her baby blues onto Angie with unexpected brevity.

"She is? Why?" As soon as she asked the question, Angie remembered why. "Is that why you guys are here?"

"No," they both answered at the same time then shared a guilty look.

"We were going to come see you anyway," Thomas explained. "After Sofia called us we just made sure to, that's all."

Angie didn't know if she was touched or angry at the fact that her friends were talking about her behind her back. She shook her head, her hair still a tangled mess from sleeping. "She doesn't need to be worried. I know exactly what's going on."

Bridget breathed a sigh of relief. "That's good to know. She said you fainted. So what's going on? Are you getting enough sleep...in that?" Bridget eyed Eckhart with suspicion.

Angie put her hand on the side of Eckhart protectively. "It doesn't have anything to do with van life."

By her expression, Angie could tell Bridget didn't completely believe that van life hadn't taken its toll on her health.

Bridget pressed, "Is it the movie? Are they working you too hard?"

"No, no, nothing like that. Working on the movie hasn't been difficult."

"Then what is it?" Bridget wanted to know.

"Bridge, let her tell us," Thomas tried to rein in Bridget's pushing.

She shot him a reproachful look. "I'm only trying to find out what's wrong. She looks thin and tired and she's living out here in a van all by herself and we have to leave in just a few hours and I'm worried, Mister."

Angie pushed her hair out of her face. "Do I look that bad?"

"No," Thomas said then, wincing at his own words, he added, "You do look a little thin."

"And tired," Bridget reiterated.

"Maybe I'm tired because you guys woke me up," Angie responded, a little short.

"We did do that," Thomas agreed sheepishly.

"Look, I appreciate your concerns, but I'm fine, really. I mean, Mercury is in retrograde, which makes things crazy, right?"

"You said you knew what was going on, though. Is that it? Mercury?" Bridget looked doubtful.

"No, not exactly." Angie took a deep breath, knowing her friends were probably going to react the same way Sofia had to her news. But they were asking, so she was going to tell them the truth. "I took an herbal tincture and it's had a pretty powerful effect on me."

"Oh, wow," Thomas looked worried now. "What was it?"

"It wasn't anything illegal, nothing like that," Angie said.

"GiGi, why did you take it?" Bridget asked.

Angie felt like she had approached the whole subject wrong. She should have simply told them outright that she had taken a love potion and been done with it. Now, with all of the build up, the whole thing was getting blown out of proportion. Now she would have to tell them everything so they would know it hadn't been a big deal and she was fine.

"I had this muscle test done at the apothecary," she started.

"What's a muscle test?" Thomas asked. Bridget shot him a nasty look for interrupting. "Sorry, just asking," he said to her. Then to Angie, "Please, go on."

Angie told them everything. From the results of the test to Stacy and Tracy's suggestions to deciding to take what was supposed to be a general love potion. Then she sucked in a deep breath and told them how she had accidentally thought of Xavier Patel when she was drinking the potion and how she had experienced a physical melt down when she saw him the next day.

When she was done explaining everything there was a long pause as Bridget and Thomas simply stared at her.

"That's why I fainted you see," Angie said. "There's nothing to worry about. It's just a love potion gone wrong because I sort of contaminated it with my thoughts."

Thomas was the first to break the silence. "And that's what Sofia's worried about? A love potion?"

Angie nodded. Thomas looked less than convinced.

Bridget's first question was, "Xavier Patel, the movie star?"

Angie nodded again.

"And he was at the apothecary when you got the…the love potion?"

"Yes." Angie noticed the coffee was done and stood up to get them all a cup.

"And you thought of him by accident when you were taking the potion?" Bridget was trying to get everything straight.

"Yep, totally by accident," Angie agreed.

"Didn't he do the voice of Peter Pineapple when we were kids?" Thomas asked.

Bridget glared at him. "That is hardly important."

"Sorry," Thomas took the coffee Angie offered him. As did Bridget.

"Yes, Thomas, he was Peter Pineapple," Angie answered politely. "He's very nice and everything, but I'm going to need to go back to the apothecary and get a cure because I can't keep fainting every time I see him."

"Right, that wouldn't be good." Bridget sipped her coffee thoughtfully.

"They've asked me to play the mermaid that the pirate falls in love with, so I'll be seeing him even more now," Angie told them.

"Really? That's awesome," Thomas seemed impressed.

Bridget was quiet, for Bridget.

"So that's what Sofia's worried about. That I've fallen under the influence of a love potion." Angie topped off her story with a sip of her own coffee.

Thomas chuckled. "I don't think Sofia's worried about a love potion."

"No?" Angie asked.

Thomas looked between the two women, searching for their understanding. "She doesn't believe in things like love potions." Thomas laughed a little, then made a sober face. "Sofia, I mean. Not us. We believe you, don't we Bridge?"

Bridget calmly turned away from Thomas and focused on Angie. "When did all of these woozy fainting feelings start happening?"

"Not until yesterday," Angie answered.

Bridget's gaze moved all the way down Angie's body and back up. "And how long have you been losing weight?"

Angie pressed on her stomach with her palm. She hadn't really been paying attention, but it was true that she may have dropped a few pounds. "The movie's really taken up a lot of time. I guess I haven't been eating as much as normal."

"Don't they feed you on movie sets?" Bridget asked.

"Yes, I don't get that hungry though. Plus half the time I'm in the scene and can't eat."

Bridget looked at her thoughtfully. "And when are you going to go back and get the anecdote?"

"I've got to be back on set tomorrow for rehearsal, so I need to run down there today sometime."

Bridget nodded slowly and came to a decision. "All right. Then we better get going if we're going go with you."

Chapter Sixteen

Visiting Polypody Cove with Bridget and Thomas was an entirely different experience than when Angie visited the tiny town on her own.

First of all, Bridget was a shopper. And though Angie enjoyed the occasional perusal of interesting shops, Bridget's style of sweeping through every inch of any nearby retail establishment and purchasing anything and everything that interested her was exhausting.

"They should put Bridge's picture next to the word 'consumer' in the dictionary," Thomas said to Angie as they waited. Bridget was searching through a group of little teapots for sale at the front counter of Leaves and Pages, where she had already picked out several books to purchase. Angie didn't know what was more amusing, his comment of the fact that he was whispering so Bridget wouldn't hear him.

"I think Tawny would love this one." Bridget held up a lavender teapot with a pattern of deep green leaves around its center.

"That is cute," Angie said. "But do you have room in your

luggage? You have those three books and you already bought the dress and shoes at the boutique."

Bridget scoffed, "I can make room. Or I can buy another suitcase." She added a mischievous smile at the end of her comment.

Thomas let his head drop back as his shoulders slouched. He gaped at the ceiling with frustrated boredom. "You already have one whole suitcase full of presents," he reminded her.

She shot an annoyed look his way. "Those presents are for the babies. I forgot to get Tawny something. She's about to be a new mother...of twins! She deserves a present."

Thomas straightened and gave her a soft smile. "Of course she deserves a present." He glanced uncertainly at the lavender teapot. "But do you really think a teapot is something she wants? Or needs? I mean, she does live in Scotland. I bet they have a lot of teapots in that drafty old castle."

Bridget scowled and put the teapot back. "Maybe not. But I want to find her something."

Angie spoke up, "Maybe there will be some nice lotions or something at the apothecary that would work."

"Yes, the apothecary!" Thomas declared. "We need to wrap up this shopping spree and take care of Angie's problem. Time's ticking."

Angie swallowed a laugh. Bridget hated it whenever Thomas said time was ticking. Today was no exception.

"Don't use that phrase. You sound like a ridiculous grumpy old man," Bridget said with a sniff.

Thomas hunched over and mimed like he was walking with a cane. "I'm turning into a ridiculous grumpy old man waiting for you."

Bridget had finally had enough. She pinched her lips together and swiftly purchased the three books. Then she motioned Angie out the door, ignoring Thomas lurching after them, still doing his old man mime.

Stacy and Tracy were dismayed to hear that Angie was having a negative reaction to their love potion. Of course, Bridget was exaggerating Angie's symptoms making everything sound much worse than Angie thought it really was.

"She's all woozy and confused, she even fainted yesterday morning," Bridget complained.

"Oh dear," Tracy shared a look with her sister.

"I'm not confused. I think I know what the problem is," Angie interjected. The twins gave her their full attention. She lowered her voice even though Bridget and Thomas were the only other two people in the Blooming Bee Apothecary. "When I was drinking the mixture I accidentally thought of someone specifically and I think all of the...*love juice*, or whatever it's called, is now getting all stirred up whenever he's around."

Stacy and Tracy blinked several times, taking in this information.

"That's why I fainted yesterday. He was there," Angie continued, hoping this would be enough information for them to suggest a fix.

Stacy's eyes slid to Thomas who was amusing himself at the scented candle display, raising each candle up to his nose and taking a deep sniff. Tracy followed her sister's gaze.

Before either of them could jump to conclusions, Bridget snorted out a laugh. "Not him! He's not the one she's having a problem with." She waved her hand toward Thomas, dismissing him as the possible reason anyone might get dizzy and faint. Thomas looked confused.

Angie felt a surge of urgency. They had spent too much of the day shopping and she needed to get her issue with Xave taken care of before she started her new role in the movie in the morning.

"Is there anything I can take that will nullify the effects of the mixture?" she asked the sisters.

"That depends," Stacy said thoughtfully.

"Depends on what?" Bridget was less than impressed with the answer. She was pretty keen on receiving excellent customer service and was obviously beginning to feel like the twins were not providing that to Angie.

Angie gripped the side of the counter, overcome by a bout of dizziness. She tried to focus her attention on Stacy, who was answering Bridget's question, but the words coming out of Stacy's mouth weren't reaching her ears. All she could do was watch her lips move and try not to fall over.

"Angie, are you okay?" Thomas' voice came through the thick fog that had surrounded her head. It sounded as if he was standing on the far side of the room, but then Angie felt his hand on her elbow. He was standing right next to her.

"Look, she's fainting again!" Bridget exclaimed, pointing at Angie as if the twins wouldn't know who she was talking about.

"I think...I think..." Angie tried to form a sentence that would make sense to the others.

She wasn't sure that was possible, however, because nothing she was feeling even made sense to her. Her head swam, her brain felt light as a feather, and the bones in her legs may as well have been jelly. It was a lot like the feeling she'd had the day before...when she had first seen Xave on the boat.

Bells jingled as the front door to the apothecary opened. Angie, who was being propped up by Thomas so she wouldn't collapse, rolled her head to the side to see who had entered. Before her eyes focused in on the tall, dark figure in the doorway, Bridget took in a sharp gasp of breath.

"GiGi, it's him!" Bridget whispered to Angie. The sound echoed in her ear.

Of course it was him. The realization that she had felt his presence nearby and that's what was causing her near fainting spell cut through Angie's brain fog. As did the vision of his perfect hair, face, and body standing in the doorway.

She tried to roll her head the other way so she could face Stacy and Tracy and let them know what was happening. But it was no use. She did not have the strength.

"Angie?" After initially pausing at the sight of her in her weakened state Xave took off his sunglasses and recognition filled his eyes. "Are you all right?" He moved toward her and Angie could literally feel her energy draining into the floor.

"Whoa," Thomas gripped her more firmly as she slumped.

Xave's eyes flashed at Thomas, like he was the one hurting her. "What's going on?"

Bridget scoffed and for a second Angie was terrified Bridget was about to tell Xave off, maybe even tell him he was to blame for her condition.

Angie opened her mouth and tried to explain that Thomas was her friend. He wasn't hurting her. But the only thing that came out of her mouth was a kind of garbled moan.

Thomas sized Xave up and seemed to decide he liked the protective way the other man was acting toward Angie. "She's not feeling well. I think she needs to sit down," he told everyone in the room, not taking his eyes off of Xave.

Xave scanned the room for a chair, but was interrupted by one of the twins, Angie couldn't tell which one, "I think she should get something to eat. Maybe you could take her next door to the pizza place. Get her some water, too."

"Yes, we never ate lunch." Bridget hurried to the door, motioning Thomas to bring Angie.

"Here, let me to help." Xave stepped to Angie's right side while Thomas took the left.

The saltwater, leathery smell of Xave rose off of him like an elixir and gave Angie a burst of energy. Sparkles filled the air around him and her lightheadedness shifted into an airy, bright feeling of joy.

Placing one foot carefully in front of the other, with one arm around each man's shoulder and their arms supporting her waist, she managed to walk out of the the Blooming Bee Apothecary and into Pie's Otta Pizza next door.

"We'll bring your order to you in a few minutes," one of the twins called after them.

Angie assumed she meant the antidote to the love potion, but with Xave at her side and the buzz he sent through her body, she had completely lost interest.

Chapter Seventeen

"So...you're Peter Pineapple?" Thomas asked once they were settled at a table in the pizza place.

Xave nodded. "That's me."

Bridget frowned at Thomas. "His name is Xavier Patel."

"People usually call me Xave," Xave interjected with a disarming smile.

That smile. Those beautiful teeth. Those lips. So warm and firm.

"Here, drink some water," Bridget interrupted Angie's obsessing over Xave's mouth. Bridget moved Angie's glass directly under her nose and continued, "We'll get you something to eat and you'll feel better."

Angie wasn't sure eating would help. She wasn't even sure that she needed to feel better. Especially sitting next to Xave. His aura and hers pressed together and melded into one made her lightheaded and woozy, but that wasn't necessarily a negative feeling.

"You're feeling faint again?" Xave asked, his gorgeous face crumpled into a frown, concern in his eyes.

Thomas and Bridget shared a look as Angie swooned slightly in her chair.

"We've kept her out souvenir shopping a little too long I think," Thomas said.

Bridget nudged Angie to drink her water. She did and the cool liquid slipped down her throat, filling her belly. A small tingle of contentment shivered down her spine.

"We'll order some pizza and you'll be good as new," Bridget told her. She looked at Thomas. "Why don't you place our order now, to speed things up. And get an appetizer too." Thomas followed her directions, waving down the waiter.

Soon Angie was sipping on crisp iced tea and listening to the others make small talk while they waited for their food.

"You were souvenir shopping? You're visiting the area?" Xave asked Bridget and Thomas.

"We're on our way to Scotland via LAX. We took a long layover and popped by to see how our GiGi was doing," Bridget explained.

The waiter returned and slipped a cold Caesar's salad in front of each of them. Bridget watched her with side eyes as Angie took a bite, but there was no need for her friend to make sure she ate. The tangy flavor of Pie's Otta Caesar dressing exploded on her tongue and Angie relished each fork full as the others made conversation.

"Where are you two from?" Xave asked between bites of his salad.

"Denver," Thomas answered.

Xave turned to Angie. "You're from Denver also?"

Angie's fervent munching paused under his gaze. Thomas and Bridget watched her as well, but it was Xave's eyes that froze her response while it was still in her throat. She swallowed. Still couldn't form words, so she nodded instead.

A glimmer of amusement danced through Xave's beautiful brown eyes. Then his brow wrinkled with a thought.

He turned his attention back to Bridget and Thomas. "Do you also know Ian and Sofia?"

Bridget snorted a laugh. "Know them? We grew up with them. Well, with Sofia at least. We've all been friends since we were kids."

This little nugget of information sparked a new conversation between Xave and her friends. Angie was once again off the hook to contribute any comments so she dove back into her salad, enjoying the luscious sensation of sitting next to Xave as she ate.

When she was almost done with the delectable Caesar salad their pizza arrived. Thick crust, bubbling mozzarella cheese covered with mushrooms, black olives and green peppers, it smelled divine.

Bridget took charge and served Angie the first piece, then Xave, then Thomas and herself.

Angie couldn't wait for it to cool down, the pizza smelled too good. Biting into the tip of her slice, the melding of chewy crust, rich tomato sauce, and toppings came together in a perfect crescendo inside of her mouth.

She pulled the slice away causing the melted cheese to stretch, connecting her mouth with her pizza. Flavors danced on her tongue and Angie was overwhelmed. A moan escaped her lips.

All eyes turned to her.

Thomas chuckled. "Were you hungry, Ang?"

Managing to break the stringy cheese with her free hand, Angie returned the other's stares with a wide innocent one of her own. Bridget cleared her throat and handed her a napkin. Angie chewed the heavenly bite of pizza carefully as she wiped flecks of sauce and oil from her lips.

She tried to care that everyone, including Xave, was watching her, but something deep and primal was taking over her senses. A particular blend of Basil and Oregano in the sauce tickled her tongue as she chewed. She let out another moan.

Amusement flickered in Xave's eyes again. He glanced down at the untouched slice on his plate. "I may have to ask for their recipe."

"It's good," Thomas added as he swallowed his first bite. He grinned. "But I don't think I'm enjoying it quite as much as Angie seems to be."

Angie giggled, covering her mouth with her hand as she chewed. The warm gooey feeling of eating Pie's Otta amazing pizza had spread past her tastebuds and into the rest of her body.

Not only was she light as a cloud, she was as soft as one too. Inside and out.

Xave smiled. A smile that reached all the way up into his eyes, into his soul. He held her gaze and a surge of heat moved through her core, both unsettling and exhilarating.

So wrapped up in the scrumptious pizza and the effect it was having on her physically, Angie lost track of the conversation. The other's voices became muted and blended together. The occasional sound of laughter rose up over the talking.

What did it matter what they were talking about while she was eating the best pizza she had ever tasted with Xave by her side? She was perfectly content to stay right there next to him, allowing the warmth emanating from his body and his aura to raise her vibration to full joy.

Xave finally bit into his slice. He paused, savoring the taste in his mouth. Then he tilted his head and chewed, an expression of pure concentrated elation on his handsome face. He closed his eyes with the pleasure of it all and, to Angie's delight, he groaned.

She laughed and patted his arm like they were old friends who had just made a miraculous discovery. "Isn't it good?"

Thomas looked at the half-eaten slice of pizza he was holding, then looked at Bridget. "Are we missing something?"

Bridget shook her head 'no' and continued watching Xave and Angie with interest.

"Excuse me." Stacy touched Angie's shoulder. She had entered the small pizzeria without Angie even noticing and stood just behind her and Xave's shoulders. "I brought you this." Stacy pushed a small brown paper bag at Angie, watching as Xave came out of his pizza daze and opened his eyes.

"Thank you," Angie managed, taking the small bag, which was heavier than it looked.

"You should take it as soon as possible...for the strongest effect," Stacy told Angie. Meaning weighed heavily in her voice, but she wasn't looking at Angie. Instead Stacy was eying the back of Xave's head as he took a voracious bite of pizza.

"Okay," Angie answered, though her heart sank a little bit at the idea.

Strangely woozy, a little bit giddy, and definitely not her normal self, Angie was surprised to realize she had been enjoying all of the unique and delightful sensations she was experiencing at Xave's side. If she took the antidote to the love potion all of the fun, odd as it was, would be over.

For a nano-second she considered not taking it at all.

"So you're all good now?" Bridget looked from Angie to the paper bag in her hand and back.

Angie cleared her throat and tried to answer nonchalantly. "Yes, I think so."

"Uh-oh," Thomas was looking down at his phone.

"What's wrong?" Bridget asked.

"If we want to make our flight we should leave right away," he answered.

"Nonsense," Bridget argued. "We have plenty of time."

"Not according to this." Thomas held up his phone where

a digital map was displayed. "It looks like traffic is getting worse."

Xave struggled to swallow the huge bite he was chewing so he could say, "Unfortunately, there's always going to be traffic problems when you're going to LAX."

"And we didn't originally factor in driving down to Polypody then back up to Angie's van," Thomas reminded Bridget.

Bridget turned her pretty mouth into a pout. "Do we have time to finish eating?"

Thomas looked at the pizza skeptically. "We could take it in a box and eat on the way maybe."

"Or I could give Angie a ride back to her van," Xave chimed in. Angie's heart did a pirouette. "That would save you some time." He added, giving Angie a questioning look. "If that's all right with you?"

Angie hoped she wasn't blushing when she nodded and stumbled a little over her words. "Sure, it's all right with me."

Half an hour later she was nestled into the passenger seat of Xave's black sports car. Unfamiliar with cars in general and completely oblivious about what made an expensive sports car worth the money, Angie discovered the luxury of the interior of the car was more than obvious, even to her.

The comfortable seat cupped her body, the wood dashboard gleamed, several dials and numbers spread out in front of the steering wheel glowed a soothing blue. After Xave held her door open and closed it softly, he jogged around the back of the car and slid into the driver's seat. When his door closed they were encased in a perfect bubble of silence.

A tingle fluttered up her spine, across her shoulders, and down her arms. Like thousands of butterflies brushing their wings against her skin as they flew by.

"Are you comfortable?" Xave asked. His voice was softened by the air tight car interior, but somehow made even deeper and sensual than usual.

Angie nodded. "Yes, very." She tried to sound normal, not like someone overcome by the intimate closeness of the sports car.

Xave smiled and Angie was glad she was sitting down. A wave of the same fluttering tingle moved inside of her this time. Through the muscles in her arms and legs, so she felt as if her body was sinking, dissolving, into the soft leathery upholstery.

"It's faux leather, by the way." Xave started the car.

Angie looked down at her hand, where she had been absently massaging the upholstery. "Faux leather..."

"I know you're vegetarian so I thought you might feel more comfortable knowing." He pulled out onto the road, the car's powerful engine sent a mild vibration up through the floorboards. He glanced at her with interest. "You're not vegan are you?"

"No, well, sometimes. I would love to be vegan all the time, but that doesn't always work out. So vegetarian is what I aim for."

"Of course, the cheese on the pizza should have told me." He looked at her, pleased. "You sound like you're feeling better."

"I am." Angie was, in fact, feeling better. Stronger. Even though she was awash with tingles every few moments. They were good tingles.

"Maybe you were hungry earlier?" Xave glanced sideways at her. "Are you sure you don't have a blood sugar problem or something like that?

"No, I don't think that's it." She thought of the little glass bottle full of antidote in her purse. Its surprising weight sat heavy in her lap.

A few awkward moments went by as Xave maneuvered the

purring car out of Polypody and onto the highway and Angie tried to keep her eyes off of his beautifully formed hands on the steering wheel.

"Would you like to hear some music?" He asked once they were on the highway.

"Sure." She was a little deflated to think he didn't want to talk with her, but equally relieved she wouldn't have to talk with him.

Suddenly the car filled with music. Pirate music. The theme from Pirates of the Caribbean poured high volume out of unseen speakers sending new vibrational sensations through her body.

"Sorry." Xave turned the music down, looking embarrassed.

"It's fine. I like that song," Angie reassured him.

"I was just, you know, using it to get into character."

Angie nodded, amused. "We can listen to it. I don't mind."

Xave hesitated then turned the volume back up, but not quite as high as it had been. The rousing music filled the interior again as the car picked up speed and he steered it expertly along the snaking highway.

Pirates of the Caribbean was followed by the song from Titanic. Angie had to chuckle at the theme of his playlist.

Xave noticed. "I know, it's a little corny isn't it?"

"No, it's not corny."

He tilted his head and narrowed his eyes at her. "It's pretty corny. I can admit it."

She laughed, which made him laugh. "Okay, maybe it's a little corny. But who says corny is bad?" Angie asked.

Xave lifted his eyebrows as if she had challenged him. Then, with a shrug, he said, "You asked for it." He hit a button and a new song began. It was familiar to Angie, but unfamiliar at the same time. There were drums and other instruments, but no singing. Xave watched her face for a reaction. "Do you know this one?

She started to say 'no' when the chorus kicked in. Still no singing, but the tune was unmistakeable. "Is this Living on a Prayer? An instrumental version?"

"Yes!" Xave laughed at her surprise. "It's the two cello guys playing Bon Jovi. It doesn't get cornier than that."

"Right! I know them. It is funny, isn't it? But very entertaining."

Happy she was still amused, he continued, "I love how they take all of these old songs and redo them with their own twist, you know?"

The cello chorus of Living on a Prayer swelled again and they both sang the words. Quietly at first, but louder when they realized the other one was singing as well. Xave kept time to the music by tapping on the steering wheel and Angie drummed the dashboard.

The sun was sinking, turning the whole sky orangey pink. Xave's sleek black car hummed, carrying them along the coast, the forest on one side and the powerful ocean on the other. Lost in the moment and in the sound of Xave's impressive singing voice, Angie all but forgot that she had to drink the antidote as soon as possible.

All of her worries about the nearly debilitating physical reactions Xave caused in her were swept away by the wind as they raced side-by-side with the sunset.

Chapter Eighteen

The sports car brought them smoothly to the entrance of the RV park where Eckhart was parked, but that was where its low clearance and powerful engine ceased to be useful. The narrow roads traversing the park weren't made for the sleek vehicle and Xave had to slow to a crawl.

"This is where you parked?" he asked as they passed huge boxy RVs lined up in camping spots, one after another.

Angie cringed. Until the final moments before she had told Xave where to turn she had pretty much forgotten that he didn't know she lived in a van. She braced herself for a negative response.

"Actually this is where I live," she said, hopefully without a trace of self-consciousness.

They passed Angie's newest park neighbor, the last RV before Eckhart. It was a rickety older RV that had seen better days belonging to an elderly couple who had befriended Angie, but mostly Fidget. Eckhart came into view, looking small and lonely and a little pathetic compared to the shiny sexy sports car.

Xave stopped the car in front of the pink van and scanned the area. "Here?"

Angie nodded and cleared her throat. "This is my home."

Xave looked at her, a little bewildered, and his voice rose in pitch. "The van?"

"His name is Eckhart." As if that would make any difference.

"Whose name?"

"The van's name."

Struggling to understand, Xave looked at Eckhart again, as if he would see an explanation painted on his tailgate.

A crazy thought occurred to her. "Would you like to see it?"

He turned back to her. "The van?"

She smiled, their awkward conversation tickling her funny bone. "Thomas built it out for me. It's pretty cute on the inside."

"Um, sure," Xave said, the information beginning to click together in his mind.

He turned off the engine and the vibration she had grown used to during their drive disappeared. Her legs felt a little numb at its loss, but she managed to get out of the car gracefully.

"Hi Angie," Fern and Albert, her elderly neighbors, called out when they saw her. They were sitting in lawn chairs under an awning on the far side of their RV.

"Hi," she answered. As soon as she spoke Angie could hear a high pitched mewing coming from underneath Fern and Albert's chairs. "Fidget!" She greeted the little calico as the cat raced to her.

"She's missed you," Albert said.

"We tried to keep her entertained though. She wasn't making this much noise while you were gone," Fern reassured Angie with a laugh.

"I'm sure she was fine. Thank you so much for keeping an eye on her for me."

"My stars," Fern exclaimed, looking past Angie. "You're the actor fella. The one from the Bandit of Death movies!"

Xave smiled quietly at her and fidgeted a little under her bright attention.

"Fern, Albert, this is Xave. He's in the movie I got a part in."

"In it? I imagine he's the whole reason it's getting made," Fern said with another laugh, this one more nervous. "Glad to meet you. You certainly are good looking. Even better looking than on the screen." Fern didn't seem to notice the way Xave was ducking his head and lowering his gaze. She just kept talking more and more quickly as each word spilled out. "It's just so crazy seeing you in person like this. My goodness, I've never met a movie star before. I'm a little flustered!" She waved her hand in front of her face like a fan.

"Let the man get a word in, Fern," Albert teased.

"It's very nice to meet you both," Xave said, all politeness.

Before Fern had a total meltdown over Xave's presence, Angie figured it was best to retire to Eckhart. She thanked Fern and Albert again, gathered the mewing Fidget in her arms, and ushered Xave over to her darling van.

Opening the side door wide she stepped in. Xave followed. A bit nervous at what he might be thinking, she kept her eyes on anything but him.

Sweeping the small space with a loving gaze as she plopped Fidget down on the floor, she said, "Here it is! Home sweet home."

Xave had to duck to enter and stay slightly ducked to not bump his head on the ceiling, but Angie heard no gasps of dismay or sounds of horrified disgust so she figured she would give him the grand tour, which took all of five seconds.

"This is the kitchen." Angie moved her arm toward the

built in cabinets and adorably tiny sink and countertop Thomas had built. "And this is the living room, which also turns into the bedroom." Suddenly very aware of how close she and Xave were standing, she felt her cheeks reddening. Clearing her throat, she gestured to the couch. "Won't you have a seat?"

"Thank you," Xave's voice permeated the space causing a shiver to move up Angie's spine. His presence was so potent she wondered if her little van would ever be the same after he left.

Fidget was making herself useful by hopping from the front passenger seat of the van, through the kitchen space and along the top of the couch pillows playfully. Mewing the entire time.

"Fidget, make room," Angie said. The cat mewed again.

Xave chuckled as he sat down on the pink and lavender cushions, filling Angie's little living room with gorgeousness. "She's happy to see you."

A little flustered over what to do next, Angie kicked into cat-Mom mode. "I think she may be hungry. She doesn't usually eat well when someone babysits her, but I can't leave her inside the van during the day. It would be too hot. And she doesn't always want to go with me in her tote bag." Angie retrieved the cat food and filled Fidget's dish. Her fingers trembled as the dry food clattered into the small ceramic dish shaped like a pink fish. She closed her eyes and took a few deep breaths while her back was to Xave. She didn't want to faint.

"This is a truly...interesting home, Angie," he said. The sound of his voice wrapped around her shoulders, bringing on a wave of wooziness.

"Get it together," she whispered to herself.

"Sorry, I didn't hear you?"

"Oh, nothing," Angie shooed an excited Fidget off of the counter and her eyes fell on the switch for the strings of solar powered white lights that were draped around the inside of the van. "I just wondered if it seemed a little dark." She flipped the switch and Eckhart's charming interior came to life under the lights.

Xave's eyes brightened. "It's really quite beautiful in here."

"I think so," Angie said, placing Fidget's dish on the floor so she could eat. "Thomas did a great job. He's a carpenter. Very talented."

"Ah, Thomas." Xave nodded, distracted. "You and Thomas have been friends since childhood?"

Angie nodded. Fidget made tiny mewling sounds as she crunched her food.

"Nothing more than friends?" Xave asked.

Angie's heart paused for a split second.

"Sorry, that's a personal question." He looked away.

The air between them glowed under the white lights. Watching Xave search for something, anything, to look at besides her brought a sense of calm over Angie. Empowered by the realization that he may, in fact, be attracted to her, she sat down next to him.

"Thomas has always been a friend," she said. Xave met her gaze. She smiled and turned to pet Fidget's back as she ate. Her cheeks threatened to blush if she looked into his deep brown eyes for too long so she shifted the conversation. "It's been me, Bridget, Sofia, Tawnyetta, Luna and Thomas for...well, forever really." A curious thought came to her. "Thomas has never been romantically involved with any of us." She wrinkled her brow. "Do you think that's odd?"

Xave considered her question for a moment. "Is he gay?"

"No, well, he's never said he was and I never got the idea that he was. He's always dated girls. Just not any of us." Xave grunted. Angie looked at him. "What?"

He let his eyes linger on hers for a long moment before answering. "I cannot imagine how he could be around you for that long, your whole life, and never be romantically interested."

Time slowed.

Angie's breath slowed. Her heartbeat slowed. She would have sworn when Xave blinked it was in slow motion.

He was staring deep into her eyes and she did not look away. All sound of Fidget's mewling crunches disappeared. Reflections of the white lights twinkled in Xave's eyes.

He moved closer. He was going to kiss her. Every nerve in her body shivered in delight and Angie was glad she hadn't taken the antidote yet.

The antidote.

The love potion.

Wait. This was wrong.

Angie sucked in her breath suddenly, harshly, as if waking from a dream. The sound broke whatever spell was pulling them to each other. At least for the moment.

He was under the influence of the love potion. So was she. Angie couldn't allow something to happen between them under false pretenses.

"I, um..." she started.

Xave pulled back from her, regret in his eyes. He opened his mouth to speak, but was interrupted by a knock on Eckhart's side panel.

"Yoohoo!" Fern called out in a high pitched singing tone. Her head popped into Eckhart's side where the door was still open. "Fidget left these at our place." She held out her hand showing them two cat toys. "Oh, good, you're still here, Xave."

They all knew there was no way Fern could have missed Xave's car still parked directly in front of Eckhart, but they all kept quiet, keeping up the facade for Fern's sake.

"Yes," Xave said, glancing sideways at Angie before

turning his full attention on Fern. "What can I do for you, lovely lady?"

Fern's wrinkled cheeks blushed under Xave's charms. She held out her other hand, which held a spiral notebook and pen. "I wonder if I could get your autograph? My kids will never believe I met you!"

Both sorry and grateful for the interruption, Angie gathered her wits while Xave graciously signed several autographs for Fern, her children, and her grandchildren.

As sorry as she was to end the evening, Angie knew what she had to do as soon as Fern left. She would feign fatigue and get Xave to go home. Then she would take the antidote. Hopefully she hadn't waited too long.

Chapter Nineteen

Before Xave left for the night he insisted on helping her with Fidget.

"Will you leave her with Fern and Albert again tomorrow?" he asked, stroking Fidget's soft calico fur.

The cat had finished eating while he was signing Fern's autographs and immediately went to investigate, licking her chops and hopping up onto the cushion next to them. By the time Fern left, Fidget was curled up in Xave's lap, purring.

Angie's heart warmed at the sight. "I suppose I'll have to. I didn't know I was going to be gone so much when I moved here. I can't very well leave her inside Eckhart in the parking lot while I'm on set all day long."

"Yes," Xave gazed down at Fidget thoughtfully. "Does she mind being on her leash?"

"No, she's pretty good about it." Angie shifted from one foot to the other.

She had gotten up from the couch to give Fern and Xave room and didn't want to sit back down next to him. That would get too cozy too fast and she didn't want to get overwhelmed by him again. Not until she had a chance to drink the antidote.

Xave held Fidget carefully in his hands and stood up, depositing her back onto the cushion in his place where she made a sleepy mew and stretched her front paws straight out in front of her.

"She's adorable. You're so lucky." He turned his eyes onto Angie with a sad smile. "My cat, well, he died a few months ago."

"Oh no! That's awful, what was his name?"

"Sem-Sem…it's Egyptian. My Mom named him."

"I'm sorry," Angie said, then realizing the possible misunderstanding, continued, "Not that your Mom named him. That he's gone."

The sadness in Xave's eyes gave way to a cozy sparkle. Angie had to fight the urge to give him a hug.

"I have a soft spot for cats." He cleared the emotion from his throat. "If you want to bring Fidget to the set, I could talk to Tillie and Brandon for you."

"Really? I don't want her to be any trouble."

"If she stays on her leash I don't think it would be a problem. Maybe she could hang out by the craft services table or in the costume trailer."

Tears welled up in Angie's eyes. She hadn't realized how concerned she had been about leaving Fidget until he made the offer. Relief washed over her and she closed her eyes, nodding.

"That would be great," she managed.

Xave watched her with concern. "I'm sorry, I didn't mean to upset you. I just thought it might be easier."

"No, no, you're right. It's a great idea." She tried to give him a shining smile. "I think I'm just a little tired."

Xave's eyes widened with alarm. "Of course, how rude of

me. You're probably exhausted after not feeling well earlier. You need your rest."

"It's fine. I'm fine," she protested.

"No, no, that was thoughtless of me. I'll go now so you can get some sleep."

And with that Xave stepped out of Eckhart and disappeared with nothing more than a quick wave.

"Thank you for the ride...see you in the morning," Angie called after him. Her words were answered by the sound of the car door slamming and its powerful engine roaring to life.

Xave was true to his word. Before she had finished her first cup of morning tea she received a text from Tillie.

Xave told me about your predicament with finding a cat babysitter. Fidget is welcome to hang out with crafty or in the costume trailer :) We could use a mascot for the movie!

When Angie arrived with Fidget in tow, Adam met her immediately and reached out his hand for Fidget's leash. "Costume wants to take the first Fidget Shift," he grinned. "If that's okay with you?"

"Sure," Angie said, happy that the gregarious costume team, Eric and Penelope, would be the first place Fidget went. "And you're sure they're okay with watching her?" She handed Adam the leash and a small sack containing her food, food dish, and a water dish.

"Okay with it? Everyone was fighting over who got to watch her first."

"Oh good, you're here right on time," Tillie greeted Angie as she and Brandon approached. Tillie gave her a big smile. "Are you ready for your new role?"

Fresh butterflies fluttered in Angie's stomach. She had gotten fairly used to being a mermaid extra, but now that she was supposed to be an actual mermaid character with longer scenes and maybe even close ups she did have a little stage fright.

"Well, I'm glad I don't have any lines, let's just put it that way," Angie tried masking her nerves with a joke.

Tillie and Brandon shared a look then Brandon placed a comforting hand on her shoulder. "You're a natural, Angie. Really. We wouldn't have asked you if we didn't think you would be great in this part."

"Plus you get your own special wardrobe!" Tillie added. "Come on, we'll walk you through everything while you get ready."

They whisked her away to makeup where Shivaun was waiting for them.

"Girl, you thought you looked like a mermaid before? Now I'm gonna turn you into a mermaid star," Shivaun laughed at her own comment and started what would turn out to be a 90 minute makeup and hair session.

For the first 30 minutes Tillie and Brandon explained her new character to her, the mysterious Mermaid Queen who Xave...or rather the Pirate Radames Drake - otherwise known as the Black Eyed Pirate - would fall head over heels with despite also being in love with the beautiful human main character being played by Elizabeth Carlton.

"And you're sure I don't have to talk?" Angie asked after listening to the elaborate emotional arcs that the characters were meant to go through by the end of the film, even hers.

"You can't talk," Brandon reassured her. "The mermaids in our movie don't have vocal cords."

"Oh," Angie nodded slowly. "Why?"

"They never developed vocal cords for speaking. They're more like sea mammals than humans." Tillie explained.

Angie looked at her reflection and caught Shivaun's eye in the mirror.

"Don't you worry, Angie, when I'm done with you, you will definitely not look like some old sea mammal."

Tillie laughed. "They can sing, if that helps. They use their gills. Think of them more like sirens than Ariel from The Little Mermaid."

"Okay, that helps," Angie said.

Tillie and Brandon were called away and Angie settled back in the makeup chair to watch Shivaun work her magic.

And magic it was. By the time she was declared "ready for the water" by Shivaun and Anthony, the hairstylist, Angie didn't even recognize her reflection.

Makeup in shades of blue and green covered every inch of her face, neck, shoulders and arms. It was similar to the makeup she had worn as an extra, but more intense. They had also added white that shimmered both silver and gold when she turned in the light. Angie's dark eyes blinked back from her reflection.

"What do you think?" Shivaun asked.

"It's interesting. It's not exactly pretty...more...I don't know...." Angie struggled for a description.

"Regal is the word you're looking for. You look like a Mermaid Queen," Anthony suggested, fussing with the ends of her long red curls that he had twisted and teased into a crown of sorts before spraying it with its own glimmering blue-green-white coating. He grunted with satisfaction. "I don't usually get to do this to someone's real hair."

"No?" Angie was confused.

"Usually it's a wig," he explained. "But not you. You've got the real thing."

Next step was getting into costume and the chance to reunite with Fidget, if only for a few minutes.

"She's such a little doll," Penelope gushed. Fidget was looping back and forth around her feet as she sat at her sewing table in the costume trailer.

"Hi sweetie," Angie bent over and made kissy noises with her mouth at her cat. Fidget stopped in her tracks and stared at Angie. "Oh, I forgot she doesn't love me in makeup."

"Really?" Penelope asked then looked Angie over with a professional eye. "Although you do look pretty different. Maybe she's just a smart cat."

"She's a beautiful kitty," Eric chimed in as he guided Angie to his corner of the trailer to get her changed. "When Xave asked us if we could babysit her we were thrilled. Such a pretty baby."

The mention of Xave's name sent tingles across Angie's arms. She tried to appear nonchalant. "Has he been here yet? Xave?"

"No, he had some choreography to work on this morning I think," Penelope answered.

"A pirate sword fight," Eric told Angie with raised eyebrows. "Yum!"

Angie had to agree, but decided not to say anything in case the love potion effect would make her seem too interested in the idea of Xave as a pirate. She was still worried that she had waited too long to consume the antidote even though she had slugged it down immediately after Xave drove away the previous night.

The antidote had been clear and tasteless. If Angie hadn't known better she would have assumed it was water. Not having looked at it when Stacy first gave it to her she had no idea if it had ever looked any different. Had it lost color as it sat in her purse on the ride back to Eckhart? Had it lost potency? She hadn't felt any physical reaction after drinking it, which was a concern.

Her worries about her love potion problem were momentarily forgotten when she realized the gorgeous blue mermaid outfits she had admired previously were now hers to wear.

Eric checked a clipboard hanging on a hook on the wall then wheeled the rack of blue mermaid costumes front and center. From ice white to a deep indigo blue, the costumes had captured her imagination when she first spied them in the costume trailer.

"Today we are using the cerulean," Eric said. He pulled a gorgeous cerulean blue bikini top embellished with tiny shimmering white seashells off the rack. Strips of wispy cloth that flowed gracefully off the bottom seam like streams of water fluttered as he held it in front of her.

Angie was thrilled to put the top on and its matching bottom, which was different than the plain fins she had been given as a mermaid extra. This costume had been cleverly designed to zip tightly around her legs when needed, but unzip and act more like a skirt when she was just walking around.

"The fins for your feet are with the water equipment. We don't need those until you're going into the water," Eric explained. Finally he pinned a sparkling mermaid tiara in the center of her hairdo.

"Look at you!" Penelope said as Eric led Angie to the wall of mirrors in her new upgraded star mermaid costume.

Angie stared at her own reflection, amazed at the transformation. Yes, it had taken a few hours, but she didn't even recognize herself. She moved her hand back and forth in front of her, verifying that she was looking at her own image in the mirror.

It was her. That was certain. But it was something more. It was her childhood dream come to life. She had been transformed into a mermaid.

She caught a glimpse of Fidget in the mirror. Her friendly, sweet, playful cat stared at her with wide eyes. She hadn't budged an inch since Angie came into the trailer.

"I get it Fidget. I barely recognize me either," she told the cat.

"Knock knock," a voice said as the door opened.

Angie and the others turned.

"We're here for our–" Kristina appeared first in the doorway, followed by Marissa. Kristina caught sight of Angie as the blue mermaid, wearing the blue costumes reserved for the star, and cut off her sentence. "Oh! Elizabeth, sorry, I didn't know–" She stopped talking again, her eyes had wandered up to Angie's red hair and were filled with confusion.

"We're just about ready for you ladies," Eric told her. "Just getting our new star into her first get up."

Confusion melted into recognition in Kristina's eyes. Her brow pinched angrily. She opened her mouth to say something, probably something snippy, but another voice rang out from the open door behind her.

"How's everything going in here?" Xave's unmistakeable deep voice filled the rapidly shrinking space inside the costume trailer.

Angie's heart skipped a beat. Fidget sprang to life underneath Penelope's sewing table, letting out a loud meow and running to Xave, leaping into his arms.

He laughed, sending a warm glow through the room. With a cursory glance at Kristina and Marissa, Xave directed his attention to Angie.

When his eyes locked on hers everyone else in the small costume trailer disappeared and Angie waited, breathless, for him to say something, do something, and break the spell.

"Angie, I–" his words caught in his throat and Angie found her heart swelling uncontrollably with emotion. "You..." he tried to continue, but seemed at a loss for words.

"She's gorgeous. Awe inspiring. Like a pirate's dream, we know," Eric said. "She's also done and we need to get you into costume ASAP." He pointed at Xave then directed the two remaining mermaid extras. "We'll get you done after Xave. Their first scene together is just the two of them so we have time."

Kristina and Marissa left, but not before Kristina cast a

nasty look in Angie's direction. Xave handed a reluctant Fidget over to Angie, as the cat was still a little mistrustful of her as a mermaid, so she placed her carefully underneath Penelope's sewing table before making her way out the door.

Angie was glad Eric had taken charge. It was good to have someone tell her what to do, because as soon as she saw Xave she lost her ability to think straight. Again.

Chapter Twenty

Disoriented after seeing Xave in the costume trailer, Angie made her way to the craft services table. Maybe she should eat something for energy. On her way she encountered several crew members and a couple of the pirate actors. All of them noticed her new mermaid costume and smiled. Several complimented her on the new look.

By the time she reached the food she was a little overwhelmed by all of the extra attention. She hadn't realized that taking a larger role in the movie would make her so *seen* by everyone else. Add that to the general loopy sensation in her head from being near Xave, and she began to wonder if she had made the right decision.

Standing in front of a large fruit tray, Angie grabbed a small paper plate and started loading it with bite size chunks of pineapple, honeydew melon, and strawberries when she felt someone touch her elbow. Startled, she turned quickly to find Sofia standing behind her.

"Hey! How's your first day as Queen of the Mermaids?"

Sofia asked, beaming. When she looked deep into Angie's eyes her smile faded. "What's the matter?"

Angie lifted one shoulder and let it fall, trying to give Sofia a brave smile. "It's good so far."

Sofia's eyes narrowed. "I don't believe you."

Angie bit her bottom lip then remembered her makeup and stopped. "Nothing's the matter. How was your trip?"

Sofia flicked her eyes to Angie's plate and muttered something in Spanish. Then in English, she asked, "Is that all you're eating? Fruit?"

"I had oatmeal this morning," Angie responded, hating that Sofia felt the need to treat her like a child, yet still not feeling totally whole and strong.

"Will you eat some eggs at least? Something with protein?"

Angie nodded, though she doubted that would help her predicament. She was pretty sure the antidote had lost its potency when she drank it, which meant she was in for a long day of fighting off dizziness and, as Sofia had so aptly called, gooey eyes.

"I'll eat some eggs, yes," she agreed.

Sofia motioned to a nearby table. "Sit down and rest. I'll bring it to you." When Sofia joined her she held a plate heaped with not only fruit, but an egg and potato breakfast burrito, tortilla ships with seven layer dip, and a chocolate walnut brownie.

"I can't eat all of that," Angie argued.

Sofia placed the food squarely in front of her. "Do me a favor and try."

Angie did as she was told and took a bite of the burrito, made just spicy enough by the addition of green chili mixed with the egg and potato.

Sofia watched her chew. "Bridget said you went back to

the apothecary and got some kind of cure." She annunciated apothecary slowly as if it was a fake word.

Angie nodded, still chewing the last of her bite. "We did and they gave me an antidote, but I don't think it worked."

Sofia leveled her gaze at Angie and relayed her displeasure without saying a word. Angie ignored her negative vibe and took another bite of her burrito, letting her eyes wander across the filming activity going on in the distance.

Sofia sighed, giving in to a conversation Angie was pretty sure she didn't want to have. "Why don't you think the antidote worked?" Sofia asked, this time annunciating antidote like it wasn't a real word.

Angie smiled softly at Sofia and her math brain. It was a stretch for her friend to discuss Angie's more metaphysical, holistic way of experiencing life and Angie appreciated the effort.

"It was several hours before I could take the antidote after they gave it to me. Stacy, the lady from the apothecary, said I should take it as soon as possible. And I didn't feel anything after I drank it, so I don't know if it worked."

Mildly frustrated, Sofia asked, "Well why didn't you take it when they gave it to you?"

Thankful for the mermaid makeup, which would cover up any color in her cheeks, Angie answered, "Xave was with me." She took another bite of burrito and did some concentrated chewing.

Sofia did a slow turn of her head and stared at her. "Xave was with you?"

Angie nodded, still chewing, scanning the set, doing anything but catching Sofia's pointed look.

"What were you doing together?" Sofia's voice was tinged with a weird stern amusement she had perfected in the fifth grade.

"He gave me a ride home from the apothecary."

"To your van?"

"Yep."

Sofia narrowed her eyes again. "And why was he at the apothecary?"

"I don't know. We ran into him and I got weird and light headed and we all went to get a pizza and then he drove me home." Angie felt like a teenager explaining why she had come home late to her parents. Although her parents had never been very severe with curfews, so she could only guess at the feeling.

Sofia stewed over this information while Angie tried a bite of the walnut brownie. Sofia took a deep breath, a precursor to what Angie assumed would be a long lecture on the lack of scientific evidence supporting natural therapies, when they were interrupted by a hard tap on Angie's shoulder.

"I guess congratulations are in order," Kristina's voice was syrupy sweet in Angie's ear.

She and Marissa stood behind the table where Sofia and Angie were seated. Angie wondered how long they had been standing there.

"Yes, congrats Angie. You're a star now," Marissa added, though Angie didn't detect well wishes in her tone.

"Thank you, but I don't think I'm a star exactly."

Kristina took a seat across from Angie at the table. Marissa followed.

Kristina shook her head and made tut-tut noises as she looked Angie's hair and makeup over. "Your part is a major role in the movie. I would call that a star, wouldn't you Marissa?"

Marissa nodded. Angie didn't think Kristina was there to pay her a compliment. She glanced at Sofia who was watching the mermaid extras coolly.

Even though nobody was clamoring for her opinion, Kristina continued, "Although my real question is what is it about you that would make Tillie and Brandon snub someone like Elizabeth Carlton?"

Angie cringed so deeply she felt it in her stomach. "What do you mean?"

Kristina gave her a sympathetic look, sorry for her complete naivety when it came to the ways of movie acting. "She was all set to be billed for both parts. The human love interest and the mermaid love interest. I mean, she has to be disappointed that you swept in and stole her role."

"Nobody stole anything," Sofia snapped.

Kristina giggled, reminding Angie of those high school movies where the pretty blonde cheerleader turns out to be the bad guy...or girl.

"I didn't ask for this role, you know," Angie said. "Tillie and Brandon asked me to do it."

With mock empathy written all over her face, Kristina answered, "Oh, I believe you. I just wonder what Elizabeth thinks about it all. It's gotta sting, someone like you taking over half of her performance."

"What do you mean someone like her?" Sofia asked, she was fast losing patience with Kristina.

"No offense, really, it's just that she's a, you know, a nobody," Kristina explained, though it did little to calm Sofia's rising irritation.

"First of all, she's not a nobody," Sofia responded with her firmest 'I'm a Professor' voice. "And just look at her." She gestured toward Angie. "She's gorgeous."

Kristina's eyebrow twitched, but she didn't drop the sickly sweet smile she had held the entire conversation. "Of course she's beautiful. But California is full of beautiful girls. What I want to know, and only because I'm interested in duplicating this kind of success, you understand. What I want to know is how did you do it?" She locked suspicious eyes onto Angie.

Incensed that Kristina or anyone else would insinuate that

she somehow did something sneaky or pushy to take a part away from Elizabeth Carlton, Angie opened her mouth to smack down the very suggestion when she had a thought. She paused, mouth half open, part of a walnut brownie still in her hand.

Could the love potion have caused some greater wave of attraction beyond Xave? Had it been powerful enough to make Tillie and Brandon think she was somehow more appealing or better than Elizabeth Carlton, a skilled actress? Had she manipulated the universe to not only get a part in a movie, which she didn't deserve, but also capture the heart and mind of its leading man on false pretenses?

Sofia was watching her. Waiting for her to tell Kristina what she could do with her theory of Angie pushing her way into the spotlight. When Angie simply sat there, shocked into silence at the possibility that she had influenced, if inadvertently, the directors into giving her the part, Sofia's brow wrinkled with indignation.

Just when Angie was sure Sofia was going to go off on the mermaid extras and tell them to mind their own business, Adam approached the table.

"I see you're all set," he said to Angie. "You look great, by the way."

"Thank you," she answered, her voice was a little thin, but at least she had found it.

"Are you ready to start?" he asked.

"Sure," she put the remaining brownie back on her plate.

"I'll throw this out for you," Sofia said, still steaming mad, but under control.

Angie couldn't look at Kristina and Marissa as she made her way around the table, yet she could feel them watching her.

"What are we doing first?" she asked Adam.

Unaware of the tension in the air, Adam was in high spirits. "Oh, you're gonna love it. This is when you save the Black Eyed Pirate on the beach and he falls in love with you at first sight."

Angie didn't have to look at the mermaid extras to know how they felt about his announcement.

Chapter Twenty-One

Angie's arm was falling asleep, yet she refused to move.

She could easily blame Tillie and Brandon for the almost painful tingling that began in her fingertips and moved all the way up her arm past her elbow. They were, after all, the ones making her hold as still as possible while they got the perfect shot. But deep down Angie knew that wasn't the real reason she refused to budge.

The real reason her arm was going nowhere was the fact that Xave's beautiful head was nestled in the crook of it. Not only his head, of course, that would have been more along the horror film genre.

Angie's blue and silvery painted arm was tenderly cradling Xave's manly, rugged pirate head that was attached to the rest of his manly, rugged pirate body as he lay on the sandy beach pretending to be out cold. His long black wig and beard were wet, as were his billowing white shirt and black pirate trousers. The wet clothing clung to his body and tendrils of wet hair roped lazily down one of his cheeks where they had stuck when he crawled through the sand.

Angie wanted with everything in her soul to reach out and

push the hair back in place, allowing her fingertips to trace his cheekbones as she did, but she had been told not to change anything about the way he looked. They needed to maintain continuity for editing. Instead, she was to gaze longingly into his unresponsive face and wait for him to open his eyes.

That she could do.

Angie gazed at Xave's face, her eyes sliding across his brow and down the perfect contours of his nose, landing on his lips where they lingered before she caught herself and raised her eyes to his again. Still closed.

"Good, Angie, good, keep doing what you're doing. Don't stop. Very slow. Take your time," Tillie called out directions from her position next to the camera.

Her arm exploding with the pinpricks caused by lack of blood flow, Angie wasn't sure she could stop when they did call cut. The object of her affection in her arms while ocean waves lapped at her mermaid tail? Please, this was the stuff of her childhood fantasies. She would stay until her arm fell off.

Perhaps sensing Angie's dedication was going overboard, or perhaps because they had gotten enough footage of this particular part of the scene, Tillie called out again, "Okay, Xave, wake up now. Nice and slow."

Xave's eyelids fluttered. Angie felt the reverberation through her whole body. She had grown used to him laying unresponsive in her arms. The sensation of seeing him open his deep brown eyes and look into hers was almost as magical as if she had actually saved him from drowning and brought him back to life on shore.

Caught in Xave's gaze, bleary as it was because he was supposed to be coming out of a near death experience, Angie sucked in her breath. His expression sharpened and he looked deep into her eyes. She opened her mouth to say...what? She wasn't sure, but she was compelled to respond somehow to the way his awakening was making her heart pound in her chest.

Just in time, Angie remembered that she was being filmed and also that the Mermaid Queen couldn't speak. Managing to close her lips without making a sound, she also closed her eyes for a split second to gather herself. That's when she remembered she was supposed to pull away from him after he woke up and disappear back into the ocean.

"Okay, Angie, go ahead and pull back now," Tillie directed.

Arm screaming in pain at being moved, heart breaking in two at having to go, Angie hurriedly released him from her embrace and backed away. As well as anyone stretched out on a sandy beach while cinched inside a faux mermaid tail could back away at least.

"Pull back more, just a little more, please," Tillie told her.

Angie leaned as far back as she could, still keeping her eyes trained on Xave, who was watching her just as intently as she was watching him.

"A little further back, Angie. Keep looking at him, but kind of lay backward then roll onto your left side so you'll be out of the shot."

Angie did as she was told, ending her first major scene as an actress positioned awkwardly on her side, facing the feet of the film crew who were standing outside the frame waiting to help her up. Xave, now out of her sight, was presumably staring in wonder at her backside.

"Cut. Great! That was really good," Tillie said with a wide smile.

Several hands reached out to help Angie up off the ground. Between pulling and pushing she was finally lifted to her feet. The costume assistant unzipped her mermaid skirt so she could move her legs again.

"Good job, Angie," Brandon exclaimed. "That was excellent. Don't you think, Xave?"

Still on his back in the sand, Xave lifted himself up on his elbows, looking far less unconscious than he had just a few moments before. "Yes, yes, I was really...feeling it." He switched his eyes up to Angie's and kept them there. "You have a strong emotional pull."

A rush of pleasure shot through her and she couldn't keep from beaming back at Xave, unable to tear her eyes from his until a realization punctured the fun.

The love potion. That's what he was feeling.

Angie glanced at Tillie and Brandon who were talking excitedly to the Director of Photography as they watched replays of the shots they had just completed. Her heart sank. It was obvious they were all under the influence of the love potion. There was no way she, a complete novice, could have been as good as everyone seemed to think she was in the scene.

Her worst fears were coming true. The love potion that she had accidentally directed at Xave had also unleashed on everyone else in her life. From the directors praising her work, to the film crew who were nothing less than fawning over her since they had helped her off the sand.

"We're good for now, guys." Tillie looked past the camera at Angie and Xave. "We're done with this scene. Why don't you two take a break while we set up for the next one."

Angie felt sick to her stomach. They were moving on, satisfied with her performance for this scene, but their satisfaction was based on an outside influence. What if, when the filming was complete and the crew and equipment were disassembled, Tillie and Brandon reviewed the footage and found it lacking? Found her performance lacking?

"Do you want to go over the next scene while we wait?" Xave asked. He had appeared suddenly at her side and touched her elbow as he asked the question.

Consumed by sudden anxiety, Angie hadn't noticed him getting up from the sand. "No," she said abruptly, turning away.

She needed to get some air. She needed to think about what she could do to stop this thing she had started. She needed to not get lost in Xave's eyes, or let his presence wrap around her and make her forget the mess they were all in because of her.

"Oh, okay." He glanced uncertainly at Adam who had approached them with a clipboard.

Adam must have picked up on the awkward vibe in the air. He cleared his throat and looked from Xave to Angie. "You've got a good 45 minute break before they'll be ready." Then directly to Angie, "If you want to rest up in your room I'll show you where it is."

"My room?" Angie didn't understand.

Adam nodded. "Since you're one of the main characters now, you get a private space. We couldn't get you your own trailer like your friend, Sofia, wanted, but we did manage a room in the costume storage trailer."

"Sofia?" Angie didn't know what was happening or what Sofia had to do with it, but she was so out of it and needed to get away to think so she let Adam take her to her room.

"I know it's not luxurious, but it is air conditioned and we'll find a little table and a lamp maybe so it's a little more homey." He said apologetically as he ushered her into a small, quiet room at the back of the seldom used second costume trailer.

He was right, it wasn't luxurious at all, but it did have a nice big window for light and what looked like a comfy love seat against one wall.

"And the best thing is," Adam disappeared from the doorway for a moment and returned holding Fidget on her leash. "It comes with a cat!"

"Fidget!" Angie was delighted to take Fidget's soft purring body in her arms. The little cat must have gotten over her mistrust of the mermaid makeup, or maybe she had been visiting so many new people on set she had overcome her shyness in general, because she showed no fear.

"Everyone is still happy to babysit her whenever you want, but we thought you might like her to hang out in here and visit her on breaks, too."

Adam left her to relax and Angie sat down with a heavy sigh on the loveseat.

Fidget hopped into her lap, cocked her head, and mewed.

"I don't know what to do, Fidget. I've really messed things up for everyone," Angie told the cat miserably.

Fidget mewed again.

"We're not in Kansas anymore, Toto," she tried to joke.

Fidget looked confused. Just as confused as Angie felt.

Chapter Twenty-Two

The next morning Angie arrived prepared. The night before she had rummaged through Eckhart and found every crystal, stone, and candle she had brought with her from Colorado and shoved them into a cloth bag. Then she had hunted along the beach and in the forest to find other items from nature that called to her, promising to use their energy on her behalf.

Her cloth bag was heavy with the additional seashells, pieces of driftwood, rocks and pinecones she had gathered together. Digging deep in the small drawer Thomas had built into the side of her couch/bed she pulled out a worn blue velvet box and dropped it on top of the other items in the bag before tightening the drawstring closed.

When she arrived at her room on set the next day she was happy to see that Adam had been busy overnight. Another chair, a small coffee table, and a side table with a lamp had been installed in the space.

"This will work perfectly," Angie told Fidget, who had already settled comfortably into the new chair. The cat yawned and curled up on the cushion. "I know, sorry we had to leave early,

but I need to get this set up to try and ward off some of the..."
Angie's voice trailed off. She wouldn't call the effects of Stacy and
Tracy's love potion 'evil'. That was too harsh. "I want to decrease
the energy of it, that's all. Dilute it." She looked at Fidget for
approval. The little calico wasn't listening. She had fallen asleep.

No matter, she would get her alter set up and do some
meditation before her scheduled time in the makeup chair. If
she could clear the energy each time she took a break in her
room she might succeed in diffusing some of the power the
love potion was wielding over Xave and the other innocent
people working on the film.

Angie covered the side table with a tie dyed scarf, placed
the lamp at the back to hold it in place and smoothed its
surface. Then she placed crystals, rocks, pinecones, driftwood,
and seashells from her bag around the edges of the table. In the
center she arranged the glass bottle which had held the antidote and was now full of ocean water she had collected last
night, three candles, a pure white feather she had found on the
forest floor, and a small green ceramic dish.

The last two items in her bag were a cotton bandana
containing a handful of rich black earth she had taken from
the ground behind her campsite and the blue velvet box.
Angie carefully poured the earth into the green dish. Then she
opened the blue velvet box.

A lump swelled in her throat at the sight of her grand-
mother's locket tucked carefully inside. Shining silver, covered
in an elaborate pattern of vines, leaves, and roses, the locket
had been gifted to her by Granny on her 12th birthday.

Angie turned the locket over in her hand and ran her
thumb gently over the engraving, *For my Felicity...Love
Forever, Daniel*

Tears pressed at the back of Angie's eyes as she thought
about her grandparents. They had passed away within one

year of each other when she was a teenager and she still missed them dearly. The immense love they had surrounded her and her parents with was a mere shadow of the enduring love they had for each other. Married for over 50 years and each other's best friend and dearest lover until the very end.

Angie sniffed and smiled sadly. She hoped one day to experience that kind of attachment, but it needed to be real, not manufactured through alchemy.

"Do your magic, Granny," she said, hanging the locket from the lamp so it dangled over the other items. She turned the lamp on and admired how the silver shined.

The locket had always been a kind of talisman of good luck and love for Angie. If anything could break the spell that the love potion seemed to have cast, it would be Granny's locket.

"Now, let's focus," Angie continued talking to her sleeping cat as she sat criss-cross on the love seat to meditate. Almost immediately, she was interrupted by her buzzing phone.

It was Sofia texting, *Were they able to get you a trailer?*

Almost, they gave me a room to take breaks in, Angie answered.

Sofia sent a frowny face.

It's okay, I like it just fine and Fidget can hang out in here when she's not visiting all of her new friends. Angie added a smiley face to punctuate that all was well.

I wanted them to give you a space to get away and clear your head.

Thanks for acting as my manager, Sof. This will work for me. I already set up an alter and everything.

There was a pause, then Sofia sent, *Alter?*

For my crystals and stuff. So I can meditate.

Right. And meditation helps you with your Xave problem?

It was Angie's turn to pause, then she answered, *Not yet, but I think the alter will help.*

Okay, well, as long as it's helping. We'll be back up to the set in a couple of days. I'm excited to see it!

Angie put her phone down and straightened her shoulders. Taking in a deep breath, she filled her lungs and closed her eyes, exhaling slowly.

There was a soft knock on the door. Angie sighed and opened her eyes. So much for clearing her head.

"Come in," she said, expecting Adam to pop his head in the door to say good morning and remind her of her call time.

"Well, lookey who's moving up in the world," Kristina cooed as she stepped through the door, followed closely by the ever present, mostly silent, Marissa.

Angie stiffened, sensing negative vibes immediately. She glanced at Fidget who had woken up and was blinking, irritated, at the mermaid extras.

"You scored your own trailer." Kristina wore a pinched smile as she scanned the small room and its furnishings, avoiding eye contact with Angie.

"It's not exactly a trailer, though, is it?" Angie tried to laugh away the tension they were putting off.

Kristina snorted daintily. Marissa offered a thin smile, but no comment. Big surprise.

Kristina's eyes fell on the newly assembled alter and paused. She slipped a look at Marissa before commenting, "What...no incense?"

"I didn't think it was appropriate since other people use the area. You never know if a scent will bother someone or if they're allergic," Angie answered.

Kristina gave an exaggerated nod as if she was in full agreement. "Right, that's very thoughtful of you." She crossed the room and stood in front of the alter, leaning over so she could study the items more closely. "So, you're a...Buddhist?"

Angie smiled. "Not exactly."

"It's fine, you know, whatever you're into is fine with us," Kristina added with a shrug.

"It's California after all," Marissa chimed in.

Angie didn't remember asking for their opinions and was silently cursing the fact that she had technically invited them into her quiet space. Next time she would check to see who was knocking before flippantly telling a visitor to come on in.

Kristina straightened and bit her lip with faux concern. "However, if you're into *really* weird stuff you may want to keep it to yourself."

"Keep it to myself?" Angie asked.

Kristina nodded, nudging Marissa to nod, too. "Yes, I mean, you have this new position and you're working with, like, a major leading man, you know?"

Angie didn't know. "I don't understand what that has to do with anything."

Kristina's mouth dropped open and she blinked her eyes in a melodramatic show of disbelief. "You don't know?"

"Know what?"

Her former co-mermaid extras shared barely contained sneers with each other before Kristina turned a too sweet smile back on Angie.

"Xavier Patel is rumored to be a deeply religious man who doesn't tolerate..." Kristina's eyes flicked to the alter and back to Angie. "Anything, shall we say, occult-ish."

Angie's stomach twisted into a hard knot. She swallowed hard.

Occult. She disliked the word. Whenever anyone used it she felt as if they were either trying to be judgmental or frightening. All it really meant was supernatural or magical. Did Xave truly despise all things magical?

"Knock, knock," Xave's voice accompanied his actual knocking on the door.

All eyes turned to him in surprise, as if the three of them had just been caught doing something they weren't supposed to be doing.

Angie heard Kristina whisper under her breath, "Speak of the devil."

"Am I interrupting anything?" Xave asked politely, though his calm, deep voice failed to whisk Angie's heart away the way it normally did.

In fact, her heart was cold, like someone had poured ice water into her chest. She blinked several times as she stared at him, at a loss for words.

Finally, Kristina answered, "No, we just stopped by to say 'hi' to Angie."

Xave glanced at each of them, a frown growing in his eyes. Angie had to fight the urge to leap off the loveseat and block the alter from his view. Luckily, Fidget saved the day.

Happy to see a familiar face, the little cat hopped off the chair and trotted over to Xave, purring.

"Oh, hello Fidget," he said, patting her head. When he looked back to Angie, his eyes were smiling again. "I just stopped by to see if you'd like to do some rehearsing tomorrow on our day off. At my place."

Chapter Twenty-Three

ngie punched the code Xave had texted her into the little box, concentrating so she would get the numbers right and not have to buzz for assistance.

"I don't know. I just don't know," she murmured as the gates swung open. She steered Eckhart carefully past them, up the winding drive through lush landscaping, wondering the whole time if this was a great idea.

Meeting with Xavier Patel alone. At his beach house. Away from the rest of the world. To anyone else from the outside world the situation might sound like a fantasy come true. But Angie knew her circumstances were different.

Not only was there all of the confusion from the love potion, but she wasn't completely sure the things Kristina had told her weren't true. Even if there was only a nugget of truth in what she had said, it raised a lot of red flags for Angie.

Her insides vibrated with uncertain anticipation as she pulled up to the huge luxury home and parked her vintage VW bus and went to the front door.

Xave opened the door, but the sight of him didn't send her into a dizzy spell. Maybe the red flags were enough to calm her reaction to him. Or maybe the sheer grandness of his house had put her into shock.

He glanced down expectantly, then back up at her. "No Fidget today?"

Directly under the gaze of his intense eyes, it took a moment for Angie to remember what she had done with Fidget. "Oh, no, I didn't bring her. She's with Fern and Albert today."

He nodded, obviously a little disappointed. "Of course, of course." An awkward pause hung between them until Xave suddenly remembered she was still standing outside. Hurriedly, he took a step back. With a gallant sweep of his arm, he ushered her into a foyer that was the size of her one bedroom apartment in Denver. "Welcome."

Angie smiled politely and followed him past a grand staircase into a gigantic open room. She wasn't sure what she expected the beach house of a movie star to look like, but she was wholly unprepared for what she encountered when she walked into Xave's home.

Vaulted ceilings featuring massive unstained wood beams stretched two or maybe three stories high. An inviting living room and fireplace were positioned on one side and a gleaming modern kitchen and dining room on the other. The west side of the room was all windows, framing an epic view of the ocean. Blue water against blue sky as far as the eye could see.

Wood floors gleamed in their natural color, unstained like the beams. An ample white sectional sofa sat in the living room. Overstuffed, it looked like a family of five could sleep on it comfortably. A puffy knit throw blanket the color of a sheep in the field was tossed across one end.

The gas fireplace surround was made of smooth white stones about the size of peach pits and rose the entire length of the wall to the ceiling. She couldn't imagine how long it must have taken someone to build that fireplace stone by stone, but it was beautiful. Almost opalescent. Each individual stone glimmered as if it was under water, making the whole fireplace look like a waterfall flowing down from above.

With the color scheme of white on white, and neutral on white, Angie would have thought the space would feel sterile. Yet somehow, with all of the unfinished wood and natural materials, plus the occasional splash of turquoise blue and sea green in the rugs, artwork, and knick-knacks, Xave's home felt warm and relaxing.

Luxurious and unique, his living space was other worldly. Rather like she imagined the home of an elf king or a fairy lord might look.

"You have a beautiful home," she said.

Xave, the pirate turned elf king, glanced down at the white marble counter top of his kitchen island where he stood. She was surprised to see he was uncomfortable with her compliment.

"Well, I've been very lucky." He lifted his eyes to hers then let them scan the ocean view. "Honestly it's too big for just one person."

Angie's heart did a flip-flop in her chest and her palms started to sweat. He didn't mean anything by that, she chided herself. He's just talking, not asking you to move in. Calm down. It's the love potion talking.

"Would you like something to drink?" he asked, interrupting the silent scolding she was giving herself.

"Um, sure," Angie responded, suddenly hyper aware of her wrinkled purple sundress and unruly red hair. She had taken a swim early in the morning and rinsed off at the outdoor shower, which normally left her feeling refreshed and clean. But standing in Xave's decor, she felt a little like a rumpled clown doll wearing a ridiculous bright costume. She tried to smile with confidence. "What do you have?"

Xave wore his signature tan shorts and off white short

sleeved shirt. The same neat ensemble she always saw him in when he wasn't in costume. He clapped his hands together and rubbed them as he turned his back to her and pulled open a massive stainless steel refrigerator.

"Let's see, there's sparkling water, sparkling water with lime, sparkling water infused with cucumber, and..." he leaned deep into the fridge, pretending to hunt for something at the back before popping back. "Citrus flavored sparkling water!"

She chuckled, which helped her nerves, and feigned deep thought for a moment before answering, "I think I'll have a sparkling water."

He grinned at her over his shoulder. "Excellent choice. Which one?"

"Surprise me."

He pulled two glass bottles out with a flourish and placed them on the island. "You can leave your purse up here if you want and we can sit on the sofa?"

Placing her woven cotton purse on the fine marble island made Angie wince inwardly. The purse had been a find at a flea market in Denver. Boho style, hand made, she had loved it right away and used it. A lot. Frayed around the edges and flopped in a sad pile on Xave's marble counter top, the purse now looked like a deflated offering made by peasants to a sleek fairy king in the hopes he might gift them a bounty of crops.

Ignoring the unusual pang of insecurity, Angie followed Xave to the sofa. The magnificent piece of furniture was as comfortable as it looked and she sank into its cushions with a quiet sigh.

"I appreciate you doing this with me." Xave handed her a bottle of cucumber infused sparkling water. Her favorite.

"No problem, I can use all the rehearsal I can get. Though I don't have any lines so I'm not sure how to even go about rehearsing."

Xave's eyes brightened. "That's exactly what I was thinking! Having a non-speaking part can sometimes be more challenging than a speaking role. And I know this is your first big role."

"My first ever role," she corrected him. "Except for a couple of plays in high school, but I only had a speaking role in one of those. Oh, and there was the one time Bridget made me play a waitress in a video letter she made for one of her boyfriends. They're no longer together. Not sure if my acting had anything to do with it." Realizing she was going on and on about being in high school plays to a man who starred in actual Hollywood movies, Angie willed herself to stop speaking.

To his credit, Xave didn't act bored. But then, Angie reminded herself, he was a skilled actor.

Still the smile in his eyes as she chattered nervously seemed authentic. Not only authentic, but inviting, magnetic...dreamy.

Ugh. Coming here had been a mistake. If she was being honest, she had known it was a mistake the moment she agreed to do it. What had she been thinking? The only explanation was that she hadn't been thinking.

Overcome by his obvious charms, weakened by the love potion still pulsing through her body wreaking havoc on her will power, and secretly amused at the reaction Kristina and Marissa had to his invitation, wild horses couldn't have kept her from accepting.

Now that she was here there was no reason not to enjoy his company. Hopefully the crazy fluttering in her stomach and general light headedness would subside. Or, perhaps she could learn enough about acting to conceal them from him.

"Angie?" Xave asked, a questioning look on his face.

He had been talking and she hadn't heard a word he said.

"Sorry?"

"Did you bring your script?"

"Oh, no, I don't have one."

"You don't have one?"

She shook her head firmly. "No, I asked for one in the beginning, when I was an extra, but the others said they don't usually give extras a copy of the script." Angie shrugged and let out a little laugh. "I don't have any lines, so I guess it's not that important."

He stood. "You should have your own script. I have some copies in my office. Hang tight."

Angie watched as Xave climbed up the staircase, two stairs at a time. She took the opportunity to close her eyes and take a few deep breaths, hoping to clear her nerves. On the second breath, she heard her phone buzzing in her purse on the kitchen island.

Xave returned with a script in his hand just as she fished her phone out of her bag to turn it off, but when she saw the screen she gasped.

"What is it?" Xave asked.

"I have 22 new texts and 11 missed calls. It looks like they're mostly from Bridget." Angie's stomach clenched. Had something happened to Tawnyetta?

"Is everything okay?" Xave's brow creased with concern. He placed the script gently on the table, forgotten for now.

"I don't know." She scrolled through her texts. They were all different variations of *Call Me!* "I'm sorry, I need to call her."

"Of course, please go ahead." He went back to the sectional to give her some privacy.

"Where have you been, GiGi!" Bridget's voice was so loud Angie was sure Xave could hear what she was saying even though he was on the other side of a huge room.

"I didn't hear my phone. I was driving." She must have been really preoccupied to not hear any of the texts or phone calls on her way to Xave's. "What's the matter?"

"Nothing's the matter. Everything's wonderful! We're going to be Aunts!"

"What, now!?"

"Yes, now! It's happening! We're at the hospital and they've taken Tawny back to prep her for surgery."

Angie squealed and hopped up and down. "How is she? How's Michael? I can't believe it! I mean, we knew it was coming, but I still can't believe it!"

"I'm going to set up a group video with everyone, so I'll call you back in a minute. But you need to answer this time."

"Okay, yes. I'll answer. Bye!" Angie's heart drummed in her chest as she ended the call. She covered her mouth with her hand and squealed again before remembering she was still in Xave's house. She whirled around to face him. "I'm sorry, I didn't mean to scream."

"That's all right," he laughed. "Good news, I take it?"

She beamed at him. "Tawnyetta's having her babies, right now. In Scotland! We're going to do a video call. She's–*Bridget's* calling me back." She turned to pick up her purse, saw the script and reached for it before stopping herself and turning back to Xave. "Sorry, I have to postpone the rehearsal. I'm so excited I can't think straight. I should go home so I can be on the call." Right after she spoke she remembered her home was parked just outside the front door.

"Of course, whatever you want." Xave stood quickly, glancing at her phone on the counter then back at her. "You're welcome to stay here for the video call. You may not be focused enough to drive if you're trying to watch your friend bring life into the world."

She hesitated, her heart racing a mile a minute, her thoughts still scattered. "I don't know what to do."

"Here, come sit down. I would be honored if you stayed here for this happy event." He came to the kitchen island and helped her to the sofa, making sure to pick up her phone. "Do you have enough charge on your phone?"

"What?" She had heard him speak, but couldn't quite process the words. Her own thoughts were floating, disconnected, above her head.

He spoke a little more slowly. "A charger for your phone? I'll plug it in for you."

"A charger," she repeated as she sat down. He placed her purse in her lap and she managed to dig out her charger, even though her hands were shaking.

"All set," he said, smiling. They both looked down at the phone in her lap. No call yet. He looked up sharply, a new idea shining in his eyes. "Would you like to watch on a bigger screen?"

Chapter Twenty-Four

Within minutes Xave had set up her phone on the mantel and connected it to his wifi so the video could be cast onto his large screen TV. Disguised as a piece of artwork on the wall, the TV was invisible to the naked eye. Still in a daze, Angie watched him use a slender remote control to make the artwork dissolve and the TV materialize in its place.

Bridget's name and photo flashed onto her phone asking for a video call connection.

"There's the call," Xave announced. He was standing near the mantel.

"How do I answer it?" Angie asked from the couch.

"I'll get it, if you don't mind."

"Please," she was relieved he knew what he was doing. Within a few moments, Bridget's face appeared up close and personal on the giant TV screen. Pieces of taupe furniture and walls showed up behind her. The hospital waiting room.

"Hello? Hello?" Bridget's pretty eyebrows were pinched in confusion. She looked away from the camera. "Mister, is this working?"

Thomas' face came into view as he punched buttons on Bridget's phone. "Hang on everyone. There." He looked into the camera and smiled. Suddenly Angie could see Sofia and Ian together in a small square of their own. Then Luna popped up in another square. "Hey guys!" Thomas said with a wiggle of his eyebrows.

Happy greetings came from all of them at once. Angie's heart warmed at the sight of her friends. She could feel the love emanating through the screen.

Thomas squinted and moved so close to Bridget's phone his face loomed on Xave's TV. "Where are you Angie? That doesn't look like Eckhart."

"Oh, I'm, uh, we were rehearsing. I'm at Xave's." Heat rushed to her cheeks and Angie knew she was turning bright red under the scrutiny of her friends.

All of them looked surprised. Thomas' face disappeared and Bridget's appeared, her eyebrows raised in shock.

Ian leaned closer to his and Sofia's phone, "Oi, Xave, how's it going, mate?"

Xave looked at Angie to make sure she was okay with him being involved. She smiled and waved him over, patting the sofa cushion next to her.

He came closer and Angie saw him appear in their square on the screen. He waved at the camera, "Hello." He started to sit down next to her then hesitated, speaking quietly he asked, "Are you sure? I don't want to intrude if it's too...intimate."

"Oh, no, you don't have to worry about that," Bridget's giant TV face answered for Angie. Apparently he hadn't spoken quietly enough. "She's having a C-section. We're only getting the PG version from the waiting room!"

Laughter rose from all of the squares. Even Angie had to giggle at the thought of Xavier Patel, movie star, watching his big screen television in shock as Tawnyetta experienced the awe inspiring event of natural childbirth, and getting to see it all up close and personal.

Xave's cheeks flushed as he sat gingerly down next to Angie. There was no way he was acting, she was certain he was embarrassed.

Thomas had reappeared behind Bridget. He was squinting at the phone once again. "Is that a beach house? I see water through the windows behind you."

"Stop it, Mister, we're here for Tawny and Michael's babies, not a home tour," Bridget scolded.

"It's for work, I'm building a house with water views." Thomas explained. "I'd love to get a video tour for some ideas."

Bridget smacked at him, but missed as Thomas ducked out of her reach.

Angie smiled at Xave, who looked like he wished he could sink into the cushions of his giant white sofa and disappear. She leaned closer to him and whispered, "Are you sure you're all right with me doing this here?"

When he turned to her, he was still a little flustered, but there was something else in his eyes that made them shine warm and bright. Admiration. Wonder.

"I am honored to be part of this," he whispered back, sending a shiver of pleasure up her spine.

At once she sensed his respect for life. His respect for Tawnyetta who was about to become a mother. Angie knew without asking that he adored his own mother. The vibrations coming off of him were clear as a bell.

In his normal voice, Xave spoke to the camera. "I'd be happy to give you a video tour later. There are some amazing views from the second floor."

"Sounds good, bud," Thomas said.

"Michael's here!" Bridget exclaimed. She turned her phone

so they could all see Michael entering the waiting area accompanied by a nurse. He held a pair of folded green scrubs and his handsome face was stiff with nerves.

"Hi Michael!" Angie called out to the screen. Everyone else shouted their greetings as well.

"Hi everyone, thanks for joining us." On edge with impending fatherhood, Michael's Scottish brogue was thicker than normal. He raised the scrubs so they could see. "I'm going in now. I won't be coming back until the bairns arrive."

They all waved and called out encouragement as he left with the nurse and Bridget turned the phone back to her face.

Sofia let out an uncustomary squeal of excitement. "I can't believe we're about to be Aunts!"

Thomas popped his head in behind Bridget's. "And Uncles!"

Laughter and excited chatter from everyone on the call filled the room.

"Give us all the details, Bridget," Luna requested.

There was nothing Bridget loved more than being the center of attention except for being the center of attention and the only one with all of the details. She filled them in on the last several days of Tawnyetta's pregnancy leading up to this moment.

Xave slowly relaxed as Bridget's monologue continued. It was nice being with him in silence, listening to him chuckle at some of Bridget's bits of pregnancy information. It was kind of him, really, to take part in what might turn into quite a long event.

At one point he excused himself to use the bathroom and Sofia took the opportunity to text Angie. Her text flashed across the TV screen.

What's going on with you, Ang? Anything new we should know about?

Angie sucked in her breath. Her eyes flew open and she looked around to see if Xave had come back into the room and read the message.

No. Thank goodness.

She stared meaningfully at Sofia in her little square and shook her head with a jerk. Sofia smiled mischievously, but gave a quick nod to let Angie know she understood not to text again.

When Xave returned he brought some hummus and vegetables to snack on and another cucumber infused sparkling water.

"Thank you," Angie murmured.

He sat back down next to her and helped himself to a carrot dipped in hummus. Sofia pressed her lips together to control a smile and Angie knew she was reacting to Xave.

She couldn't blame Sofia too much, because Angie was also reacting to him. It was difficult to ignore his presence. His good looks were distracting and the fact that he was basically inside their little friend group, participating in one of its biggest moments ever, made it feel like he was one of them. A little like he and Angie were a couple, like Sofia and Ian.

Angie closed her eyes momentarily and took a steadying breath. She didn't need to go down that road at the moment. So far, she had been able to overcome the powers of the love potion and remain pretty normal with Xave in his beach house mansion. It would be great if she could keep it up for the rest of their time together, no matter how long that was.

"Like Bridget and Thomas," she said under her breath. She opened her eyes, surprised at the sound of her voice.

Xave turned to her. "Did you say something?"

Angie shook her head 'no' and reached for a piece of celery to dip into the hummus, but her mind was turning. Bridget and Thomas weren't a couple. They were friends. But watching them together in the hospital waiting room, one might think otherwise.

Not every couple that spent time together had to become romantic partners.

She snuck a peek at Xave's handsome profile. Warmth squeezed her heart. None of this had to become anything other than it was, two people who happened to be acting in a movie together and may possibly become friends over time. That was real. That was what she needed to focus on. They weren't going to be in this situation forever, after all. The movie was scheduled to wrap in just over a month.

Xave glanced over and caught her staring at him. Angie smiled quickly. He responded just as quickly with a blinding smile of his own.

See? No problem. Friends it was.

"I can't go back there," Thomas explained to Bridget.

"But it's taking so long. What if something's wrong?" Bridget's big blue eyes were wet with worried tears.

Angie had lost track of the main conversation, but caught up pretty quickly listening to Thomas and Bridget bicker.

"Michael will be out as soon as he can," he reassured her.

"She could text me or something just to let us know," she complained.

Thomas looked at her in disbelief. "She's in surgery, having babies...two babies! I'm sure she has other things to worry about."

Smiling at Thomas' struggle to control Bridget, Angie reached over to dip her carrot in the hummus. Just as Xave did the same. Their hands bumped together. The touch of his skin against hers sent a jolt through her arm into her heart, making it jump into high gear.

He caught her eye and didn't look away. Stunned. Had he felt the same shocking buzz through his body as well?

"Michael's coming!" Bridget called out.

Everyone on the call jerked to attention. There was a squeal of delight, voices talking over each other in the waiting room, and a blur of video as Bridget dropped her phone.

"Thomas, what's going on?" Sofia asked, hoping he would hear her over the chaos in the waiting room.

"Show them, show them!" Bridget's voice commanded.

The phone was picked up, scenery of the waiting room whipping by in a blur. Then, suddenly, there was Michael. He stood in the doorway still in his scrubs, flanked by two nurses this time.

He held two tiny bundles, one in each arm.

Angie gasped. Babies. Those were Tawnyetta's babies!

"Their mother is doing fine. She'll be ready to receive visitors soon." Michael beamed with pride and joy. "In the meantime, here they are. They're both strong and healthy She wanted you all to get a look at them right away."

Luna was laughing and crying in her square. Ian had his arm around Sofia holding her close as she clapped her hands together, laughing and crying as well.

Angie realized she was crying, too. She covered her mouth with one hand and looked down. She wasn't sure how it had happened, but she was holding Xave's hand with her other hand.

He looked at her, his eyes soft with emotion. He squeezed her hand warmly. She didn't pull hers away.

"Oh my God, they're gorgeous!" Bridget cooed, moving her phone in closer so small pink faces swaddled in soft cotton blankets took up the whole screen.

"They're darling!" Luna exclaimed, still sobbing happily.

"What are they, Laird Michael?" Ian asked.

In all the excitement Angie had forgotten that Tawynetta and Michael had not wanted to know the sex of their twins before they were born.

"Right, right," Michael laughed, a deep throaty laugh.

Angie could picture him laughing in the gardens at Claymore Castle surrounded by his children, giving them piggyback rides. "I forgot to announce that, didn't I?" Michael chuckled again. He lifted his right arm. "This is our strapping lad. And this," he lifted his left arm, his voice noticeably softening. "This is our wee little lass."

More tears, more laughter, and more congratulations filled the airwaves before Michael left to return the *wee bairns* to their mother's arms. With a promise to let everyone know when Tawnyetta was up to being live-streamed, Bridget ended the official part of the video call and everyone else hung up.

Thomas, on the other hand, had more questions for Xave about his second story views. Angie handed her phone over to Xave so he could do a video walk through of his house.

She followed, moving through the beautifully decorated rooms, but still wrapped up in the miracle of life they had just witnessed.

What must Tawnyetta be feeling at this moment? Angie couldn't take a guess. She had been overwhelmed with love and adoration when she brought Fidget home. How much more would the joy of giving birth to your own children be? Two little precious souls to cherish.

And Michael, what a wonderful husband, and what a magnificent father he would be in the future. Having the kind of relationship Tawnyetta and Michael shared was the perfect way to start a family.

A pang of longing struck her right in the stomach and she stopped walking, allowing Xave to continue on without her. She wasn't sure how long she had been standing there when she heard his voice.

"What do you think?" Xave was asking her a question.

Angie looked around and noticed they were in a bedroom. A bedroom about five times bigger than any bedroom she had ever had, but a bedroom nonetheless.

"Do you like the view?" Xave was standing on the far end of the room, looking back for her reaction.

Her mind, which had so recently been blown with the birth of Tawnyetta's twins, had a hard time catching up to what was going on around her.

King sized bed, bleached wood furnishings, thick blue rugs, and French doors leading to a wide balcony, all came into focus. Pictures on the dressers. A stack of books on one side of the bed. This bedroom wasn't a spare room. This was Xave's bedroom.

"Is it amazing in person, Angie?" Thomas' voice came through the speaker of her phone in Xave's hand. "It's amazing from my end. It must be out of this world in person."

Xave watched her, a strange look on his face. Neither of them budged an inch and Angie couldn't bring herself to answer Thomas. Her voice stuck in her throat. Her eyes could not leave Xave's.

A breeze came through the French doors and tickled her arms, brushing against her face with a kiss of salty air. The ocean stretched out behind Xave. So close she could hear the waves rushing against sandy shores somewhere below the balcony.

"Are you there? Did you hear me? A balcony with a view like that off the master bedroom has got to be amazing," Thomas' speaker voice said.

Angie cleared her throat. "I'm–I'm here." She didn't look away from Xave. "The view is amazing."

The side of Xave's mouth twitched up into a grin. Then the grin turned into a smile that moved into his eyes. Heat filled Angie's cheeks. Still, she did not look away.

"Say, Xave, what kind of square footage is your master bedroom?" Thomas asked, blissfully unaware of the electricity sparking between her and Xave.

Xave answered without taking his eyes off of her, "I'm not

sure of the square footage. It's big, though. Much, much too big for one person."

Chapter Twenty-Five

"Girl, I swear, you are literally becoming the Mermaid Queen." Shivaun admired her handiwork in the large makeup mirror.

Angie smiled. She appreciated everything Shivaun and the others had done for her during this transition into the Mermaid Queen role. It was their skill that made her look like a mermaid.

"You do all the work, Shivaun. I just sit here!"

"I don't know, Angie," Anthony twirled his chair around until it faced her. Shivaun nodded, giving her the go ahead to leave the makeup chair and get into Anthony's chair to get her hair done. "We can do a lot, you're not wrong. But!" He held one finger in front of her as she sat down, shushing her arguments before she even thought about speaking them. "It still takes something special, a kind of mermaid sparkle in your eyes, to take it over the edge." He turned her toward the mirror and leaned down so his face was even with hers in their reflection. "I saw some of the dailies and you look absolutely amazing in them!"

Angie flinched at the idea. She was sure the residual effects of the love potion was skewing his opinion, but there was nothing she could do about it at this point. At least, that's what she had decided.

The damage had been done. The film directors and the crew, in addition to Xave, continued to be quite taken with her and she had determined all she could do was be responsible with that power. Especially after Xave's attentions had increased exponentially since she spent the day at his beach house.

It had taken every bit of willpower she possessed to leave his gorgeous master bedroom, gather her things, and drive away after bonding with him over Tawnyetta's twins being born.

"I've got to get home to Fidget," she had said, knowing full well that Fern and Albert would happily watch Fidget for as long as she needed. No questions asked.

"Oh, of course," Xave had seemed disappointed. How could he be otherwise? Angie had basically drugged him into thinking that he wanted to spend time with her and that he found her overwhelmingly attractive.

She had drugged herself, too. So much so that whenever she even thought about his dark good looks her heart went into palpitations.

That was the worst part. The pain that ripped through her core every time she had to push him away. But she had no choice. The honorable thing was to make the best out of the situation and try not to use her advantage to manipulate anything or anyone.

"I just want to do a good job," she admitted to her hair and makeup team.

Shivaun snorted a laugh. "You're doing a fantastic job. And this being your first role, you should be proud of yourself."

Angie fought to control a cringe and tried to smile

graciously. Her phone buzzed for the fifth time that morning. Still fighting the cringe, she flipped it over to see Xave was texting her. For the fifth time that day.

Anthony's eyes grew wide. He had caught a glimpse of the name on her phone when she flipped it over. Their eyes met in the reflection and he gave her a wily grin. "Our favorite pirate seems to have taken notice of you as well."

It was Angie's turn to snort out a laugh, but hers came across a little too fabricated. She watched in the mirror as Anthony and Shivaun shared a knowing look behind her.

"It's nothing," she blurted out, realizing immediately how defensive she sounded.

Anthony patted her shoulder reassuringly. "Don't worry, it's not unusual for romance to filter off the camera and into the set."

Shivaun nodded. "We won't tell anybody."

Glad her heavy makeup hid the flush in her cheeks, Angie shook her head. "No, no, it's nothing like that."

Anthony raised his eyebrows. He didn't believe her. Neither did Shivaun. Neither did she, actually.

"He's just...we're just, you know, rehearsing and stuff. We've been going over the scenes and everything. For the movie." Angie couldn't think of anything else to defend her contact with the star of the film. She couldn't exactly explain that he was inexplicably drawn to her because of a love potion and that she was doing her best to fend off his texts and phone calls and keep everything at a friendship level.

"Well, that explains why the dailies looked so good then, doesn't it?" Anthony joked. Thankfully, he sensed she didn't want to talk about Xave anymore, so he moved on to the next topic, her hair.

Angie didn't check Xave's text until after she was completely done with hair and makeup and on her way to the costume trailer.

In addition to the three early texts that were mostly good morning, how's your day going kind of messages, and to which she had answered promptly in the most friend-type way she could devise, there were the last two texts, which were much more specific.

First...*We have the same lunch break today :)*

Then...*Are you going to lunch in your room or at crafty's outside tables?*

Angie's stomach flopped up and down, twirled around, and landed with a thump. He wanted to eat lunch with her, that was clear. The part of her that was drawn to him was ecstatic. The part of her that knew she should keep her distance was distraught.

Before she could come up with an answer, Kristina and Marissa appeared out of nowhere and sidled up next to her.

"How are you, Angie? It seems like we haven't seen you in forever." Kristina was, as always, the only one out of the two to speak.

"I'm fine, how are you guys?" Angie responded politely. She had been raised to be kind to everyone, even those who may not seem friendly on the outside.

Kristina definitely didn't feel friendly, but Angie had other things to worry about. Xave in particular and the rest of the film crew as well. She almost welcomed Kristina and Marissa's odd negative vibes, at least they weren't looking up to her under false pretenses.

Then again, why weren't they looking up to her?

Angie peered at Kristina more carefully. Still short. Still blonde. Sans makeup, because she was on her way to get it done, but still fairly pretty without it. Kristina was just an average young woman. Marissa as well, except taller and a brunette.

So why hadn't they fallen under the spell of the love potion? They obviously didn't like her. What was their secret?

"Where are you off to?" Kristina asked, oblivious to the fact that Angie had suddenly become much more interested in her as a person.

"I'm going to my room to check on Fidget before I get dressed."

"Oh," Kristina shot Marissa a sideways look then smiled at Angie. "Mind if we join you?"

Pleased that she might get a few minutes to grill Kristina on her lifestyle and find some clue as to why the love potion had had little to no effect on her, Angie smiled broadly. "Sure, that would be nice."

It was easy to get Kristina to talk about herself, not so much Marissa, but that was okay. Angie was gleaning a lot of good information about Kristina's eating habits by pretending to ask her what she was planning on eating for lunch.

About halfway into Kristina's explanation of why she was naturally trim and had never had to watch her figure, the sounds of jingling metal came from behind them.

"Hey, Angie," Xave's voice reached her ears before she could turn around, but not before Angie caught her two companions sharing a bitter look about his arrival.

Ignoring them, she greeted Xave calmly, which was quite an accomplishment considering he was already in his pirate costume and cutting quite the figure in the morning sunshine.

"Hi," she said, taming her smile to low beam.

It didn't matter that she was trying to remain cool, Xave's eyes were warm and shining as he slowed to a stop right in front of her. Angie's heart pounded harder in her chest. He carried the scent of leather, crisp linens, and spice, which mingled with the fresh morning air and salty breeze off of the nearby ocean. Enough to send her over the edge into la-la-land if she wasn't careful.

Xave reached out and touched her elbow, not seeming to

notice the other two women at all. "Did you get my text about lunch?"

"Oh, yes," Angie pretended she had just remembered his message. "I'm probably going to eat at the outside tables. It's such a nice day."

"Yes, it is," Xave hadn't taken his eyes off of hers once. Now he let them wander up to her wild mermaid trusses and back down with a grin. "You're looking exceptionally beautiful today."

Angie looked down coyly, unable to contain her reaction to his compliment. She could feel Kristina stiffen next to her. Xave must have felt it too, because he glanced over and finally noticed the other two mermaids.

"Good morning, ladies," he said, all politeness. He looked back at Angie. "Are you all going somewhere now?"

"To her room," Kristina injected.

"To check on Fidget," Angie added.

"Mind if I join you?" Xave asked.

She couldn't exactly refuse his request, nor could she somehow get rid of Kristina and Marissa. So they went as a group to the second costume trailer. A somewhat misfitted group. One fully dressed pirate, one Mermaid Queen wearing a pair of cutoffs and a tank top, and two women who looked perfectly normal despite the fact that at least one of them was seething with jealousy.

When they reached the trailer Angie went in first, followed closely by Kristina and Marissa. Xave held the door open for them and entered last.

As she made her way past the racks of clothing and stacks of shoes and boxes to get to the hallway leading to her private room, Angie sensed a change in the atmosphere. Kristina's palpable jealousy had morphed into something else. Anticipation. She was so close on Angie's heels it seemed as if she was trying to get in front of her. Angie could hear her small pants of breath as they reached the hallway.

So distracted by Kristina invading her walking space, Angie didn't see the string of garlic hanging on her door until she was almost upon it. When she did see it, she stopped short and tilted her head, studying the fat garlic cloves that had been woven into a long rope and hung on her door from a thumbtack.

Spite rippled through the air. Angie suddenly knew why Kristina and Marissa had asked to accompany her back to her room.

Kristina let out a guffaw of laughter so loud, it made Angie jump.

"We found it in the props room and they weren't using it!" Kristina said. Again, much too loud. She elbowed Marissa in the ribs who was only sniggering, not laughing so hard she was snorting like Kristina. "We thought..." more snorts..."We thought you could use it to ward off evil spirits!" She gripped Marissa's arm for support as she laughed and Angie understood why Kristina hadn't made it in Hollywood yet. She couldn't act.

Angie looked past the two mermaid extras at Xave who seemed as confused as she was, if not more, but was still smiling.

"Like a...vampire?" he asked.

"No, silly!" Kristina turned completely around to face him and smacked him on the shoulder.

"For your little alter thingy," Marissa added, flapping her hand at the closed door.

Angie's ribs tightened and her breath was shallow. She kept a placid smile on her face, though she didn't think their joke was very funny. It smacked more of ridicule than a good natured joshing. She glanced at Xave. His smile was dimming.

Glad once again that she had enough makeup on her face

to cover the reddening of her cheeks, Angie fumbled for words. She didn't want to overreact, but their attempt at a joke had fallen flat. First, it wasn't very witty. And second, they weren't actually friends. Random jokes only worked between friends.

Mewing came from the other side of the door. Suddenly Angie was afraid to let them in. She didn't want Kristina and Marissa in her space and she didn't want Xave to see her alter. Maybe he did have a problem with metaphysical spirituality. From the look on his face he wasn't keen on finding out more about her 'alter' or 'warding off evil'.

"On second thought," he said curtly. "I forgot I've got a meeting with the stunt coordinator." He backed up, nodding politely at Kristina and Marissa then catching Angie's eye. "Say 'hi' to Fidget for me."

Then he was gone and she was left with her two co-mermaids, though there was definitely no camaraderie between them.

Fidget's mewing grew more urgent, but Angie didn't want to open the door. She didn't want the other two inside her room or near her cat. The tightening in her ribs increased and she took a thin breath, trying to fill her lungs yet falling short. She glanced up at the garlic.

"Don't worry, I'm sure he didn't know what this was about," Kristina said, reaching past Angie and snatching the garlic string from the door so hard the thumbtack flew off and skittered across the floor. With a roll of her eyes she added, "It was just a joke. These aren't even real. They're plastic." To prove her point she tapped one of the garlic bulbs with her fingernail and it made a hollow plastic sound.

Fidget stuck her paw under the door, reaching for Angie's feet. All three women looked down and watched in silence.

Finally, Angie took a deep breath and said, "It might be better if I go in by myself. She's a little high strung today."

Kristina blinked at her. Marissa did too, Kristina's silent shadow.

"Fine," Kristina sniffed. She glanced down at Fidget's paw then looked up at Angie with a smile that showed all of her teeth. "Your cat's so cute. We'd love to babysit sometime, wouldn't we, Marissa?" Marissa nodded on cue.

Angie shrugged noncommittally, but didn't say yes. There was no way she would allow either of them to take Fidget anywhere. Their whole vibe was just too negative.

Giving them a quick wave and a false smile, she watched as they disappeared down the hallway and waited until she heard the door to the trailer close before she turned to open her room. She had the key in her pocket and was surprised to find her fingers trembling slightly as she retrieved it.

Was she really that upset over a stupid joke? She hadn't thought so, yet the tightness in her ribs didn't go away. It wasn't that the joke wasn't funny, it was more that she suspected it hadn't been meant as a joke at all.

For whatever reason, probably her connection to Xave and her being offered the Queen Mermaid role, Kristina and Marissa didn't like her. Kristina especially. Angie wasn't used to that kind of animosity. Maybe she had become too comfortable with the adoration the love potion brought to her. Either way, it was a problem she would have to deal with for another five weeks. That's when they would be done shooting the film.

She managed to get the key out and into the doorknob. Fidget's mews turned into loud meows.

"Hush, hush, I'm coming," Angie said softly. It would be nice to cuddle with her cat in peace and solitude.

Just when she was about to push the door open, someone came out of nowhere and tapped her hard on the shoulder, startling Angie so much she cried out in surprise.

Chapter Twenty-Six

Angie whirled around, ready to confront Kristina more firmly this time. "I need a few minutes alo–" She stopped short when she saw it wasn't Kristina who had tapped her on the shoulder. Her eyes flew open. "Luna!"

"Surprise!" Luna raised jazz hands high in the air.

"What are you doing here?" All of the tension left Angie's body and she was filled with joy at the sight of her friend.

"I'm surprising you!" Luna gave her a big hug then held her at arms length and took in her Mermaid Queen look. "I almost wasn't sure it was you, but then I got closer and saw your hair. You look amazing!" Angie laughed, but Luna was searching her eyes more closely, looking past the makeup. "Is everything all right? You seemed a little...brusque."

Angie was delighted at the question. Luna was a writer and always using unusual words. "Brusque?" she asked with a grin.

"You know, abrupt, annoyed." Luna furrowed her brow and looked down the hallway as if the culprit of Angie's previous bad mood would be found there. "You never get annoyed." She looked back at Angie. Are you being treated well? Are they working you too hard?"

Fidget's full front leg stretched underneath the door. She batted at their toes with her paw.

"Fidget's here?" It was Luna's turn to be delighted.

"Come on, we can hang out in here for a little while," Angie unlocked the door.

Settled on the loveseat with the door closed to the outside world and Fidget happily pacing across their laps so she could be petted equally by both of them, Angie filled Luna in on her little drama. The story poured out easily as Luna was a sympathetic listener.

When she was done, Luna's light brown eyes were full of understanding. "So you don't think you can trust your feelings."

The words were posed as a statement, not a question, and they hit Angie square in the face. She pulled her head back slightly, surprised at the accuracy. Not that she should be totally surprised, Luna knew her well and was a solid judge of emotions.

"Well, yes, I think you're right. I think you've hit the problem right on the head." Angie's mind was swirling. If Luna was on the right track, did that mean she had real feelings for Xave? Not just love potion induced feelings?

As if she could read her mind, Luna asked, "Do you have romantic feelings for him, Angie?"

The question squeezed her heart. A knot swelled in her throat and Angie suddenly found herself staring wide eyed at Luna while blinking back hot tears. Her bottom lip was trembling, but she managed a choked response. "I don't know."

"Oh, honey," Luna pulled her in for a hug, careful to stay clear of her rather large Mermaid Queen hairdo as she patted her back.

"I'm so confused," Angie admitted with a sniffle when the hug was over.

"Of course, it's a confusing situation."

"I mean, on one hand, who wouldn't have feelings for him? He's nice and caring. Fidget likes him." Angie reached out and stroked Fidget who had curled up and was purring happily in Luna's lap.

"That's always a good sign," Luna agreed.

"Plus he's Xavier Patel, you've seen him," Angie added.

Luna nodded emphatically. "Yes, gorgeous movie star. He's so attractive he makes a living at it."

Angie chuckled even as she carefully dabbed tears away from her eyes, trying not to disturb her makeup. Luna watched her with such a curious look on her face Angie asked, "What's the matter?"

Distracted by her own thoughts, Luna said, "I've never seen a mermaid cry."

Angie paused her dabbing and they stared at each other for a beat. A smile crept onto Luna's face. Mirth tickled Angie's tear filled eyes. One moment later they both burst out laughing.

After they were done cracking up, Angie patted Luna's knee affectionately. "How long are you visiting?"

"I've got four days here before I'm leaving with Sofia and Ian to Scotland."

"Right, they'll be back up here tomorrow, yes?"

Luna nodded. "Yes, she told me Ian has to wrap up a few things with his part of the film before they leave America. I'm hoping you have at least one day off while I'm here." She gave Angie a meaningful look. "I wouldn't mind going by that apothecary with you if you want. Maybe they have something else that could help you out."

Relieved that at least one of her friends was open to the world of herbal healing, tinctures, and possible love potions, she nodded emphatically. "I'm off again in three days. You'll love Polypody Cove, too. It's an adorable little town."

"Polypody Cove?" Luna giggled some more.

"I know, funny name, but it's cute."

The time over the next few days spent filming with Xave during working hours and socializing with Luna, Sofia and Ian in the evenings flew by. Angie managed to keep Xave at arms length using Luna's visit as a reason to fend off any attempts on his part to get together outside of the film set. And she was so caught up with spending time with her friends, she was able to push thoughts of Xave out of her mind when she wasn't on set.

By the time she and Luna drove into Polypody Cove in Luna's rental car on Angie's day off, she was almost numb to having any feelings whatsoever for Xave. She had grown adept at putting aside her emotions in order to get through the day.

"You were right, this is an adorable little town." Luna looked around appreciatively as they strolled down Main Street to The Vanilla Bean.

Angie smiled, letting the charm of her favorite hideaway combined with the companionship of one of her favorite people lift her mood.

She hadn't been in a bad mood over the past few days per se, but she been experiencing some disconnect. The need to separate from her feelings was casting a bit of a shadow across everything. Stepping away from filming on her day off at least gave her a little breathing room.

She pointed out the mechanic shop where she had brought Eckhart and first discovered the town. They walked by Pie's Otta Pizza and the Firedancer Bar & Grill, which weren't open yet, before reaching The Vanilla Bean. Angie tried to ignore all of the memories of Xave flooding back to her.

Him buying her coffee and a scone when Eckhart broke

down. Running into him at the Blooming Bee. Eating pizza with Bridget and Thomas and the resulting drive home.

"Are you okay?" Luna held the door of The Vanilla Bean open, waiting for Angie to enter.

Angie blinked. She'd been spacing out again. The delectable smells of fresh brewed coffee and baked goods wafted out of the open door and surrounded her. Not a bad way to be brought back to the present.

She smiled. "You are in for a treat. Their lemon blueberry scones are magnificent!"

After filling up on the treats The Vanilla Bean offered, including Maggie's friendly chit-chat, Angie and Luna made their way to the Blooming Bee Apothecary. Angie couldn't help but keep one eye out for Xave to suddenly appear, as he so often had before. The thought of it sent several tiny butterflies flitting through her stomach.

"Good morning, Angie! So good to see you again," Stacy greeted them. Or maybe it was Tracy. She was too far away for Angie to read her name tag.

"Good morning," Angie answered.

Luna didn't waste any time. She tugged on Angie's arm just as she was about to stop and check out a shelf full of scented candles, and led her toward the counter. "We were wondering about the, um, herbal mixture you created for Angie a few weeks ago?"

"Are you still having troubles with that?" Tracy, name tag front and center, stood up on the other side of the scented candle display where she had been unpacking boxes.

Angie nodded. "I took the antidote you gave me, but I don't think it worked very well. There's still a lot of..." she searched for a word to describe what she had been feeling and witnessing in others. Moving her hands in circular motions, she continued. "A lot of *intensity* flowing through me and everyone I come into contact with."

Tracy looked at Stacy behind the counter who was shaking her head and clucking her tongue against the top of her mouth, making a tsk-tsk sound.

"Come tell us about it." Tracy led Angie and Luna through the store to the counter where it had all begun.

"This is my friend, Luna, from Colorado," Angie said.

Both of the twin's eyebrows lifted and they made small satisfied sounds.

"Beautiful name," Stacy said. Tracy nodded in agreement.

"Thank you," Luna answered, amused. She let her eyes wander across the shelves and shelves of glass jars behind the counter as Angie explained her continuing predicament.

When she finished telling Stacy and Tracy all about her mounting attraction to Xave, his apparent reciprocation, the unusual amount of kudos and attention she was receiving from others on the film, and her concerns that the original potion was somehow manipulating those around her, Stacy and Tracy shared a look.

Stacy was the first to speak. "We wouldn't give you anything that could possibly make you or anyone else do something against their will. It might magnify feelings or merely open up pathways of connection between people, but it wouldn't be powerful enough to change someone's emotions completely."

Angie exhaled quietly, grateful for that bit of news. "So that explains the girls who don't like me."

"Come again?" Tracy asked.

"I didn't understand how everyone else seemed to be seeing me through rose colored glasses while two of the girls I work with definitely do not like me. I thought maybe they were immune or something."

Stacy smiled warmly. "How could anyone not like you, dear?"

"Is it really possible your product had such a dramatic effect?" Luna asked.

For a moment Angie was afraid Stacy and Tracy might be insulted at Luna's blunt question, but they took it in stride.

Tracy gave them both a sincere smile and placed her palms on the counter in front of Angie. "There is the possibility, Angie, that your co-workers, and your gentleman, genuinely like you. Perhaps our original mixture only opened you up to what was already there."

Angie's heart skipped a beat at what Tracy was implying. "So you're saying my feelings are...real feelings?"

Stacy and Tracy nodded in unison.

"They might be amplified or more noticeable because the pathways were opened up between you and someone else, but we couldn't make you feel anything you didn't already feel." Stacy reiterated.

The bells on the Blooming Bee's front door jingled. Angie's heart skipped a beat again. She had gotten so wrapped up in listening to Stacy and Tracy that she had forgotten to keep on the look out for Xave.

Heart pounding so hard she was afraid the others might hear it, Angie put on a nonchalant smile and turned slowly toward the door.

Two young women entered and headed straight to the glass cabinet full of crystals. Angie's pounding heart quieted and shrank inward. She swallowed hard, trying to regain her composure.

When she did turn back to the others her voice was full of false cheer. "That's great news, actually. It seems that I don't have anything else to worry about then."

Stacy, Tracy, and especially Luna, did not look like they believed her drama with Xave was over.

Chapter Twenty-Seven

Angie, Luna, and Sofia sat at a patio table overlooking rolling hills of grapevines. Lunching at a winery was high on Luna's to-do list for her visit and Sofia had found the perfect location.

The winery, along with the attached wine tasting room and restaurant where they were eating, were all built of stone. A wide pergola over the patio area provided enough shade to keep them from baking in the sun while a constant breeze brought the scents of rich earth and growing vines right to their table.

"When do you think you'll make it to Scotland?" Sofia asked Angie before taking a sip of the Pinot Noir she had chosen for their first bottle to share.

A pang of sadness brought a frown to Angie's lips. "I've still got over a month of filming before I can plan on going anywhere."

Then there was the problem of her lighter pocketbook, but she didn't mention that to her friends. Her financial challenges weren't a fun topic of conversation for this little getaway and she was determined to stick to light and entertaining conversation. Throughout their morning in Polypody Cove, Angie felt like she had already burdened Luna with more than enough of her Xave sorrows. It was time to focus on someone other than herself.

As if on cue, all of their phones pinged at the same time. Sofia was the first to reach hers. "Baby pictures!" She exclaimed, turning her phone around so they could see Tawnyetta with the twins in her lap.

"Awww," Luna put one hand on her heart as the image popped up on her phone, too.

Angie dug her phone out of the bottom of her boho bag and got a look at the image up close. "Look at Tawynetta's smile. She's so happy!"

Indeed, Tawnyetta's joy was obvious. Her eyes shone with love for her children. Her family.

"Nothing," Sofia said, frustrated.

"What nothing?" Luna asked.

Sofia plopped her phone down on the table, screen side up so the image remained visible, and picked an olive off of the charcuterie board. "They haven't named them yet. I thought she might be letting us know their names."

It was true, Tawnyetta and Michael had not named their babies. Tawnyetta had said they wanted to get to know them first.

"I think it's sweet that they want to name them according to their personalities," Angie said in Tawnyetta's defense.

"And I think there are historical things to consider because he's a Lord and everything," Luna suggested, reaching for a slice of brie from the board.

"Ugh. I wouldn't think it would be that difficult," Sofia argued.

"Yes, you I could see picking out the names right after you found out you were pregnant," Luna teased.

Sofia chuckled. "I would. Then I could have all of their personalized baby wear ordered."

They all laughed at that. If anybody in their friend group was going to have personalized baby wear made for her children, it would be Sofia.

"So, all baby talk aside, I want to know what's been going on while I was gone. How do you liking acting?" Sofia again turned a questioning look on Angie.

"How am I liking it?" Angie hadn't put a lot of thought into her role over the past few weeks. She'd been so preoccupied with other things, mostly her emotional entanglement with Xave. She considered the question before answering, "Well, it's pretty tedious, actually. I spend a lot of time in hair and makeup, a lot of time waiting for lighting adjustments and for costume to get my tail right in the shot. And, of course, a lot of time waiting in between scenes that I'm *not* in."

"Not the glamour world you thought it would be?" Luna asked.

"I didn't know much about acting, really, so I had no idea what to expect. But, you are correct. Definitely not a glamour world." Angie shrugged. "The people are nice though." Kristina and Marissa rushed into her mind. "Most of them anyway."

She took a sip of wine and ignored the expectant looks on Sofia and Luna's faces. She wasn't going to go down the rabbit hole of talking about Xave when she didn't even know what to think about the situation herself anymore.

"Would you consider doing more acting if any offers came in?" Sofia's manager personality emerged as she snapped off the corner of a cracker and ate it.

"I hadn't thought about that either," Angie answered honestly.

"You should. You're in a movie with some pretty big stars.

Someone's bound to notice that you make a beautiful mermaid."

"You do make an amazing mermaid, you know. Your makeup is gorgeous and so mythical," Luna added. "Have you had a chance to see what you look like on screen?"

Angie tilted her head and winced at Luna, not sure she enjoyed thinking about what she might look like on film. "No, I haven't. I don't know if I want to."

Luna was surprised. "You have to watch the movie when it's done, don't you?"

"Do I? I mean, what if I'm a horrible actress?"

Sofia waved that possibility away with a flick of her wrist. "I thought you were good when I was watching the filming. And Tillie and Brandon wouldn't have asked you to play the part if they thought you were horrible."

Angie wasn't so sure. Even with Stacy and Tracy's assurances from earlier in the day she still had a gnawing feeling Tillie and Brandon had overestimated her acting abilities.

"Besides," Sofia added with a sly grin. "You can always find a mentor. A more experienced actor who could offer you some tips. Right?"

Angie ignored Sofia's obvious reference to Xave and looked out over the beautiful vineyard, sipping her wine to keep from having to answer.

Sensing it was time to move on to another subject, Luna turned to Sofia. "Are you and Ian going right up to Claymore Castle with me when we get to London?"

Sofia shook her head, her straight black hair rippling as she did. "I've got three days of meetings at the college before we can come up. Summer planning sessions with the professors and such. And Ian has some work to do with the band, too." She looked down as her phone buzzed with a text. "Speaking of..."

While Sofia was distracted reading Ian's text, Luna looked

out over the vineyard. "California's gorgeous. Are you happy you made the move here?"

An interesting question. And another one Angie didn't have an immediate answer to. What exactly had she been doing since she got here? She had driven here in Eckhart to fulfill her dream of living by the ocean and experiencing all the natural beauty of California. But thinking back, she couldn't remember fully experiencing much of anything in her new life except for her crazy feelings for Xave.

Staring at Luna, Angie tried to think of what to say, but nothing came to mind.

"Ian wants to take us out to dinner," Sofia interrupted.

"That's nice of him," Luna smiled.

Sofia continued, half looking at them and half reading his text, "Since we won't be back up here before they're done shooting, he invited Tillie and Brandon." She switched her gaze to Angie. "And Xave and Elizabeth, too."

Hyper aware that both Sofia and Luna were watching her for a response, Angie kept her expression calm.

"That's nice," she said, but the words came out strangled. She cleared her throat and reached for her wine. "That's nice," she said again to prove that she had not been rendered speechless by this news.

She smiled serenely, but her attempt at remaining cool didn't last long. Betraying the nervous butterflies that had risen in her middle at Sofia's news, her hand fumbled, clumsily knocking over the wine glass. Deep red wine spilled out over the white table cloth.

"Oh! Sorry," Angie said, flushing madly as she righted the glass, even more sorry that this time she didn't have mermaid makeup to cover up her red cheeks.

"It's okay, Ang." Luna tossed her own napkin over the red stain. "That's why they use white, so they can bleach things out. Besides, a winery has to be used to the occasional spilled glass."

"That's right," Sofia added, raising the half full wine bottle from its place near her side of the table. "And the other thing about wineries is they have an unlimited amount of refills!"

Chapter Twenty-Eight

The fact that Angie had not interacted with Elizabeth until Ian asked them all to dinner struck her as odd. She pondered the curiosity of it as she and Luna rode in the back seat in Sofia and Ian's car to the restaurant.

Being the lead female star of the film, Elizabeth had been around the set, but Angie had always seen her from a distance, in passing, or during one of Elizabeth's big scenes when Angie was an extra in the background. Why they had never crossed paths otherwise was strange. She was already wrestling with what to do about her feelings for Xave, seeing as they may be based in more truth than she had been willing to admit. All of these thoughts whirled together in her mind, making her stomach mildly upset and giving her a low level of anxiety as they got closer to their destination.

The Crow's Nest Seafood Emporium was a famous fine dining establishment nestled on a cliff overlooking the ocean. Known for delicious food, excellent service, upscale clientele and, of course, epic views, Sofia explained to Angie and Luna she had chosen it mostly for Xave and Elizabeth's sake. Apparently, it was the kind of place used to hosting big celebrities.

"Plus the name is brilliant, don't you think?" Ian asked. He glanced over his shoulder from the driver's seat at Angie. "I only wish I could have convinced you to wear your mermaid gear and Xave to come as a pirate."

Everyone laughed, including Angie, though maybe not as heartily as the others. It would have been fitting to be in fins, as much as she felt like a fish out of water on this outing.

Ever since she had learned of their evening plans, she'd been unsettled. Distracted. Unsure. But she had kept her vibration high so as not to ruin their fun afternoon. After the lengthy winery lunch, Angie returned with Luna to her hotel, a small boutique establishment which boasted an organic, earth friendly spa.

"Let's get ready for dinner together," Luna had suggested, inviting both Angie and Sofia to her room for some girl time. "I can order some fun things from the spa!"

It was in the middle of giving each other rejuvenating facials that Angie had taken note of the rather sad condition of her green cotton sundress. "I should have brought a change of clothes, my dress is looking pretty worn out."

Luna frowned, cracking the drying face mask on her cheeks. "Should we go back to your van to get something else to wear?"

"It's no use. I don't have a lot of closet space in the van so I pared down my wardrobe quite a bit. I don't really have anything for a very nice restaurant." Angie straightened her shoulders, determined not to bring the others down. "It's okay. I don't mind. It'll be dark, right?" She laughed, but Sofia and Luna watched her doubtfully.

"You can borrow something of mine," Luna jumped up and went to the hotel closet. "I always pack too much and we're about the same size, aren't we?"

They were the same size, but Angie's red hair and fair skin made it hard to find a dress in Luna's closet that was a good color on her. Finally, they landed on an off the shoulder ankle length dress in orange.

Orange wasn't usually Angie's best color, but this dress was a deep orange with small flecks of cream throughout the fabric, and somehow that combination gave her a healthy glow without blending with her hair and making her look like a carrot. With draped sleeves that exposed her shoulders and a ruffled hem the dress was feminine and had a lovely flow. Perfect for a nice evening out.

Angie smoothed the front of the orange dress after she stepped out of the car at the restaurant. Ian handed the valet his keys and linked arms with Sofia and Luna, then Luna linked arms with Angie.

"I'm gonna be the envy of every man in this place," Ian said happily. "And some of the women, too."

The three women giggled, pleased at his compliment and happy to be out with each other. Angie took a deep breath and exhaled slowly as they entered the building, willing her nerves to shift from anxiety into anticipation of a good time.

Luckily, they were the first ones to arrive. Ian being a celebrity in his own right, of the rock star variety, had scored a beautiful table on the furthest edge of the outdoor eating deck overlooking the ocean.

The view was breathtaking and seeing the water stretch out to the horizon with the great yellow orb of a sun inching closer and closer to its edge appeased Angie's senses. So much so she could almost forget anyone else was joining them.

Tillie and Brandon were the next to arrive.

"I've heard of this place," Tillie said as she sat down. "They say their specialty drinks are really amazing."

"Let's get started on a round then, shall we?" Ian suggested, looking to make eye contact with the waiter.

Angie decided to try the Passion Fruit Mai Tai, mainly because she had never had one and thought it might match nicely with her dress. It was bright and fun looking, plus delicious. She was glad to have downed almost half of the potent mixture by the time Xave arrived.

Maybe it was the Mai Tai or the sensation that they were hanging off of a cliff over the ocean, or maybe it was fatigue from her long day of frolicking with her friends, but from the moment Xave appeared on the other side of the restaurant Angie's whole world went into slow motion.

Black slacks, white shirt, dark skin, perfect hair, gorgeous face, magnetic eyes, his exquisitely masculine frame stood out immediately as he moved confidently through the room. Heads turned as he passed. People parted in front of him. An electricity filled the inside of the restaurant and spilled out onto the deck when it became obvious he was headed in their direction.

Too late, Angie realized the two seats left open were between her and Brandon. She carefully placed her half empty Mai Tai down on the table to avoid knocking it over and concentrated on breathing in and out as she wondered who would sit by her, Xave or the elusive Elizabeth. She didn't know which one would cause her more discomfort.

"Hello, sorry I'm late," Xave said as he gave Angie a quick smile and sat down in the chair next to her, sending her stomach into a flip-flop and filling the air between them with the scent of his cologne.

Her palms began to sweat, but she managed to return his smile with a quiet one of her own. She didn't try to speak.

"Glad you could make it, mate," Ian said.

"We're just waiting on Elizabeth...as usual," Tillie said with a laugh.

Angie glanced in the direction Xave had just come. She had assumed Elizabeth would arrive with him.

Xave chuckled, "She's a wonderful actress, but someone needs to teach her how to set an alarm on her phone."

The conversation continued without Angie's input, which was for the best. She kept her hands in her lap, clasping her fingers together and watching Xave's profile as he joked and laughed with everyone at the table.

The crisp cloth of his shirt was neatly pressed and bright white. Occasionally, when he moved, the cloth pressed against his bicep and she could see the formation of his muscles underneath. She longed to touch his arm. Slide her finger along the cloth and feel his warm strength. Angie clasped her hands more tightly together.

There was a sense of comfort between them. Having spent so much time filming with each other, Angie pretending to be in love with him, Xave pretending to be in love with her. Then the time they had spent together at his beach house waiting for the twins to be born. They were more than just acquaintances at this point. The question was, how much more?

Sofia had a lot of questions for Tillie and Brandon about finishing their film and how they would go about distributing the film when it was complete. Their lively conversation took over the table for a while, during which time the waiter brought Xave his drink. Something called a Dark and Stormy.

He took a sip then turned his head to look at Angie more closely. His eyes wandered quickly over her hair, which Luna had primped into red curly perfection, and down to her shoulders peeking out from the draped fabric of the dress. When he lifted his eyes to hers they were their own kind of dark and stormy. Angie was glad she was seated, because all feeling in her legs disappeared under his gaze.

Xave bent his head toward her so he could speak without being overheard. "You're quiet tonight."

Heart erupting into a million sparkles inside of her chest, she gripped her fingers together even harder. "Am I?"

He paused, his eyes staying on hers, his hand flexing where

he held his glass. He spoke even lower than before. "You look beautiful."

She wondered if she turned into jelly would Luna, who sat on the other side of her, be able to keep her from sliding off of her chair and underneath the table.

"There she is," Tillie announced, looking toward the inside of the restaurant.

All eyes turned to find Elizabeth following a slightly flustered waiter through tables of gawking diners as he showed her to their table.

Elizabeth was thin and graceful. Her blonde tresses were long and undulated in loose curls, reminding Angie of fairy tales where the princess had flowing golden locks. She wore pale blue. A good color for her it would seem, as she appeared to be glowing. It was as if a soft white light emanated from within her and Angie, like everyone else, was drawn to it like a moth to a flame, unable to look away.

Xave had turned in his seat to watch Elizabeth's entrance, his back toward Angie. As she watched Elizabeth, popular movie star and Xave's on screen love interest, get closer and closer, Angie sensed something change in Xave.

A softening came over his whole body. Tension left and a comfortable kind of warmth took over. Angie could literally feel him change with every step Elizabeth took in their direction.

With every shift in his body more of the sparkles that had filled her chest just moments before went dark. By the time Elizabeth arrived at the table and they were properly introduced, Angie was left with nothing inside but a hole where her heart used to be.

phen Twenty-Nine

<h1 style="text-align:center">Chapter Twenty-Nine</h1>

When dinner was over Angie went to the water for solace.

The cliff on which The Crow's Nest Seafood Emporium perched was equipped with a steep, rather teetering set of wooden stairs leading to a small private beach below.

Angie excused herself before the rest of the party had decided what to order for dessert, concerning Luna and Sofia.

Sofia's eyebrows pinched. "Where are you going?"

"Are you feeling all right?" Luna asked.

"I'm fine," Angie brushed off their questions and avoided eye contact with everyone else at the table, especially Xave and Elizabeth. "I want to go walk around a little bit before we make the drive back."

Luna pushed her chair back and started to stand. "I'll join you." This prompted both Ian and Xave to start to stand as well.

"No, no, have some dessert," Angie waved away their attempts to come along. "I also need to call Fern and check up on Fidget, too. I won't be long."

With what she hoped was a breezy smile and a light step, Angie made her way quickly out of the restaurant's front door and into their landscaped gardens. That's where she discovered the stairs leading to the beach.

Not worrying about the long climb back up, Angie descended the steps eagerly, looking forward to communing with the ocean during this dark moment of her day. A swift breeze off the waves swept up the face of the cliff, carrying salt spray and the promise of something wild and unreachable.

At the bottom, Angie stepped into warm sand, remembering at the last moment to slip off her sandals. She carried them dangling from one hand as she made her way to the edge of the water. She took in a deep breath, letting the breeze push her hair back from her face, lift it into the air and tangle the ends together.

"Mother, give me strength." Angie had always looked to the power of nature for spiritual guidance. Adopting her own mother's tendency to speak to Mother Nature during troubling times.

Not that these times were especially troubling. Everything was going smoothly...on the outside.

"But inside," Angie admitted to the water. "Inside, I'm a mess."

Watching Xave and Elizabeth interact during dinner had been excruciating. Like a thousand tiny needles piercing her heart in waves. Every time Elizabeth placed her thin hand on his arm to laugh at one of his jokes, every time Xave turned his shining eyes away from Angie and looked at Elizabeth, Angie sank further and further into a pit of despair.

She took in another deep, cleansing breath and let the riveting sunset hold her gaze. Childhood memories of her first visit to the ocean drifted over the waves and through her mind.

Nine-years old. Scrawny and pale. Tall for her age. Long, skinny legs. Wild, disheveled red curls escaping their hair tie. A light blue polka dot bikini that her mother had found at a thrift store. All of it came flooding back as she watched the golden ball of the sun drop completely off of the horizon.

Angie wrapped her arms around herself as the temperature on the water's edge began to dip, but she didn't move. The carefree feelings of childhood filled her struggling adult soul.

Why did anyone ever have to leave those times behind? Children didn't have financial problems or wonder what they should do with their lives. The didn't get wrapped up in romantic attachments. They didn't get their hearts broken by some man they just met.

"How did I let this get so out of hand?" she asked the water. The waves lapped closer and closer to her feet, but didn't answer. The pain of dreams discarded throbbed in her chest.

As a child Angie had been obsessed with becoming a mermaid, which she knew was impossible. She had thought playing a mermaid might be interesting, but in truth her experience as an actress had been less fun than expected. She was pretty sure acting wasn't something she enjoyed enough to want to do it again.

That skinny little girl in her polka dot bikini who played in the waves and the sand wasn't impressed with acting. Her dream wasn't makeup and costumes and long days of shooting. That little girl craved powerful waves, warm sand, the thick forest along the shore, tall trees and all of the plants, animals and birds who thrived in beautiful, natural places. That was what fascinated her. Had always fascinated her.

"That's why you moved here, Angie! That's what you should be doing. Exploring nature, taking it in, letting Mother Nature guide you. Definitely not worrying about a romantic relationship with a movie star," she chastised herself.

Since when had she ever cared about that kind of thing,

anyway? She had never had crushes on celebrities. She barely watched enough television or movies to even recognize celebrities when someone else pointed them out.

Everything had gotten way off track. She needed to return to her original plan. Sure, she had this mermaid gig, which, given her childhood obsession, was pretty ironic.

"Ironic, but not real," she reminded herself out loud. "I need to get back to what's real. That's the only thing that's going to make things right again."

A thrill whispered across her skin as the ocean breeze chilled under the setting sun.

She could fix this. It wasn't too late. She could re-focus her energy onto the beauty of nature, spend more time on the beach and in the surrounding forests, and spend far less time worrying about the likes of Xavier Patel.

"Angie?"

The voice snapped her out of her thoughts. She turned quickly, startled at the interruption.

There was Xave standing at the foot of the stairs. The glow of the setting sun turned his white shirt gold and washed him with the magical end of day light.

Angie sucked in her breath at the sight of him. She couldn't respond. Neither, it seemed, could Xave. He held perfectly still, an ache in his expression.

No. She would not let her feelings, or the love potion, or whatever was going on, take control. Not anymore.

Angie clenched her hands into fists and released, bringing her back into reality. "Is it time to go?" she asked curtly.

Xave's words caught in his throat. He swallowed, then nodded.

"Great!" Angie declared with more energy than necessary. "Let's go."

She walked to where Xave was still standing, immobile, and leaned over to slip her sandals back on. When she straightened, they were face-to-face. Angie looked him directly in the eyes, bringing all of the power of her convictions to the forefront of her mind.

His eyes dropped to her mouth then quickly back up. For an instant she thought he might try to kiss her. Part of the strength she had mustered up began to crumble.

"Oi, are you ready to go?" Ian, who had climbed halfway down the stairs, called from above.

Angie tore her eyes away from Xave and looked up at Ian and the others, waving. "Yes, I'm ready." Then she brushed past Xave and hurried up the stairs, not looking back to see if he was following.

Chapter Thirty

"Are you sure you're going to be okay?" Luna asked, her eyes troubled.

"Me?" Angie acted surprised. She brushed aside the question with a definitive shake of her wild Queen Mermaid locks.

Luna and Sofia stood together, their eyebrows drawn into a concerned wrinkle in exactly the same way, showing off their family resemblance. They had stopped by her trailer to say goodbye before they left with Ian to the airport. Off to Scotland to see Tawnyetta and Michael's precious babies.

"You're doing that cousin thing where you look so much alike it's weird," Angie tried to change the subject.

"We're serious," Sofia said, her gaze flicking toward Angie's alter set up in the corner. "I think maybe your whole situation here has gotten a little weird."

"It feels like maybe you're not completely okay," Luna said, a little softer and more accepting than her cousin.

Angie blinked. Her Queen Mermaid mascara weighted down her eyelashes making her blinks overly dramatic. She tried deflecting again, pressing a finger to her chest and coughing out a laugh. "Me?"

Sofia gave a little roll of her eyes. "Stop saying that. Seriously, are you going to be okay for the next few weeks doing this?" She waved her hand up and down in front of Angie's mermaid bikini top. Angie was in full costume and makeup waiting for someone to come get her for the next scene. "Or do we need to–"

"Need to what?" Angie interrupted. "Not go see the babies? Don't be silly. I'm fine!" She stretched her arms out wide, showing off her mermaid look with confidence. "Everything's fine."

They continued watching her, unconvinced.

Angie dropped her hands to her sides and sighed. "Seriously, I think the whole love potion stuff has worn off. It just took a little time. I feel fine. I am fine. Everything's fine."

Her friends shared a look.

"You can't not go see Tawny's babies! That would be horrible. They're waiting to meet you. I don't want to be the reason you stay here." Angie hated the idea of her instability keeping her friends from making their trip.

Luna's resolve began to crumble. "Will you be able to go to Scotland soon to meet them? When you're done with the movie?"

"Yes," Angie lied. Well, only half lied. She would love to go to Scotland, but needed to figure out what to do with Fidget and Eckhart while she was gone. Not to mention fit it into her budget. "Don't worry about me, you guys. I only have a few weeks left of filming and then all of the *weird* stuff will be behind me and I can go to Scotland to see the babies."

Her words seemed to convince her two friends that they were safe to go on their holiday. They were almost enough to convince Angie, too.

"Are you ready?" Adam poked his head into the room and she was saved from any further discussion of the matter.

With a quick and careful hug, so as not to muss her hair or makeup, Luna, Sofia, and Ian were off and Angie was left to face her remaining time as an actress alone.

Well, not completely alone.

Surrounded by the camera crew, Tillie and Brandon, Adam, the script supervisor lady, and the costume and makeup assistants who rushed in to touch her up between takes, she managed to keep what she thought was a healthy emotional distance from Xave during their scenes together.

In a nice turn of events most of her remaining shots were of the The Black Eyed Pirate admiring her from afar, which meant much of her day was spent with a wall of filmmakers aiming the camera lens and multiple lights at her while she preened and pretended to ignore or make eye contact with Xave, who wasn't actually there.

Staying busy helped assuage the grief of missing out on seeing the newborn twins with all of her friends, too. She was worried that by the time she was able to go to Scotland the babies would be walking and talking. Sadness over this fact permeated her mood for the rest of the work week and, apparently, added to her believability as a distant, lonely Queen of the Mermaids.

"Great work today, Angie," Tillie complimented her as Adam and another crew member helped her down from a rock jutting out into the ocean where she had been perched for her last shot on Friday.

"Really?" Angie could hardly believe them, she had barely moved for the past hour and a half.

Tillie and Brandon both nodded enthusiastically and Tillie continued, "Really. You totally nailed the sort of aching longing look in your eyes that we wanted for this scene. I don't know how you do it without any lines, but it looks great."

Angie didn't want to admit to the directors that the aching longing look in her eyes was real. What she did want was to gather Fidget up and get back to Eckhart where she could spend some time meditating and planning a weekend trip. She had decided to drive into the Redwood forest and absorb some of the ancient wisdom from the trees to try and get over her glum mood.

"Hello, stranger," Kristina fell into step next to her as she made her way to her trailer.

"Hi." Angie smiled politely in return.

"Done for the day?"

Angie nodded then glanced at Kristina's street clothes. "You too?"

"Yep," she answered.

Hoping their conversation had reached its inevitable end, Angie opened her mouth to make some excuse that would keep Kristina from following her all the way into her trailer when Kristina interrupted her thought.

"Some of us are going out for drinks. Kind of a Friday thing."

Angie smiled again. "Sounds nice."

"We were wondering, well, I was wondering if you might want to come with us?"

Surprised at the invitation, Angie looked sideways at Kristina as they walked, trying to get a better reading on her expression.

"I thought I could buy you a drink. Kind of an apology for teasing you the other day," Kristina added.

"Oh, well, that's nice–"

"I mean, it's just me and Marissa and a few of the other extras. None of the actors with lines. So you might feel weird being seen with us."

Angie scowled. "I wouldn't feel weird being seen with you."

Kristina flashed a smile. "So that's a yes?"

Angie stopped walking and faced Kristina. She wasn't going to go out with them, but she wanted to make it clear that it wasn't because they were extras.

Just as she opened her mouth to explain, she caught movement out of the corner of her eye and glanced over to see Xave heading their way. He was also dressed in street clothes and Angie had a feeling she was going to get involved in some kind of awkward interaction between herself, Xave, and Kristina.

She did not relish that idea.

She wished she was sitting on a plane with Luna and Sofia, not trying to avoid Xave to protect her somewhat fragile emotional state or rebuff Kristina's superficial attempt at friendship. All she wanted was to get out of her costume and makeup, take her cat, and escape this pressure. She made a snap decision to try and side step both Kristina and Xave.

"Sure, I'd love to go out with you guys," she said, smiling widely to distract Kristina from noticing Xave's approach. "Do you have my number? I've got to get changed, but if you text me where you're going I can catch up with you in a little bit."

Kristina was almost comically surprised. "Sure, yeah, I can do that. What's your number?" She pulled out her cell phone.

"I'll put it in," Angie suggested, taking the phone out of Kristina's hand and punching in her number as she started walking again, this time in the opposite direction of where Xave was coming.

Just as she turned away from him, she could sense Xave's forward motion decreasing. Maybe he had caught the hint that she wasn't interested in talking to him. Or maybe he thought she and Kristina were involved in a conversation he shouldn't interrupt. Either way, her tactic worked and he fell back, which allowed her to finish with Kristina's phone and send her on her way before they reached her trailer.

"Mommy got rid of everyone else but us for the night," she told Fidget when she stepped into her private room. Fidget looked at her from where she was curled up on the chair and released a sleepy mew. "Now, I'll get cleaned up and we can go home. By ourselves. We're taking a trip tomorrow, Fidget." The cat yawned.

Angie locked the door then pulled off her costume and hung it up on the rack the costume department had moved into her room just for the mermaid outfits. She was in the middle of pulling her bra off of its hanger to get dressed when there was a soft knock on the door.

"Angie?"

Xave's voice, unmistakeable even through the door, sent a shiver up her naked spine. She froze in place. Fidget raised her head and looked at the door.

"Hi, um, I'm changing," Angie replied.

"I'm sorry, I don't mean to interrupt. I was wondering if you were busy tonight. After you get changed?"

Angie crossed her arms, covering her nakedness. She closed her eyes against the onslaught of feelings that enveloped her at his words, pushing the feelings back. Hadn't she watched him spend an entire dinner flirting with Elizabeth? He was a handsome celebrity, used to getting whatever woman he wanted. Probably a playboy type. Hadn't she already decided he was not the man for her?

Yes, she had decided she would not be on his long list of discarded lovers. She was taking her life in the direction she had always intended and she didn't need or want to be distracted by Xavier Patel any longer.

Unfortunately, all she could see in her mind's eye was Xave leaning casually against the wall by the door, waiting for her to answer. In her mind's eye he looked amazing.

She shook her head, trying to rid herself of the image.

Fidget watched her with lazy curiosity. Angie bit her lip. She was taking too long to answer.

"Actually, Xave, I've got a...a *thing* tonight." She spoke in Fidget's direction, using eye contact with the cat to sound more natural. "Yeah, I'm getting together with some friends right after I leave here." She winced at the lie.

"Oh, I see. Right...well, another time perhaps?"

She could hear the disappointment in his voice and was glad she was nearly naked. Otherwise she may have weakened and opened the door, and once she was face-to-face with him she may not have the courage to persevere with her plan to move on with her life.

"Sure, sure, another time would be nice." Angie tried to sound as casual as possible.

With any luck this would be the last time she had to refuse him during filming. In a few short weeks they would no longer be working together and she was certain he would forget about her. And she would do her best to forget about him.

Chapter Thirty-One

Angie finished wiping her bowl and coffee cup dry and placed them securely in Eckhart's cupboard before locking the cupboard door so it wouldn't open while she was driving.

Birds chirped outside and several yellow butterflies flitted in front of the open window. The sounds of an RV park waking up had already begun and were only getting louder. It was time to go.

"Come on, Fidget," she called out the window.

The little cat sat serenely in the gravel next to Eckhart watching butterflies with the nonchalance of a feline planning a secret attack.

Angie picked up Fidget's fish shaped food dish and tapped it gently on the window frame to get her attention. "Here kitty, kitty," she called lightly. Fidget snapped to attention, racing under the van and into the open side door. "Good girl." She placed a few kitty treats into the dish and set it on the floor, closing the side door and windows to ensure Fidget didn't get outside again. "Now we can get going," Angie announced happily.

After texting Kristina the night before to let her know she couldn't meet them for drinks after all, Angie had grown more and more excited about her plans for the weekend. She had returned to the RV park to relax and plan out her route to see the famous Redwood trees.

The twinge of guilt she felt about cancelling on the extra's night out needled her a little, but she had pushed all of that aside. In the end, her mental health and spiritual cleansing were more important. And what would be more cleansing than soaking in the vibes of an old forest and its 300 foot tall trees?

With that in mind, Angie had gotten up early to spend some time on the beach while the sun came up. After taking a quick swim in the water to wake up, she washed the salt off in the RV park showers, fixed some breakfast, and was ready for her weekend outing.

Waving to Fern and Albert as she passed, Angie maneuvered Eckhart through the RV park to the main entrance and stopped. She peered down the road both ways, waiting for a significant break in the traffic before she pulled out. Eckhart had a lot of great qualities, but fast acceleration was not one of them.

As she watched the cars coming down the road, one of them stood out against the rest. Among all of the SUVs, RVs, trucks pulling campers, and family cars filled with vacationers, one luxurious sports car screamed Los Angeles. Or, more specifically, Hollywood.

Angie's heart thumped inside of her chest as she watched the sleek, black car grow more and more clear the closer it came. If she didn't know better she would guess that it was Xave's car.

She squeezed the steering wheel, her palms sweaty, and chastised her wild imagination. "Have you lost your mind? Are you that incapable of having two days to yourself that you have to fill your brain with thoughts of him the whole time?"

Fidget stopped preening in the passenger seat and stared at her, probably wondering what in the heck she was going on about. Angie clamped her lips together. She was not going to spoil her time with the ancient Redwood trees by obsessing over some man.

She flicked Eckhart's blinker on and glanced in her rear view mirror. A massive RV pulled up behind her, also wanting to leave the RV park. She looked back at the approaching traffic. The Hollywood car was almost upon them.

The car's dark windows made it impossible to see who was driving. Angie wished she paid closer attention to makes and models of cars so she could know for sure, but with every passing moment she grew more and more certain it was Xave's car. What in the world was he doing here?

In answer to her question, the sleek sports car slowed down and made a swift turn into the RV park, stopping right next to Eckhart.

A whimper escaped the back of Angie's throat.

The passenger side window of the car lowered, revealing Xave leaning over from the driver's seat, smiling up at her.

"Hi!" he called out.

She waved and smiled, too freaked out to form words yet.

"I was stopping by to say 'hi'," he said, rather awkwardly. "But I see you're on your way out."

Angie nodded. The RV behind her inched forward impatiently.

Xave noticed the RV, checked behind him to make sure nobody else was turning into the park, and looked up at her again, uncertain.

She could leave. She didn't have to put her plans on hold for Xave. It wasn't like she had known he was coming.

She bit her lip, feeling the pressure to make a decision and make it quick. Curiosity about why he had come to the park won. She pointed at the shoulder of the road just past the main entrance. "I'll pull over up there."

Xave nodded. The sports car engine roared as he drove into the RV park in order to turn around.

Within minutes they were standing outside their vehicles on the side of the road. Fidget peeked at them through Eckhart's windshield, opening and closing her mouth in muffled meows. Traffic raced past. Not the most romantic circumstances Angie had ever been in and, yet, Xave's presence automatically raised the vibration.

In his khaki shorts, a sage green short sleeved shirt, sunglasses, and his hair in casual waves, Xave was the image of a hot weekend lunch date. Wearing a pair of cut-offs, a faded Colorado T-shirt, her hair pulled up in a high pony tail, Angie didn't quite match his look.

A few car horns screamed as they whizzed by. She wondered if they were honking in protest because they were parked on the side of the road, or at Xave's good looks, or because they recognized him.

"Sorry for intruding," he said.

"No, no, don't worry about it. I'm glad you caught me before I left." Angie was all friendly smiles, though her palms were still sweaty and she had to swallow hard to squelch the butterflies in her stomach.

"Where are you going on such a fine day?"

"I'm taking a day trip to see the Redwoods."

Xave's knees buckled slightly and he tipped backward, like the horse he bet on had just lost. "Oh, bummer. There's no way I can compete with the Redwoods. They're amazing."

She kept her eyes locked onto his, unable to contain her interest in why he was there. "Why would you be competing with the Redwoods?"

Suddenly, Xave was at a loss for words. He did a quick

search of the gravel around his feet for the best response, then looked up. "I was wondering if you might want to go for a drive. Get lunch somewhere along the way?" He shrugged one shoulder, giving up on the idea before she had a chance to respond. "Just a whim. I should have called first."

She smiled, automatically pleased that he had wanted to spend their day off together, despite the fact that she had been planning on using the weekend to get over him.

A wild idea popped into her head and she asked the question before taking time to think about it. "Do you want to come with me?"

The instant she said the words Angie was kicking herself. What in the world would possess her to invite him along?

It was too late. Xave had broken into a wide smile. She couldn't see his eyes behind his sunglasses, but she knew they were twinkling.

"You would be okay with that?"

Angie swallowed, hoping she would be okay. "Yes, sure, why not?"

Why not, indeed?

She would handle the situation like an adult. There was no reason bringing Xave along on her Redwood trip needed to change anything between them. She would still be in the midst of the ancient trees. In fact, she told herself as she waited for him to park his car in the RV parking lot, maybe having him along would allow the vibes of nature to wash them both clean of the whole love potion fiasco. Maybe having him along would mark a new chapter in their relationship and everything would be a-okay from now on.

It wasn't more than a few minutes into their drive that Angie all but forgot her reservations about asking him along.

"Cassette tapes!?" Xave couldn't contain his excitement when Angie offered him her basket of tapes to pick some music.

"Eckhart's sound system is a little old fashioned." She patted the dashboard gently, not wanting to offend the little van.

"I haven't seen a cassette tape in...I don't even know when. Maybe my parent's car?" He lifted each plastic tape container to admire them individually.

Angie laughed. "Sounds about right. My parents gave me most of those tapes."

Xave read the names of the bands out loud. "The Mama's and the Papa's, The Doors, Bob Dylan, Cream, The Grateful Dead. You know, I don't think I've ever actually listened to a Grateful Dead song."

"Really?" Angie was astonished. Her childhood had been permeated with the band. "It's perfect to drive to if you want to listen to it now."

With their soundtrack chosen and Xave volunteering to take on navigation duties, the two hour trip to the Redwood National Forest went by in the blink of an eye. In between sharing stories of their childhood vacations they stopped a few times for gas, snacks, and extra water and protein bars for their hike.

Xave had agreed that going to see the biggest trees they could, which were located in the Tall Trees Grove, was a great idea. Getting to the grove required them to hike about five miles in and out of the forest.

"A small price to pay to see them," Angie had said. "Do you like hiking?"

"I do," Xave nodded. "And even if I didn't, I would never keep you from going where you planned just because I hitched a ride." He glanced down at his phone and announced, "We've officially entered the Avenue of the Giants."

Following the road named for its famous evergreen residents was already a delight. Angie thrilled at every turn as they drove deeper and deeper into the woods. Eckhart was already dwarfed by some of the specimens they passed, she couldn't imagine what it might be like to stand next to the biggest Redwoods in the Tall Trees Grove.

Xave made a show of breathing through his nose then blowing the air out of his mouth several times. "It smells amazing here."

"It does, doesn't it?" Angie agreed, enjoying the cool and refreshing smell of the forest. "It feels healing. Like with every breath I take the air moves through my body and does something magical." Xave was silent and Angie looked sideways at him. "Does that sound a little weird to you?"

"Not weird, I've just never thought of it that way."

"No? I think nature has special healing powers. Our bodies need to be surrounded by trees, open sky, lakes, the ocean. I mean, it's where we all came from, right? We didn't start out living in cities."

"That's true. When my parents took us camping as a kid, my father used to say, *Just living is not enough...one must have sunshine, freedom, and a little flower.*"

"I like that."

Xave smiled as he remembered. "And at the end he'd always hand a wildflower to my mother that he'd picked secretly and hid behind his back."

Angie's heart melted. "How sweet!"

"It was sweet. My mother always blushed like a girl when he did it."

"It sounds like they were very happy."

Xave nodded. "Always."

The Grateful Dead cassette had come to an end and they hadn't picked a new one, choosing to chat and look at the scenery. Now they drove in silence. Xave watched out the passenger window as the trees went by while Angie drove and occasionally snuck a look at his profile.

She wondered what his father looked like. Was he as devilishly handsome as Xave? What would it be like to have a man like that making small, precious, romantic gestures towards you throughout a whole lifetime of marriage?

Like a dream, that's what it would be like.

Xave glanced down at his phone. "The turn is coming up."

She followed his direction and they drove along an even narrower, more winding road until they came upon a gate. Which was closed.

Angie put Eckhart in park and turned off the engine. There wasn't a soul around as they both got out and read the sign next to the gate.

"Permit required?" Angie read out loud, a sinking feeling in the pit of her stomach.

"It says they only allow so many visitors each day. You can get the permit online, but it has to be at least 24 hours in advance," Xave paraphrased the rest of the sign's information.

They both looked over the gate at the lush forest beyond, then at each other.

"I didn't see anything about that on my phone," Xave said.

"It's not your fault." Angie didn't know if she was more disappointed about missing out on the biggest Redwoods or if she was embarrassed because she hadn't made better plans. "I should have noticed that when I was looking everything up for the trip."

"I never would have thought you would need a permit," Xave tried to make her feel better.

A hard knot appeared at the back of Angie's throat. Silly, really. There was no reason to cry, yet the knot was forming because she was holding back tears. It was foolish to allow something so small to bring her down. Though it was definitely one of those times she wished she was more of a planner, like Sofia or Bridget. They would have never missed any fine print about permits.

"We can still enjoy the forest," Xave suggested softly.

Angie dared to look at him. He was watching her with a pained look on his face, afraid she was about to burst into tears. She gave a frustrated shake of her head, willing the knot in her throat to disappear so she could respond. It refused. She mustered up a weak smile instead, but could see his distress at her reaction.

"I hate to see you upset," he said. "We could come back another time. Get the permit for next weekend maybe?"

On the verge of speaking and risking her words coming out in short bursts of sobs, Angie was distracted by a whirring noise approaching from the road behind them.

Xave heard it, too, and turned his attention in the same direction she was looking. Concerns over the locked gate were forgotten as the whirring grew louder.

Chapter Thirty-Two

"Sorry, folks, you can't get in without a permit." The park ranger told them even before she climbed out of an impossibly small EV pickup emblazoned with the Redwood National Forest logo on the side. The pickup's battery powered engine had been the source of the whirring sound.

"We saw that when we got here a few minutes ago," Angie confessed, giving the ranger a polite wave.

"Is there any way we could get a late permit now? I'm happy to pay any extra fee," Xave offered.

The ranger unfolded her long body from the tiny pickup, chuckling and shaking her head as she did. "You don't know how many times I've been asked that question." She was tall, taller than Xave, and intimidating. Full of confidence, she adjusted her leather belt and flat brimmed hat before joining them at the closed gate. "I'm afraid I can't–" She stopped short when she got a good view of Xave.

Xave hesitated, then shot a quick look at Angie. He pushed his sunglasses up so they sat on top of his head, completely revealing his face. Then, with no shame and more than a little dazzle, he gave the ranger a wide, charming smile.

"Are you...are you Xavier Patel?" The ranger asked, her voice rising at least one octave.

With a duck of his head Xave feigned embarrassment, but lifted his magnetic gaze quickly back to the ranger, locking onto her widening eyes. "Guilty."

Angie suppressed a smile.

"Oh my goodness! Oh my goodness!" The ranger covered her mouth and made a giggly squealing sound, still staring in amazement at Xavier Patel in the flesh. She bent over slightly and turned around in place, stomping her boots with excitement.

Xave shifted uncomfortably on his feet, but remained focused on the ranger. Angie wondered how often this kind of thing happened to him.

"I'm sorry, I'm sorry," the ranger was trying to compose herself. "I don't normally get star struck like this."

"Of course not," Xave said politely, understanding written all over his face.

"It's just you are my all time favorite actor...of all time!" She exclaimed, then snorted out a laugh. "Did I say that twice? Oh my God, this is so embarrassing!"

"Please, don't be embarrassed," Xave said kindly.

"You must think I'm crazy," the ranger exclaimed.

"Of course not," Xave reassured her. "Many people get a little freaked out when they see what I actually look like in person."

The ranger laughed at his joke. So did Angie.

"For real, I think I need to sit down," the ranger said. She fanned her face with both of her hands and breathe in and out rapidly.

"Here, allow me," Xave assisted her back to her work

pickup and settled her into the driver's seat. When she had caught her breath, he asked, "May I ask your name?"

"Cassandra, Cassandra Mills."

Xave stuck out his hand. "Nice to meet you Cassandra." He beckoned Angie over. "This is my friend, Angie Levine."

"Nice to meet you." Cassandra shook Xave's hand then Angie's. She looked between both of them. "You were wanting to see the Tall Trees Grove today?"

"Yes, a spur of the moment kind of trip," Xave answered. His face fell a little. "Unfortunately, we didn't notice the permit requirement until we got here."

Cassandra looked back and forth between them again, pitying their predicament. "That is too bad." She glanced at Eckhart. "You two doing some camping around here?"

"A few hours south of here," Angie answered for both of them.

"Actually, we're on break over the weekend from filming," Xave added.

Cassandra's eyes widened again. "Get out! You're making a movie right now?"

Xave nodded, looking to Angie for support. She nodded, too.

Cassandra shook her head in amazement. "That is too cool. I'm talking to Xavier Patel and his co-star about their new movie. My sister is never going to believe me."

Xave smiled warmly again then took a step back. "Well, I guess we'll turn around and get out of your way, since we can't get a permit today."

"Wait!" Cassandra held out one hand, her long fingers bearing very un-ranger-like polished nails. Xave paused as Cassandra gushed, "I can't get you a permit this late, but I can take you with me. I was about to go on my rounds to some checkpoints on this loop, take some measurements. I can show you two around. Kind of like a ride-along."

A true smile, which was almost identical to the extra charming smile he had given Cassandra minutes before, spread over Xave's face. He looked to Angie. "What do you think?"

"That sounds great," Angie answered, energized by the turn of events.

Cassandra directed them where to park Eckhart on the side of the road then they all squeezed into her EV mini-pickup, which meant Angie had to sit on Xave's lap and Fidget had to sit on hers. Cassandra entered a key code at the gate and it swung open. They were off.

The drive from the gate to the trailhead only took a few minutes, but they were long minutes for Angie. As Xave answered all of Cassandra's questions about their current filming project, Angie marveled at how neatly she fit on his lap. He had edged over a few inches so she could sit almost sideways and face Cassandra while leaning back into the crook of his shoulder. A comfortable and, she supposed, enviable position to be in.

Cassandra seemed to notice their snug seating arrangement. Angie wasn't sure if she saw jealousy in Cassandra's eyes or if it was simply a fan's keen interest, so she kept her attention on Fidget and the massive trees they were driving past. This also helped her to ignore the way Xave's body felt next to hers.

Warm. Strong. Muscular. Words kept popping into her mind as they drove. She stared hard out the window, hoping the fluttering in her heart would stop when they got out of Cassandra's pickup. It didn't, but in Xave's defense, not all of the fluttering was due to him.

When Angie climbed out of the vehicle and breathed in the damp, cool, piney scent of the deep forest, she was treated not only to major heart flutters, but to several waves of shivers moving up and down her spine.

This place held a serenity she had never experienced. A

quiet majesty. A silence that wrapped around her and made her think that maybe there really could be such things as faeries, gnomes, and elves.

No matter the issues they had faced on the way there, the descent into Tall Trees Grove was worth all of it. With Fidget following dutifully on her leash, Angie entered the grove in a state of euphoria. Xave's lap a pleasant, yet fading, memory.

These were not just trees. They were massive Redwood trees whose bases were bigger around than Eckhart, with trunks that stretched straight up into the sky disappearing out of sight like Jack's fabled beanstalk. There were also ferns and other fauna growing under the trees. Taller than Cassandra, the ferns increased the optical illusion that they were all shrinking. As if they had been suddenly reduced to the size of mice scampering across the forest floor.

"We can walk through it!" Angie declared as they approached a Redwood fallen across the path. Instead of trying to remove the tree, they had carved a tunnel into it. A tunnel large enough they didn't have to stoop to move through.

"Yes, when one of these babies falls it can take centuries to even start to decompose," Cassandra explained. "We leave them where they are so they can become part of the forest again. The way they were meant to be."

Goosebumps covered Angie's arms. She and Xave followed Cassandra through the fallen tree and when they emerged on the other side, Angie didn't feel like the same person. Her very being felt changed. As if she was now an honorary forest nymph or some other creature of the leaves and branches.

As Cassandra told them facts of interest about these amazing trees, Angie felt like she was hearing about her ancestors. Like she belonged with them. Like she was a small part of something much larger, much older, and much more awesome than she could ever imagine.

The emotional roller coaster she had been on for the past several weeks fell away as they moved deeper into the trees. Angie's shoulders relaxed. Her muscles warmed from the exercise and she took deep breaths of the sweet, cool air. It was enough to be among these giants, walking through them, communing with them, and allowing them to bring her peace. Nothing else mattered.

A hushed reverence fell over all three of them. Xave was in step beside her. Something was different about him as well. He emanated strength, as usual, but also a calmness that was new. Not that he had ever come across as scattered or nervous, but he seemed more centered in this place.

He saw her looking at him and smiled, catching her hand in his and squeezing it warmly.

To her surprise, Angie didn't melt and lose control of her senses. She merely smiled back and squeezed his hand in return. A shared moment under a canopy of trees that had witnessed countless shared moments over the centuries. Theirs was no more or less important than any of them.

Later, they sat on a bench carved out of a huge chunk of a fallen tree and waited for Cassandra to finish her ranger tasks so they could go back together.

"Makes you feel kind of insignificant, doesn't it?" Xave peered up into the towering tree tops.

"You mean not like a famous movie star?" she teased.

Xave gave her an amused look. "Definitely not like a famous movie star." He watched Cassandra busily going about her duties while humming a song from one of his action adventure films and sighed. "The strange thing about acting is it's not real."

Angie lifted her eyebrows. It was her turn to be amused.

"I know that sounds obvious. But it's more than that," he said.

"What do you mean?"

"Well, for instance, I'm not really a pirate."

Angie chuckled. "Really?"

Xave tried to explain. "Of course I'm not, that goes without saying. But I couldn't even begin to do the things a real pirate might do. I don't know how to sail a ship or navigate by the stars or even sword fight." He listed each item on his fingers, then dropped his hand back into his lap. "I do know how to make it look like I'm sword fighting, although not really. The fight choreographer knows. I just do what they tell me to do."

Angie didn't say anything, because his confession made her sad. Mostly because she got the feeling it made Xave sad.

He looked into the middle distance. "I've played a doctor, a pilot, an Ancient Greek mathematician, a teacher, an astronaut, an explorer, a scientist...but I don't actually know anything about any of those things. Only enough to pretend. I'm not really any of those things."

Angie nudged him gently. "Do you mean to tell me you aren't Peter Pineapple either?"

Xave's eyes brightened and he laughed. "Peter Pineapple." He shook his head, remembering. "That was probably one of the most satisfying roles I've ever played. All in fun. Nobody ever saw me so nobody recognized me." He eyed Angie apologetically. "Not that I'm complaining. I'm grateful for the people who like my acting, who like me, and go see my movies." His gaze returned to Cassandra. "But that's kind of what I'm talking about. They don't truly like me, because they don't truly know me. They can only like who I'm pretending to be."

His words squeezed her heart. A quiet ache for him grew

in her chest as she watched Xave drop his eyes to the ground in front of the bench.

She suddenly realized that she felt sorry for him, which was counterintuitive. On the outside he had good looks, money, fame, many things a lot of people sought in life. But it was clear to her Xave wasn't happy.

Regret about her interactions with him bubbled to the surface. From using the love potion on him in the first place to her failed attempts to stop its effects to disregarding his humanity because he was famous. Even though her manipulation had been accidental, she had still messed with him inappropriately, and she was sorry. He wasn't an object to be gawked at and mooned over. He was a human being with his own thoughts and feelings as well as a right to find happiness, just like anyone else.

Angie wanted him to be happy. As happy as she felt in this grove of Redwoods. As happy as she always felt on the ocean shores. Deep in nature is where she belonged and where she would build her future, not on a film set and not in a metaphysical book store like the one back home. She wished Xave would find the place where his soul soared, too.

Angie reached over and placed her hand on his. "I hope the universe brings you what you're looking for, Xave."

His eyes softened. Turning his hand over, he interlaced his fingers with hers. "Thank you, Angie."

The moment stretched on.

They were rooted in place, eyes locked, holding hands. Sun rays broke through the tree tops and shone on their bench. Light bits of dust and the tiniest fluffiest seed puffs danced in the air around them, enchanting her senses so she lost track of how long she gazed into Xave's shining eyes.

If they were in a movie, this would be the moment he would kiss her, Angie realized. The fluttering in her heart returned. Xave opened his mouth to speak.

"Say, cheese," Cassandra called out, jarring them back into the present moment.

The spell between them broken, Angie slipped her hand out of Xave's. They turned toward Cassandra who had her phone raised in front of her like a camera, holding it up in their direction.

"Don't move, now. You look straight out of The Princess Bride or The Lord of the Rings or something like that."

Angie stole a look at Xave. He had straightened up and had his charming actor smile in place again. Angie's positive mood sank a little bit. Whatever true connection they had experienced was gone now.

Cassandra didn't notice. "Okay, now, ready? One, two, three, cheese! My sister is gonna be so jealous!"

Chapter Thirty-Three

Angie moved through the following days detached from everything and everyone. It was challenging to fulfill her role as the Queen of the Mermaids after deciding acting was definitely not in her future, but she showed up and did her best.

Keeping herself emotionally distant was an unfortunate necessity if she wanted to stay sane. Sitting in the makeup chair for hours each day before shooting her scenes for at least another ten hours was hard work when all she wanted to do was climb into Eckhart and drive away. Disconnecting from the drama made it easier.

Ditching drinks with Kristina and Marissa the week before had put an even bigger rift between her and her former co-mermaids. They had actually taken to acting like they couldn't see or hear her whenever she was in their vicinity and, unfortunately, so did the other extras. Angie was sure Kristina was spreading stories about her snubbing all of them, but she didn't know how to fix the problem, nor did she have time to figure it out. All of it seemed so childish and unnecessary. She would just have to grin and bear it for a few more days.

Life on set was crazy busy. They were in the last few weeks of production and everyone was stressed out. Tillie, Brandon, and the rest of the crew had all they could handle trying to fit all their planned scenes into the time they had left. Angie felt like she was barely keeping her head above water and was sure everyone else felt the same.

She and Xave were only scheduled to shoot a few more scenes together. Being the star of the movie, he was the busiest of all, on set from before dawn until nearly midnight every day. They had very few instances to interact one-on-one and Angie was grateful for that. The day was fast approaching when she would leave all of this, including him, behind. The less they saw of each other up until that point the better.

Or so she told herself.

"You okay today?" Shivaun asked as she put the finishing touches on Angie's makeup.

"I'm fine," Angie reassured her. Shivaun raised one eyebrow, questioning her answer. "No, really, I'm fine. Just tired I think."

That wasn't a complete lie. Long hours on set combined with the emotional strain of working with people she wasn't friendly with was taking its toll. Plus there was the fact that all of her dearest friends had congregated at a beautiful Scottish castle to welcome two precious little babies into the world and she wasn't with them.

Angie sighed. "I'm just missing my friends. Feeling a little worn out."

"Girl, you're not the only one." Shivaun leaned heavily on the back of the makeup chair, feigning exhaustion. "These last weeks of shooting are liable to kill me!" She snorted out a laugh, making Angie smile. "We'll get through it. Are you here every day until the end?"

Angie shook her head 'no'. "I've got tomorrow off, actually. Then I'm here for the duration."

"That's good. Doing anything fun tomorrow?"

"Probably catch up on some sleep."

"To quote my dear departed Grand-daddy, 'I'll sleep when I'm dead'!" Shivaun cracked up laughing again.

"Hopefully it won't get that bad," Angie laughed.

"Well, make sure to treat yourself nice tomorrow. That's what I'm telling everyone who has any time off at all. I think Xave's got a short day tomorrow, too. Then he's on full time again until we're done. Poor man."

Angie's stomach tightened at the mention of Xave's name. She managed to hold her expression so Shivaun didn't misinterpret her reaction. She was no longer affected by Xave the way she had been when the love potion had taken over her senses. She was, however, hoping to avoid too many potentially intimate or awkward moments with him before this whole film shoot was over. It would be easier to go on her way if she kept her distance.

With that in mind, Angie decided to don sunglasses and a baseball cap when she drove to Polypody Cove the next day. Taking Shivaun's advice to treat herself, she planned on spending some relaxing time at The Vanilla Bean while she had Eckhart's oil changed. She could recharge and Eckhart would be ready for whatever adventure she wanted to go on as soon as the movie wrapped. With her hair in a baseball cap and sunglasses on she might be less noticeable if Xave happened to go to Polypody Cove during his time off, too.

With Fidget snuggled inside the cat-tote bag at her feet, a hot cup of coffee and luscious raspberry cream scone on the table in front of her, Angie looked wistfully around The Vanilla Bean's charming decor. Leaving this part of California behind would mean she wouldn't be stopping in Polypody Cove anymore and that made her sad. She had started to think of the darling little town as her new stomping grounds.

"But that can't be helped," she murmured. If she was

going to get on with her life then she needed to make some plans. "No time like the present."

Giving Fidget a quick rub behind her ears, she pulled a notebook and pen out of her tote bag and placed them on the table. Inside the notebook was a map of the west coast, which she had used when initially planning her move from Denver. Today she was going to use it as inspiration to help her decide where she should go next. Perhaps someplace further North, like Oregon, might suit her plans.

A familiar buzz of excitement filled her chest. Her most recent adventure hadn't turned out exactly as expected, but that didn't mean she couldn't try again and have an even better experience next time. This morning was another new beginning and the start of the rest of her life after all.

She pressed the map flat on the table and squinted as she read the names of the cities along the Pacific coast. Gold Beach, Dunes City, Rockaway Beach, Ocean Shores...that was in Washington. Maybe she would move to Washington. She had always heard good things about Washington.

Lost in her own thoughts, Angie barely registered the sound of a man clearing his throat behind her. There was a tap on her shoulder and a question before she had time to turn around and face him.

"Excuse me, Ma'am, I was wondering if I could have your autograph?"

Chapter Thirty-Four

"Thomas!" Angie stood up so quickly her chair almost fell over.

Thomas caught the chair deftly in one hand then wrapped his other arm around her shoulders in a half bear hug. "Angie!"

She held tightly onto her friend to get the most out of the hug as possible. Breathless and exuberant she finally held him at arms length. "What are you doing here?"

His good natured laugh faded when he got a look at her face. He tilted his head to the side, his eyes worried. "Are you doing okay, Ang? You look thin."

Angie let go of him and pulled at the front of her oversized sweatshirt nervously. "I'm doing fine. Just a little worn out." She finalized her point with a bright and confident smile.

Thomas nodded slowly, opening his mouth to say something else when a loud mew rose out of Fidget's cat-tote.

"Hey, Fidget," Thomas bent down and picked up the cat then sat down in the spare chair at Angie's table holding Fidget in his lap. He eyed Angie as she took her seat. "What's with the incognito look? Are you getting pestered by the paparazzi already?"

Fingers flitting to the brim of her baseball cap then back down into her lap, Angie let out a high pitched laugh. "I'm not incognito."

His suspicions raised, Thomas leveled his gaze on her. "It's me, Angie. You can tell me what's going on."

"I know that." She waved her hand in front of her face, dismissing his concerns. "What I want to know is why you're here! Is Bridget here too?" She glanced around the small coffee shop as if she could have missed their blonde bombshell buddy.

"I had to get back to work. Can't do everything online in my business." Thomas shook his head and chuckled. "And I'm pretty sure Bridget is never leaving Claymore Castle again, unless it's to bring the twins back with her to Denver."

Angie laughed. The thought of Tawnyetta's new babies wrenched at her heart. "Are they adorable?"

His face softened. "They are. They don't do much, though."

Angie laughed again. "What were you expecting?"

Thomas shrugged and readjusted in his chair. "Oh, I don't know. I thought they would at least smile."

"Hmm, I guess that all comes later."

"I thought the 'wee little lass', as Michael calls her, smiled at me once, but Bridget said it was just gas."

Angie patted his hand. "I bet it was a smile. Bridget was probably jealous."

He grinned. "Probably." He scanned the cozy coffee shop. "You're here alone?"

Inexplicably, Angie's stomach tightened at his question. "Yes, waiting for Eckhart to get an oil change."

Thomas nodded. "How is the ol' camper van running?"

"Good, really good," Angie nodded, tapping the bottom

of her coffee cup with her finger tips. "I'm getting ready to take off after the movie's done shooting."

"Yeah?"

She nodded. "That whole scene really isn't for me."

"I can understand. It seemed kinda crazy when I went by there this morning to look for you."

"Is that how you knew I was here? At the coffee shop?"

"I made an educated guess that you were somewhere in this town after they told me you had the day off. So I hunted you down. I was trying to use my noggin before I caved and texted you. I wanted it to be a surprise."

She leaned back in her chair, smiling warmly. "I am one hundred percent surprised. And happy. It's good to see you."

"You too." He glanced at her nearly empty coffee cup and the empty plate which had held her scone. "Are you hungry? I'll take you to that pizza place we went to last time. Put some meat on your bones."

She agreed and they gathered up Fidget and strolled down the street to Pie's Otta Pizza. After ordering a large pizza with all of the vegetable toppings it could hold and getting a cheesy garlic bread appetizer, Thomas directed the conversation back to where it had started.

"So, are you gonna tell me what's bothering you?" he asked.

Angie paused as she reached for the cheesy garlic bread. "Nothing's bothering me. Why do you think something's bothering me?"

Thomas cocked his head and shot her a skeptical look. "I've seen you sick, I've seen you depressed, I've seen you tired and I've seen you stressed. But I've never seen you quite like this." His eyes brightened. "Hey, that sounded like song lyrics, didn't it?"

"A little." Angie lifted a piece of garlic bread to her mouth to take a bite. "What exactly is wrong with how I look?"

Thomas studied her for a moment, considering her question. "It's hard to describe, really. But you kind of look...lost."

Angie's stomach sank to the floor, pulling her down with it. Carefully chewing the bite of garlic bread she had just taken, Angie wasn't sure she was capable of swallowing it. Her throat was thick with emotion.

Lost.

The word echoed through her body. Through her soul.

Lost?

Thomas took a voracious bite of garlic bread. He hadn't noticed the affect his words had had on her yet.

Discarding the uneaten bread onto her plate, Angie covered her mouth with her hand. Chewing had become impossible. Her eyes were rapidly filling with tears.

Thomas swallowed, finally seeing she wasn't okay. "Are you choking?"

She grabbed a paper napkin and discreetly spit out the cheesy garlic bread then took several deep breaths to try and calm down.

"Sorry, I don't know what's the matter." Tears slid down her cheeks.

"Jeez, Ang, no wonder you're so thin," he said tenderly. He reached across the table and put his hand on hers. "Does this have anything to do with the movie star?"

"Xave." His name stuck in her throat when she said it.

"Yeah, him." A flicker of anger sparked in Thomas' eyes. "Has he done something to you?"

She shook her head. "No, nothing bad."

"Why don't I believe you?"

She shook her head more vehemently. "It's not him, Thomas. It's me."

"Is it that herbal store? Did they give you something that made you sick?"

He was really going off the rails. She took his hand in hers and held it firmly. "No, they're fine. All of that's over with. I mean, the tincture I took wore off and now I'm just dealing with the mess it left behind."

"What mess, exactly? You need to talk to me, maybe there's something I can do to help."

Angie doubted Thomas could do anything to help the way she was feeling, but she did her best to fill him in on everything. Some of it she had told him before, some of it was new, all of it came out in a rush because she needed to get it out before she started crying again.

She went over the love potion, the physical way she reacted to Xave, and how Stacy and Tracy told her the potion could never make anyone do anything they didn't want to do. She told him how the mermaid extras had reacted to her taking on the role of Queen of the Mermaids and how she struggled on set working closely with Xave, but maintaining enough distance to not lose control of herself in his presence.

Finally, she told him about the time she had spent alone with Xave. When he had waited with her for Tawnyetta's twins to be born, which Thomas already knew about, and when they had gone to the Redwoods together, which Thomas did not know about.

It was a great relief to confide in someone. The weight on her chest grew lighter and lighter the longer she talked. Her fear of bursting into tears disappeared. As she spoke the anger in his eyes vanished and they became more animated. The corners of his mouth twitched with a slight smile.

"So that's what I've decided to do," she announced with finality. "When the movie's over I'm getting out of here, away from all of the weird vibes, and go north. Maybe Oregon or Washington. I'm going to find a good ecological group that's working to keep the oceans clean and the forests healthy and I'm going to work for them. It's what I'm meant to do."

Thomas nodded slowly. "You could be right about that."

Comforted by his reaction, Angie felt calmer. Confidence stirred inside of her, replacing the sickening sensation of falling she had experienced just minutes before. "I can't tell you how wonderful I felt in the Redwood forest. Everything was so light and fresh and beautiful. It was magical. Absolutely magical. And I just want to have that feeling all the time, you know? I want my life to be magical."

Thomas nodded in agreement. The waitress brought their pizza and for a few minutes they were distracted dishing up their slices. Angie felt well enough to take a bite. In fact, she was so famished that she took a big bite.

Thomas watched her chew and swallow before saying, "Can I ask you something?"

Angie nodded. "Sure."

"How do you know for sure that you felt magical because of the forest? Could it have been because Xave was with you?"

Angie had been about to take another bite. She paused and lowered the slice back to her plate. "I hadn't considered that."

"Maybe not, I'm just asking because you kind of light up when you talk about him."

"I light up?"

Thomas mimed an explosion with his hands.

Abandoning her pizza completely, Angie snorted out a laugh. "I don't light up when I talk about him."

Thomas raised his eyebrows and mimed the explosion again, this time more slowly and with a wiggle in his fingers. "Like a firefly."

Angie pressed her palms against the table and pushed back into her chair, shaking her head. "Xave didn't make it magical. It was the place. The trees! You should have seen the trees." She scoffed and looked away from him.

"Maybe you're right. I'm only saying it's a possibility," he said.

She looked back, hoping she had convinced him, and herself, that she knew what she was talking about. He picked up another piece of pizza.

"I've just always been of the opinion that love can feel magical when you're with the right person," he said, then took a bite.

Angie blinked at him. Her heart and mind were fixed, unable to move on from his words.

Thomas. Silly, funny Thomas, the ultimate romantic with the loyal heart of a beloved brother, munched happily away on pizza while his words reverberated through her body.

Could he be right? Could she have been so wrong? She didn't know.

What she did know was he had rocked her perception of everything that had been going on with Xave from the beginning. The certainty she had convinced herself of was replaced with vague whispers of fear...and of possibility.

"Are you gonna eat?" Thomas asked, oblivious to the predicament he had caused. Ignorant of his own romantic soul.

"Thomas?"

"Yeah?"

"Why have none of us ever fallen in love with you?"

He halted the devouring of his slice of pizza at the question and looked her square in the eye. A few beats went by then he broke into a wide grin. "Monumental bad luck on my part I guess."

<h1 style="text-align:center">Chapter Thirty-Five</h1>

Angie's last days of being the Mermaid Queen were miserable.

Exhausted from non-stop work, surrounded by the other cast and crew who were also exhausted from non-stop work, she moved through the days like a zombie.

Constantly being so close to Xave, yet separated by cameras, lights, makeup assistants, directors, sound guys and other actors. Wanting to talk to him, not knowing what to say. Feeling something wonderful at her fingertips, watching it slip away. All of it was getting to her and she was drained.

She could barely eat. She slept only fitfully. Her heart grew heavier with each passing day, but she didn't know what to do to make it all better.

If Thomas had thought she looked lost before, she was afraid of what he would think now. Not that she would see him. Thomas had gone home to Denver after their pizza lunch and wouldn't be back any time soon.

Angie was on her own again...and she was tired.

Tired of the long hours. Tired of finding blue and green makeup on her clothes and everything she owned because she could never quite seem to scrub every bit of it off. Tired of relegating Fidget to spending twelve hours or more each day to the tiny trailer room where Angie had hoped she could go to relax and meditate, but never seemed to find the time.

Tired of thinking, of wondering, of feeling.

She couldn't wait for Tillie and Brandon to wrap the filming of the movie. And she dreaded the moment it all would come to an end.

"Are you set, Angie?" Tillie called out to her.

For what felt like the thousandth time since she had become a pretend mermaid, Angie was in the ocean. Standing in waist deep water, waiting for Tillie and Brandon's direction, the waves pushing her forward as they rolled past, making her worry she would miss her mark and they would have to start from the beginning.

This was their last day. Everyone's last day, actually. The movie would be wrapped after this one remaining scene. They were shooting the Mermaid Queen's big moment when she rises up out of the sea and shows herself completely to the Pirate Radames Drake. Otherwise known as the Black Eyed Pirate. Otherwise known as Xave.

Her instructions were to submerge herself under the water right after Tillie said 'action' then stand up fast, arch her back dramatically, and reach for Xave with one hand, all while looking particularly mermaid graceful.

Angie's push up out of the water would be aided by a stone platform they had placed in the sand right at her feet, which she would step up on during the dramatic display of leaving the water. The platform would give her extra stability and height so she would almost seem to be leaping out of the water. Or so that was the plan.

Xave, for his part, would be wet and shirtless on the beach, having just fought off a legion of mermen who were the Mermaid Queen's enemies along with various other water beasts. Panting from exertion, still wielding a bloodied pirate sword, Xave would stare in amazement as Angie the mermaid came out of the water and revealed her full mermaid glory to him. Then he would run into the water toward her and she would move to him by walking on the unseen platform, trying to make it look like she was floating or swimming more than walking, because she wasn't supposed to have legs.

The ambitions of the filmmakers for this scene seemed a little high from Angie's perspective. Possible complications were multitude. She didn't know if the end result would look like what they wanted, but she was determined to do her best for them. They had planned this scene as her last in case the constant submerging due to multiple takes ruined her costume. She may as well make it a good one.

"You ready?" Adam had walked knee deep into the water to check on her, concern about her lack of response written all over his face.

"Yes, sorry, I'm ready," she answered.

"You sure you can hear us over the waves?"

She gave him a strong nod. "I'm sure. I'm ready."

"Okay, everyone at one. Let's get this show on the road," Adam called out.

As he made his way back to shore and out of the shot, Angie tried to maintain her footing and keep her mind on what she was supposed to do next, not on a shirtless Xave watching her from the beach. She had never seen him without a shirt and found the sight more than a little distracting. Wide muscled shoulders, six-pack abs, the kind of body that was well built, but not overly muscular. The most perfect male body type that existed in her opinion.

Knowing they would soon be moving closer to each other, the water between them no longer an obstacle, but rather the place where they would meet, and he would take her hand in his, was almost more than she could bear. Thank goodness the script didn't call for them to embrace or kiss at the end. Thank goodness the Mermaid Queen and the Black Eyed Pirate shared the same destiny she and Xave did in real life, never to be together.

Because if Angie thought for one moment that Xave would take her up in his arms and hold her against his bare muscled chest, she thought she might actually faint.

"Sink, stand, step up, arch back, reach out, float forward," she whispered to herself. That's all she had to do. All she had to remember.

"Angie," Xave's voice came to her, snapping her out of her meditation. He had cupped one hand next to his mouth so his voice would carry over the water to where she stood. "You've got this!" He gave her a thumbs up and a brilliant smile. A soft sensation moved through her legs and she thought that she probably did not 'have this' at all, but the show must go on.

She gave him a weak smile then looked down into the water, the soothing ebb and flow of the current wrapping around her legs, reminding her where she was. Angie released a heavy sigh. The ocean would hold her up and move her forward when the time was right. The ocean would take care of her. It would give her the strength to finish the last day of filming then move on with her life.

Suddenly, all time for thinking was over.

"Action!" Tillie's voice rang out.

Angie took a deep breath and dropped straight down into the water until she was completely submerged. Blue and green engulfed her body, lifting her red locks so they floated in a billowing mass around her face and neck.

Mesmerized for a long moment by the mystical sensation of flying which being under water always gave her, she watched the light penetrate the surface and filter through her floating red locks, dimming more and more until it touched the tops of her bare feet and the stone platform in front of her.

Reminded by the stone platform of her current task, Angie pressed her feet firmly underneath her body and pushed up, taking care to be as graceful and mermaid-like as she could while finding the stone platform step with one foot. Right before breaking through the surface she tilted her head back, letting the water push her hair out of her face as she emerged.

"Beautiful, keep going," the distant sound of Tillie's directing comments met her ear.

Angie arched her back, felt too unstable, and lessened the pose. She blinked several times, but managed to control the urge to rub water out of her eyes. Realizing too late that she probably shouldn't have opened her eyes while submerged, Angie looked toward Xave on the beach. He was nothing more than a blurry figure.

Her eyes couldn't focus. They were burning. Saltwater or makeup or the combination of the two was irritating them to distraction.

Nobody yelled 'cut' so Angie kept moving. Trying not to blink furiously or squish up her face by squinting, she stepped gracefully, she hoped, onto the stone platform. Her body rose further out of the water. She reached out her hand in the general direction of the blurry, blob-like figure of Xave on the beach.

The figure moved closer, wading into the water towards her. She tried to emulate floating, though as she moved she wasn't sure what exactly she needed to do to look like she was floating. Waves hit the backs of her thighs. The fin costume was loose from her knees down so she would be free to walk through the water, but it had been pulled as tight as possible at her waist and down her thighs, which made her unstable.

Keeping her arm outstretched, she inched along the platform, attempting to stay in a straight line as she did. Xave's fuzzy, half naked form, was growing closer and closer.

A larger than normal wave hit the back of her thighs so

hard that water sprayed up against her back and over her head. Angie stumbled, but caught herself before she fell back down into the water.

"Go to Xave, Angie. To the right." Tillie's voice.

She must be off course. Blind to her surroundings, unsteady on her feet, uncertain on how to 'float', she turned more to the right to try and correct the problem.

"Uh-oh," Xave's voice came to her. He was close. He grabbed hold of her hand.

Angie used his grip to steady herself. Mindful that they were still filming, she turned her gaze toward his blurry image and tried to look like a Mermaid Queen in love.

"Uh-oh!" He said again, his voice filled with alarm.

She didn't have time to wonder what was causing his concern, because right at that moment a wall of cold water smashed into her back, sending her flying forward. Straight into Xave's arms.

The strength of the wave overtook her physically, lifting her off of her feet. She lost all sense of anything except the weight of rushing water and her desperate need to breathe.

Xave's grip on her hand intensified then released. Something grabbed her. When the wave was past she found that Xave had his arms wrapped around her, protecting her from being swept away. Huddled into his bare chest with her eyes closed she thought she could feel his heart beating.

Tillie shouted, "Hold the roll! If you two are all right, keep going. You look good!"

Angie pulled her head back, but stayed in Xave's arms. She was grateful Tillie wanted them to keep rolling, because she didn't want to break away.

"Are you all right?" Xave whispered in her ear.

As a mermaid she wasn't supposed to speak, so Angie nodded. Not seeing him clearly, it was difficult to know if he understood, but he didn't let go.

Without thinking, Angie let her hand slide up Xave's arm. Though saltwater still burned her eyes and his form was nothing but a blur, her fingers moved over the contours of his muscles. A burst of warmth filled her body.

Another large wave and Angie was pushed further into his arms. Their bare stomachs pressed up against each other. Xave's arms tightened so she couldn't pull back, even if she had wanted to. Her breathing was fast and shallow. The exertion of fighting to stand up against the waves, or something more?

Bending his head down, Xave moved close enough to kiss her. His warm breath on her cheek. His muscles flexing under her fingers. She wished she could see into his eyes. See what he was feeling. See if he was only acting.

They stayed that way for what seemed like an eternity. An eternity spent in heaven instead of hell. Body against body, the ocean pushing them together, insisting they hold fast and never let go. Angie would have happily kept rolling until the camera batteries ran out. In fact, she dreaded returning to reality when Tillie called 'cut'.

"Cut! That was great!" Tillie's voice sliced through their embrace.

The bubble of passion burst. Disappointment twisted Angie's heart. Then abruptly stopped.

Xave hadn't let go.

"Guys, you're good. I liked that better than just holding hands," Tillie continued, but her voice seemed farther and farther away with every word.

Another wave, this one gentler. Xave pulled her in to him again. He didn't need to hold her so tightly. They didn't need to be pressed together, chest-to-chest, stomach-to-stomach. The scene was over. The danger was past.

He didn't want to let her go.

Angie sucked in her breath. Her heart beat faster, harder,

and blended with Xave's. She closed her eyes and lost herself in the feeling of their hearts beating as one.

Xave's warm breath moved from her cheek to her neck. Tingling instantly shot down her neck and shoulders. She shivered.

"Are you all right?" he whispered into her ear, only intensifying her shiver.

"Hey guys, you're good. We're cut." Adam's voice broke through, clear and strong, closer than Tillie's.

Angie and Xave turned together. Adam had walked into the water to get their attention.

"Right," Xave said.

His embrace loosened and Angie regretfully pulled away from him, letting her hand drop from his shoulder where it had been resting. She couldn't resist letting her fingers trace his muscles one last time as they separated.

"They like this version better. It looks more vulnerable, Tillie said," Adam relayed the directors' message.

"Okay," Xave said.

Was her hearing playing tricks on her or did he sound out of breath? Angie silently cursed her blurred vision.

"Let's go to the beach and get your makeup touched up." Adam took hold of Angie's elbow. "We'll get you both back to one, then we're gonna do it again."

They trudged to the shore, Adam and Xave on either side of her, each holding an elbow.

"How many more takes do you think we'll have of this?" Xave asked.

"It's hard to say. We'll get these and then we'll have to move the camera to get a different angle."

"I wanted a general idea of when we'll be done for the wrap party," Xave said.

"The wrap party?" Angie didn't understand.

"Yes, didn't I tell you?" Xave asked.

"No." This was the first Angie remembered hearing of a party.

"Xave's having the wrap party at his house. I was gonna double check everybody knew before we packed up later." Adam said.

"You're coming, right?" Xave asked.

"Well, I don't know." Angie had thought she could escape after they were done filming. Because of the intensity of the past several minutes, she felt like escape was mandatory if she was going to get past her feelings for Xave.

"Oh, you've gotta come, Angie. You'll have a blast," Adam insisted.

"Please come, it won't be the same without you," Xave added.

"I...I have to take care of Fidget," she answered weakly.

"How about I'll have Jewell or someone who'll be done earlier than you take Fidget over?" Adam offered.

"Yes, several people are going early to get things set up," Xave said.

With the Fidget excuse shot down, Angie's mind flew to the next issue. "But I'll have to shower..." Her voice trailed off. She didn't want to get into the challenges of van life with the two men, but it would be exhausting to drive all the way back to the RV park to take a shower then down to Xave's house for the party. "I'm not sure I'll be up to it tonight."

"This is a pretty exhausting scene," Xave agreed.

They were nearing the shore and it was getting easier to walk through the ankle deep water. Angie didn't know if she was relieved or disappointed to be off the hook for the wrap party. She didn't have too long to consider it before Xave spoke up, his voice full of delight that he had come up with a solution.

"I know, you can shower at my place!"

Chapter Thirty-Six

"Angie! You made it!" Shivaun greeted her at Xave's front door. "Congratulations, girl, your first movie is wrapped." Angie entered as the makeup artist let out a hearty laugh and gave her a side hug.

Unlike Angie's first visit to Xave's home, the large entry hall and living room was brimming with people. All of the cast and crew seemed to be there as well as other people she didn't recognize.

"How was your last scene?" Anthony asked, taking in her ruined tresses, still wet from the multiple times she had risen up out of the ocean and into Xave's naked chest.

"I think they liked it," she said, searching the room for the directors. "Are Tillie and Brandon here?"

"They'll be a little while. Xave's finishing up with them. He texted and said you were going to use his bathroom to get cleaned up when you arrived," Shivaun said.

Angie nodded. Still a little chilled from her afternoon in the ocean, she was looking forward to washing all of the sand and seawater off in a nice hot shower. She had shoved her teal sundress into her purse to change into. All she had to do was work her way through the crowd to the bottom of the stairs.

Shivaun walked with her, telling her where she could find the snacks and, most importantly in Shivaun's opinion, the bar. Angie noticed Elizabeth Carlton leaning casually against the back of Xave's couch and wondered how many times the actress had been there to rehearse with him.

The thought made her feel a little sick, but she managed to return Elizabeth's wave of hello. The two women flanking Elizabeth turned to see who she was waving to, and it was none other than Kristina and Marissa. Angie kept the smile plastered to her face as she waved at them as well.

"Do you know where the bedrooms are?" Shivaun asked, loud enough that Angie knew Kristina could hear.

"Yes, I'll just be a few minutes," she answered, grabbing the stair rail. She had to admit she felt a spark of delight at the flash of envy in Kristina's eyes when the actress realized Angie was already familiar with Xave's house.

Upstairs was quiet. Nobody from what she was pretty sure would be a wild party by the end of the night had yet ventured onto the second floor.

Angie hesitated. She had toured most of the house when Xave was showing Thomas the layout on her cell phone. The room she had found most appealing on the second floor had been the master bedroom.

Xave's room.

Walking softly down the hall to the door of his bedroom and finding it ajar, she paused, looking up and down the hallway as if someone might stop her from entering. But there was nobody. She was alone.

What had Shivaun said? Xave was finishing up with Tillie and Brandon. Who knew what they were doing, but in her experience nothing moved very quickly with the brother and sister directors.

"Do I dare?" she whispered, glancing up and down the vast hallway again to make sure it was empty.

With a fluttering stomach, she pushed the bedroom door all the way open. There were no lights on, yet the room was awash with gold and pink from the sunset off its private balcony. Drawn to the view, Angie stood in front of the French doors that opened onto the balcony, mesmerized by the beauty of the white sand, blue water, and sinking sun.

Surrounded by peaceful silence and pure luxury, her damp hair in red unruly curls, her worn sandals and rumpled clothes, the scent of saltwater on her skin, none of it fit.

What was she doing here? At this party? In this house where everything felt like a dream? A dream she was stumbling through, pretty sure the floor was about to give way.

Xave's world was a world beyond hers, beyond what she could imagine. A surreal fantasy come to life. But not real life. Not her life.

Still, she could not bring herself to leave the bedroom.

Moving quietly through the space she admired the artwork on the walls, inspected the books on the nightstand, and ran her hand over the sumptuous comforter on the bed. When she came to the open door of the master bath, Angie stopped.

The bathroom was immaculate. Huge. Elegant. But the thing that gave her pause was the magnificent freestanding soaker tub. Glowing a pristine white on display in front of a picture window with its very own view of the ocean, the soaker tub was dazzling.

She stared at it for a long moment, deciding.

Finally, with a backward look at the empty bedroom, she sighed, "You only live once." Then she drew herself a hot bath.

It had been a long time since Angie had soaked in a tub. And she had never been in a tub quite like Xave's.

The water was perfectly warm and the contours of the

porcelain were flawless, well suited for a person to lean back and unwind. Actually, the tub was large enough to easily hold two people, but she managed to scrub that thought out of her mind as she washed and conditioned her hair then sank back and allowed the water to soothe her sore muscles and tired mind.

The sunset was on full display in the picture window. Angie watched the brilliant colors in the sky deepen and darken, growing more and more drowsy. She would get out and get dressed when the sun had set completely then join the party downstairs. It seemed like a pretty good plan. Until the unexpected part when she drifted off to sleep.

"Hello?"

A deep voice penetrated her slumber.

"Angie, is that you?" The voice again, this time accompanied by a soft knocking.

Angie opened her eyes, confused about her surroundings. She was cold. The room was dark.

"Angie?" The voice again. Xave's voice.

"Oh," she croaked, her throat thick with sleep.

Water moved around her. Cold fingers and toes. She looked down in surprise. Her movement was causing the splashing. She was sitting in a tub full of cold water in a dark bathroom. Xave's bathroom.

Light exploded around her. She let out a yelp, covering her chest with hands whose fingertips were water logged and turning blue.

"Sorry!" Xave was in the doorway. He shielded his eyes from the sight of her with one hand and found the wall switch with the other, flicking the lights back off.

She pushed up, trying to stand, but her calf muscle cramped and she slipped, falling back into the water. This caused a small tide wave which hit the side of the tub and splattered loudly onto the floor.

"Are you okay?" Xave's silhouette lowered his hand slightly to check on her.

"Don't!" She held her palm up to stop him. The cramp in her calf knotted into a Charlie Horse and she cried out in pain.

"Here, let me–" Xave moved toward her.

"Stop!" She raised her hand higher to keep him at a distance. The cold water was not helping the Charlie Horse, but she was not ready for Xave to help when she was completely naked. "My leg is cramping," she whimpered.

"The floor is slippery when it's wet. I'm going to turn on the light so you can see to get out." The lights flicked on again. "I promise I won't look."

Angie sucked in her breath as her calf muscle twisted harder. She had to pant to overcome the pain, but it wasn't working and she was filled with anger. She shot a mean look at Xave. "What are you even doing here?"

He paused at the cabinet where he was pulling out a towel. His mouth twitched into a smile. "It's my bathroom."

Angie scowled as another cramp rendered her leg useless. Of course he was right, but it didn't make her feel any less annoyed.

"Step on this so you don't slip." Xave tossed a towel on the large puddle next to the tub. Keeping his eyes averted he asked, "Can you get out by yourself?"

"Yes, yes, just go." Hurting and shivering from cold, all she wanted was to end this humiliating experience as quickly as possible.

He stepped out of the bathroom without a word. Carefully, Angie climbed out of the bathtub and onto the sopping wet towel, noticing too late that there was not another towel in sight.

"Are you all right?" Xave asked from outside the door.

Thoroughly mortified and near convulsing in full body

shivers, Angie's anger dissolved. She groaned with frustration. "Where are the towels?"

"Right, I'll get you one."

She didn't have the energy to warn him not to look. Balancing most of her weight on her non-cramping leg, it was all she could do to hold steady while Xave felt along the wall of the bathroom with his eyes closed until he found one of two slender linen cabinets.

Eyes still shut tight, a fluffy turquoise towel in his hands, he turned in her direction holding the towel up between them like a curtain. "Hold still. I'll come to you."

"O-o-okay," she stammered.

When he reached her and wrapped the towel around her shivering body, his fingers brushed against her arms. "You're freezing."

Without asking, he took hold of her shoulders and guided her into the bedroom onto the dry plush rug next to his bed. Angie held the towel around her body with trembling fingers. Xave disappeared for a second and returned with more dry towels, unceremoniously plopping one on top of her head and rubbing her wet hair and shoulders like she was five-years old.

Angie didn't complain. She was so cold she couldn't have if she wanted to, but the vigorous rubbing was doing a great job of warming her up. After a few minutes he stopped and tossed the used towel aside, handing her a new dry towel.

"You can wrap your hair in this if you want. You have clothes to change into?"

Angie nodded.

"Get dressed and I'll grab a blanket."

She nodded again and watched him step into a large walk in closet. Bending over, she wrapped her wet hair up in the dry towel then finished drying off the rest of her body and pulled her teal sundress over her head.

A knock sounded from inside the closet. "Are you dressed?"

"Yes."

Xave stepped out of the closet with a blue and white blanket. When his eyes landed on her he froze. For the first time since she had woken up in the bathtub Angie got a good look at him. He was only half changed out of his pirate costume. The billowing pants and knee high boots had been replaced with faded jeans and dark sandals, but he still wore the Black Eyed Pirate's white shirt, untucked and unbuttoned enough to show off the top of his abs.

A different kind of shiver rushed through her.

Xave's eyes slipped down her body until they reached her feet and he was struck with an idea. He turned on his heel, went back into the closet, and came out with the blanket and something small and black sitting on top of it.

"This will warm you up." He flung the blanket up and over her head then pulled it around her, closing it at her chest. "Have a seat." He motioned to the bed behind her and Angie obliged, too grateful for the soft blanket to think about whether or not she should be on his bed.

Xave dropped down to his knee in front of her, gently picking up one foot and sliding a heavy black sock onto it. "These are wool. You're not allergic, are you?"

"No, I'm not."

"Good." He put the second sock on her other foot and looked up. "Which leg is cramping?"

"My left," she said feebly. "It's not as bad as it was a minute ago."

Despite her report, Xave moved his hand gently up from the sock on her left leg and rubbed the back of her calf. Pain shot up her leg when his hand pressed on the angry muscle. She winced.

"That's a huge knot. I can work it out if you want?"

She managed a high pitched, "Okay."

The pain in her leg dissipated as Xave massaged the back of her calf. The socks and blanket began to do their job and her chilled body started thawing out. After a few minutes she felt almost normal again, except for the stinging embarrassment.

"I'm sorry about all of this," she said.

Xave lifted his eyes to hers and her heart skipped a beat.

Words spilled out of her, "I know you said I could shower here, but I shouldn't have used your personal bathroom. That was rude. I don't know why I did it. I know there are other bathrooms up here. I didn't even try to look. I just barged into your personal space and made a big scene." She covered her face with the hand that wasn't holding the blanket closed.

He stopped kneading her calf muscle and put both of his hands on the tops of her feet. "If you had used another bathroom how would I have found you and saved you from freezing to death? Or drowning?"

"It's not funny. It's embarrassing."

"Don't be embarrassed. It's not a big deal, I promise."

She lowered her hand to see if he was telling the truth. He seemed to be. She sighed, her cheeks still burning.

Xave caught her eye and grinned. "In fact, you're one of the nicer surprises I've ever found in my bedroom."

She laughed. "Is it normal for you to find random people in your bedroom? In your bathtub?"

"Not in my bathtub, no. That's a first." His eyes twinkled with fun. "But I am a movie star, you know. It's not abnormal for people to lay in wait for me in odd places just to get an autograph."

Angie laughed again and some of the awkwardness subsided. "I am both surprised and relieved to hear that."

"Good." Xave nodded in emphasis then looked up at her again. "Actually, Angie..." He stood and took a seat next to her on the bed. "I've been wanting to find some time alone with you." He rubbed his hands on his thighs. "There's something I wanted to, um…" His words caught in his throat. He tried again. "I've been wanting to talk to you about–"

"Come here, kitty. Where are you, kitty?" A voice called from somewhere down the hall.

Confused, they both turned to look at the bedroom door.

A whistle came from somewhere else in the house, like someone calling a dog.

Then a different voice came from right outside the door. "Where do cats like to hide?"

Whoever had asked the question had a companion who answered, "I don't know, but we need to find her before Angie realizes she's missing."

Angie's heart dropped into her stomach.

She looked at Xave who was already getting to his feet. "Fidget! I forgot about Fidget!"

Chapter Thirty-Seven

Angie didn't know what the party guests found stranger, her racing down the stairs wrapped in a blanket with Xave's extra large black wool socks flopping on her feet, or her frantic calls for Fidget as she tried to be heard over the party noise.

Sick with worry, Angie didn't care what she looked or sounded like. All she was concerned about was finding her cat. Poor Fidget. She was timid and not used to so many people or loud music. She must have been terrified without Angie nearby.

"I can't believe I forgot about her." Her eyes flew around the room noticing each door and open window. There were too many places where a cat could escape.

"It's all right, we'll find her," Xave said.

Shivaun and Anthony had followed them downstairs when Angie burst out of Xave's room. They had been the ones talking right outside the bedroom door.

"Adam's at the front of the house looking," Shivaun said, her brow bent with worry. "She's only been gone a few minutes."

Angie didn't want to waste time on blaming anyone. Besides, it was her fault for not taking proper care of her own pet. She spied the open door to the back deck, which was dark and quiet compared to the party atmosphere inside the house.

"Maybe she ran out there." She hurried through the crowd toward the deck, not caring who followed. When she stepped through the door into the cool night air, she was almost certain Fidget would be there. With potted flowers along the edge of the deck and palm trees stretching up on either side, it was exactly the kind of place a cat would try to hunt at night. "Fidget, here kitty, kitty," she called softly into the dark.

"We haven't seen her out here," Elizabeth stepped out of the shadows at the edge of the deck followed by Kristina and Marissa.

Angie gave them a scathing look. She had no doubt Kristina was enjoying her suffering, though the blonde mermaid extra's expression appeared to be of genuine concern.

"Maybe she'll come if you're calling her," Elizabeth suggested.

Angie straightened, suddenly remembering she was still wearing the blanket and floppy socks. She tugged the blanket together in front of her chest like it was a queen's cape and joined them at the edge of the deck.

"Here Fidget, come here, kitty. Here kitty, kitty," she called into the night. Nothing but the sound of waves rolling onto the beach in the near distance came back.

"Angie, I'm really sorry," Kristina said.

Angie called to Fidget again, not wanting to engage with Kristina at the moment. But something about the girl's face in the pale lighting of the deck made her pause and look closer.

Kristina squirmed uncomfortably under her gaze. "I only had her for a minute."

Angie's heart, which had been sitting heavily in her

stomach like a stone, unexpectedly rose into her throat and became a throbbing ball of wrath.

"*You* took her?"

"I was holding her for Shivaun for a minute."

"You *lost* her?"

"It was an accident."

Hot anger replaced all of the worry that had filled Angie when she realized Fidget was missing. She narrowed her eyes at Kristina, "Did you lose her on purpose?"

"What? No!"

Angie didn't believe her. "What did you do with my cat, Kristina?"

"I didn't do anything with her. I dropped the leash by accident and she ran into the crowd."

"Maybe it wasn't an accident."

Kristina scoffed. "What's that supposed to mean?"

"It's no secret you don't like me."

"That's not true."

"It is true. You haven't liked me from the beginning. And you especially haven't liked me after I got the part of the Mermaid Queen."

Kristina let out a caustic laugh.

"Plus you're mad because I didn't come to your stupid little party," Angie added.

Kristina's blue eyes flashed and her face reddened. "Fine, you know what? You're right. I thought it was rude of you not to show up for drinks when you said you would. And I don't think you deserved to get the part of the Mermaid Queen." Her eyes bulged as she spoke, her voice shaking with emotion. "You don't even have any acting experience. How is it fair that you get a top role in the movie? Plus you've got the star following you around, panting after you like a puppy." Kristina stopped short, deciding she had said enough. She took a shaky breath and added, "But I would *never* hurt a defenseless animal out of jealousy."

Nobody moved. Her words hung in the air. The truth. Finally. And it was an ugly truth.

Angie raised one hand and splayed it across her chest, sputtering out her answer, "I–I never wanted any of this. I didn't ask for it. None of it. It all happened by–by accident."

It was Kristina's turn to narrow her eyes. She shot a vicious look at Angie. "That makes it even worse."

Angie pulled her head back, shocked. She flicked her eyes to Marissa and Elizabeth, who were staring uncomfortably at their feet. Kristina rolled her eyes and turned away from all of them, hurrying to the open deck door and past Xave, who had been standing in the doorway watching.

Flustered, Angie opened her mouth to say something then closed it again. All of her anger was gone, replaced with a new wave of humiliation. Hot tears filled her eyes.

Xave stepped onto the deck and reached out his hand as if to lead her back inside. "We're having everybody look for Fidget. I'm sure we'll find her."

Angie backed away from him to the top of the stairs that led down to the beach. With a sharp shake of her head she said, "I shouldn't have come." Then she turned and escaped down the steps.

Chapter Thirty-Eight

For once in her life the sound of the ocean did nothing to calm Angie's nerves. Wracked with guilt over letting her precious Fidget down, allowing her to get lost in a strange place with strange people, perhaps never to be found again, Angie paced back and forth along the line where the waves swept in and out over the sand. She had discarded the black wool socks on the bottom of the deck stairs, but kept the blanket around her shoulders.

She called for Fidget along the shore line as she walked back and forth, but saw no signs of the little cat. Gradually her hope crumbled and she succumbed to the tears that had forced her away from the house. Away from Xave.

As she cried the whole scene with Kristina ran through her mind on repeat.

She had never thought much about how heart wrenching it must have been for Kristina to watch her become the Mermaid Queen. Kristina and Marissa and all of the other extras were working actresses, trying to make a living in Hollywood. For her to waltz in and take the role without even considering their feelings had been tone deaf.

And knowing the role had gone to her because of the love potion made her actions even more unforgivable. Abusing the power of the universe was doubly insulting to the other actresses on set who would have loved the chance to be the Mermaid Queen.

Then to accuse Kristina of losing Fidget on purpose. Angie shook her head, trying to erase the memory. "I'm a better person than that, aren't I?" She asked the ocean. It didn't answer.

Obviously not. She was petty and immature, remarkably out of touch with the feelings of others, and willing to use the powers of the unknown to manipulate those around her. The whole situation was shameful.

Angie let out a heavy sigh. "So Kristina was another victim of the love potion. Just like Xave."

"Just like who?"

Angie whirled around at the sound of his voice.

The night sky was bright enough she could see him walking across the sand, his pirate shirt rippling in the ocean breeze.

"Xave." Her voice came out as a whisper. The wind caught his name and carried away.

"I thought I might find you down here."

With every step he took in her direction, Angie had to fight the urge to run and meet him. But that wouldn't do. She had to release him from the bonds of the love potion, from all of the confusion that surrounded them, not encourage him. She gripped the blanket tighter together at her chest, creating a cocoon of detachment.

"I found something of yours," Xave said.

A glimmer of hope rushed through her heart. Before she could ask, a small mew came from somewhere inside his billowing shirt.

"Fidget!" Immediately forgetting her cocoon of detachment, she threw off the cumbersome blanket and raced to him. "You found her."

"Yes, she seems fine," he said with pleasure, carefully placing the calico cat in Angie's arms.

"Where was she?"

"Apparently Fidget is a bit of a dumpster diver."

"Dumpster? You looked through your garbage?"

He nodded, brushing his hands off as if he had just climbed out of a dumpster. "The recycling bin on the side of the garage. I wasn't going to leave any stone unturned."

"Thank you, Xave. You're very kind." Relief and joy tumbled together with guilt over the distress she had caused since she came to California, causing hot tears to flow down her cheeks again.

"What's the matter?" Xave touched her elbow, concerned at these new tears.

"This is all my fault. Everything." She threw her arm up and around, encompassing the beach, the ocean, and Xave's beach house towering in the background.

Xave looked in all the places she was pointing then back at her, his expression softening. "I don't think it was anybody's fault, really. It was an accident."

"Not just losing Fidget." Angie kissed the top of the cat's head then let out a heavy sigh. "I mean everything. I invaded your bathroom, your space, and I yelled at Kristina, and I've been mean spirited this whole time. I've been acting so crazy lately."

"Crazy?" Xave didn't seem to agree.

"Maybe not crazy. But definitely deceitful."

"Deceitful? Mean spirited?" He repeated each word in disbelief and shook his head 'no'. "You couldn't be deceitful and mean spirited if you tried, Angie. You're the kindest most emotionally available person I've ever met."

Angie scoffed. "You don't know what I've done." Stopping herself from saying too much, she pressed her lips together and straightened her shoulders, holding firmly onto Fidget. "But that's okay. Because it's going to end. Nothing good comes from all of my metaphysical manipulation. I'm done with all of the woo-woo fairy magic stuff. It's caused too much pain. I've made a decision and I'm quitting it."

Xave's wide shoulders dropped. He raised his palm as if to stop her. "No, no, no, don't do that."

"I need to give it up. It's caused so much negativity and...other things."

Xave's eyes pleaded. "But it's who you are. All of your crystals and–and your hippie van. The way you look at the world. It's one of the things I love about you."

Angie's thoughts ceased abruptly. She stared at him, his words slowly sinking in. Xave held her gaze. His chest rising and falling like an animal about to be released from a cage.

She swallowed hard and spoke in a clear, steady voice, "No, you're wrong. You don't love that about me. You just think you do. And I let you think that because...well, because you're..." Here words failed her. She clamped her mouth shut, afraid of what might spill out if she lost control.

Xave breathed out and rubbed the back of his neck. "Look, I have something to tell you. Something I wanted to keep a secret, because it's, well, it's pretty embarrassing. But I think I should tell you. I think you should know. Honesty's the best policy, right?"

Angie stepped back, fearing what he was going to say. "No, don't tell me. It's not real, whatever you're feeling. You might think it's real, but it's not–"

He raised his voice and talked over her. "I got a love tincture at the apothecary, kind of a love potion, and I think it's affected you."

Everything stopped. The ocean. Fidget's wriggling. Angie's heart.

Her mouth fell open. She stared at him with wide eyes, not sure she had heard him correctly. "What did you say?"

He dropped his chin to his chest and let out a heavy sigh. "The ladies at the apothecary convinced me to try something to boost my chances at finding real love. Something that's eluded me for a long time." He lifted his eyes to hers then ran his hand through his hair, confessing, "I didn't mean to, but I sort of aimed it at you. You were so beautiful and ethereal. All of my thoughts kind of drifted in your direction when I drank the stuff. And ever since then you've had all of these fainting spells and I can't think straight when you're around. I've been trying to keep my distance, but I can't. I just can't."

Angie's mind raced with his confession. She tried to answer, but had to close her eyes and get the question right. Finally, she asked, "*You* used a love potion on *me*?"

He winced, looking miserable. "I didn't mean to. I didn't know it was going to work...or be so strong."

Angie paused. Blinked. Then burst out laughing.

Xave lifted his eyebrows in surprise, a hint of a relieved smile on his lips. "Yeah, it's kind of silly I guess."

She shook her head and tried to say that's not why she was laughing, but the irony was too much. She laughed so hard she had to bend over, which made it impossible to speak.

Xave shoved his hands into his pockets and looked down at his feet. "You don't believe me. I get it. I don't believe me either." He raised his eyes to hers. "I thought out of anyone I know, you might believe me."

"No, it's not that," she managed to say. "I believe you!" The words came out in a squeak as another bout of hilarity hit.

He leaned back and studied her. "You don't look like you do."

"I'm sorry, I'm sorry," Angie got control of herself. She

wiped tears of laughter from her eyes with one hand while managing a wiggly Fidget in the other.

"Yeah, well, I probably shouldn't have told you. It all sounds pretty stupid when you say it out loud." He said miserably.

"That's not why I'm laughing," she corrected. Angie pressed the palm of her hand against her chest. "I believe you because I did the same thing. I went to the apothecary and they gave me a love potion, too."

"They did?"

She nodded emphatically.

"You took a love potion?"

"Yes, they called it a tincture, but I call it a potion. And I, um, well, I sort of accidentally thought about you when I took it." Angie was too embarrassed to look at him as she explained. "I had all these reactions and I saw you reacting to me. I saw everyone reacting to me, giving me jobs, being so friendly, and I thought the potion must be too powerful. It must be manipulating everyone around me. I couldn't get it to stop. I went back to the apothecary and they gave me an antidote, but it didn't work. I still...I still..."

"You still what?" He took a step toward her, closing the distance between them.

Angie's breath quickened. She forced herself to remain outwardly calm when she looked up into his eyes. "I still have feelings for you. Feelings I can't control."

Xave looked into her eyes. She couldn't look away. In fact, she could barely breathe. He reached up and traced the side of her cheek with the back of his fingers.

"Me too," he said softly.

Angie could not back away from him. His touch lingered on her cheek as he moved his hand into her hair and wrapped a curl around his pinky.

Her words faltered, "Really? Wh-what kind of feelings are you having?"

He dawdled with her hair, pushing it back over her shoulder one tendril at a time, his eyes glittering. When he spoke, the words were sensual and moved over Angie's bare neck and shoulder as if they were physically touching her, leaving trace tingling behind.

"Sometimes..." he began. "Sometimes when I look at you I can't breathe. The air leaves my lungs and the rest of the world shuts down. I can't remember what I was doing. I don't know my own name anymore. All there is is you."

"That sounds familiar," she answered softly.

Xave let his eyes drop to her mouth then her neck. The hand that wasn't in her hair reached around her waist. "Angie?"

"Yes?"

"Maybe we should go with it."

"Go with the love potions?"

"Yes, I mean, why fight it?" He bent down and spoke into her ear. "If we both took one they kind of cancel each other out, don't they?"

She couldn't bear it anymore. His fingers in her hair. His hand on her waist. His breath on her neck. She had fought her feelings for so long. The battle, it seemed, was lost.

"Maybe you're right..." she whispered.

Xave touched his lips to her neck. She gasped. His hand gripped her sundress at the small of her back.

Careful not to squish Fidget, she ran her free hand up the arm of his pirate shirt and into his thick dark hair. With an urgency that matched her own, his mouth met hers and they kissed.

A passion she had never known before pounded through Angie's heart, setting her blood on fire. Xave pushed his hand further into her hair, holding her firmly, sweetly, as their kiss lingered. They drank each other in, finally and completely connecting after so much time pushing away.

He pulled back, his eyes twinkling with love. A powerful surge of emotion moved between them and Angie knew without a doubt it could not have been made in a bottle. Nothing made by a human hands could create a bond as strong as she felt, as strong as she saw in Xave's eyes.

Angie ran her finger along the open collar of his shirt and sighed happily. "You know, a friend of mine told me that sometimes love can feel like magic."

Xave smiled down at her, showering her with adoration from the depths of his soul. "You'll always be magical to me. You are a mermaid after all."

Months went by and Angie and Xave fell even deeper in love. They only had eyes for each other and were so completely wrapped up in their relationship that whenever they were together nothing else seemed to matter. At first.

The paparazzi jumping out of bushes to take their picture didn't usually bother them. When they went to an event the flashing of cameras were like so many stars in the night watching over their love story. That's how Angie decided to look at it anyway. Even the tabloid stories questioning Angie's past as a metaphysical bookstore employee and her penchant for wearing crystals suggesting that she had performed some kind of witchcraft on one of the most eligible actors in Los Angeles made them laugh, most of the time.

"If they only knew," Xave chuckled as he read the most recent tabloid article, which the head of his PR team had texted him.

Angie was busy stirring a batch of oatmeal cookie batter with extra raisins and dried cranberries. "What did it say?"

Xave left his phone on the coffee table and joined her in the kitchen. "Nothing as interesting as the real story."

She laughed, moving a tendril of curly red hair that had escaped her pony tail with the back of her hand. "No? And what would you say was the real story?"

Xave stood behind her and wrapped his arms around her waist, leaning down and letting his lips brush her bare neck. "That we both fell under the spell of a love potion for which there is no cure."

"Ooh, that does sound intriguing," Angie giggled. She smacked Xave's hand lightly as he reached into the bowl to take some of the cookie dough. "If you eat all of the dough we won't have any for the road trip."

They were taking Eckhart on another drive to the Redwoods. This time they would be staying for four days. Angie had been looking forward to the trip for weeks.

Xave sighed dramatically. "I wish we could stay longer this time."

"You don't think four days is long enough in Eckhart? It's a little cramped for you, isn't it?" Angie thought about the extension to the fold out bed that Thomas had helped Xave rig up the last time he'd visited California, and how Xave's feet stuck out at the bottom when they slept.

"You know what? I would rather spend eternity crowded into Eckhart with you than one day in this house without you." Xave swept his arm in a wide semi-circle, encompassing the entire great room of his beach mansion.

Angie followed the sweep of his arm. It was a beautiful home, that was for sure. The decor was magnificent and even with some homey touches, like the fresh flowers Xave had brought in every few days just because she loved them. The most recent was a huge vase of white daisies, one of her favorites.

Still, there was something about the freedom of the open

road that was van life. No ties, no commitments, nobody watching them or snapping pictures of them wherever they went.

"Agreed. Not that this isn't nice, but Eckhart is special, isn't he?"

Xave turned her to face him. "He is, but he's not as special as you, my heart."

His words warmed her. As always. She knew their relationship was only months old, but every time Xave spoke sweetly to her it was like honey running through her veins. With one hand holding the mixing spoon, she placed her other hand on his cheek and gave him a kiss.

Fidget hopped onto the bar stool next to the island to see if she could inspect what was in the bowl. She mewed in the shaky way she did when she had been sleeping.

"Fidget's jealous again," Xave said with a chuckle. Ever since the night Xave had found her in the recycle bin, Fidget had been extra needy. Especially when Angie showed too much affection for Xave.

"She's working through her feelings." Angie reached over and stroked Fidget's orange and black ears. "And I think she's been getting better since Hawthorn came along."

As if he had been waiting to be called, Xave's new rescue cat, Hawthorn, jumped onto the stool next to Fidget's. Named for the Hawthorn plant, an herbal remedy frequently used for matters affecting the heart, Hawthorn was a large white cat with an extremely laid back attitude. He yawned and watched them all with calm green eyes. They had chosen him in the hopes that he and Fidget could be friends. Their plan had worked, for the most part.

Xave sighed. Again.

Angie looked up at him more carefully. "What's bothering you?"

For a moment she wasn't sure she wanted to know the

answer. She could see in his eyes that he wanted to say some-thing and the vibration in the room felt like a relationship changing vibration. Angie was well aware that relationship change didn't necessarily mean a good change.

Xave closed his eyes and took a deep breath, but he didn't let go of her waist. When he did open his eyes they were shin-ing. "I've been thinking."

"Okay...what have you been thinking about?"

"I've been thinking that all the things I love are these kinds of things." He looked at the bowl full of cookie dough.

Angie followed his gaze. "Cookies?"

He laughed, squeezing her gently into him. "Not just cookies. Making cookies." He thought for a second. "Not just making cookies. Making cookies with you."

"I like making cookies with you, too." Was he going to ask her to move in with him? She wouldn't say no. She practically lived there as it was, but they had never made anything official.

He shook his head. She wasn't getting it. "Not just that, Angie. It's you and me, cooking together, the cats, being home, going on silly road trips, that's all I want. I don't want all the other stuff." He glanced at his phone, which had buzzed several times since he left it on the coffee table, and scowled. "I'm not saying this right."

"Try again then. What are you trying to say?"

He looked back to her, his dark eyes sparkling. "I'm saying I want to go with you, and Fidget and Hawthorn of course. Go somewhere where nobody's looking for us. Somewhere people will forget about my movies. Maybe back to the Redwoods," his voice rose with excitement. "It was amazing there. I want that every day with you."

"You want to give up acting?" She was surprised, but not disappointed. "I didn't know you felt that way." She studied his face. "Are you saying you want me to move in with you?"

He chuckled, a sound that was contagious. "I want to

drive away in Eckhart and never come back. Go out and see the world with you. Experience all of it outside of the bubble I've been living in. So I guess it's the opposite. I'm asking if I can move into Eckhart with you." He raised his eyebrow in question. "If you'll have me."

A whole new world opened up inside of Angie. One without restrictions, without public relations people and reporters, without cameras and makeup. A world where she and Xave could explore the wonders of the universe together.

As she looked into Xave's eyes a peace settled over her like she had never known. After all of her searching and wandering, she suddenly understood without a doubt that she was home as long as she was with him.

She reached up and touched his face, marveling at the amazing man standing in front of her, asking to drive away with her into the sunset. "Of course I'll have you. And you'll have me. From this moment to the next, and to the next, and on and on forever!"

His smile lit up his face. He twirled her around and danced her across the floor, dipping her dramatically next to the bouquet of daisies. Angie laughed and Xave reached over, pulling one of the daisies out of the vase. Then he brought her gracefully back into a standing position, keeping the daisy hidden behind his back.

"After all, just living is not enough...one must have sunshine, freedom, and a little flower," he said, presenting the flower to her.

Angie took the flower and the love he was offering and they never looked back.

The End

Also by Darci Balogh

Dream Come True Sweet Romance

1. Her Scottish Keep

2. Her British Bard

3. Her Sheltered Cove

The Mighty Aphrodite Writing Society

1. Beach Retreat at Turtle Cove

2. Beach Wedding at Turtle Cove

Lady Billionaire Series

1. Ms. Money Bags

2. Ms. Perfect

Sweet Holiday Romance Series (Box Set - great value!)

Want a quick escape over the holidays? These feel-good romances will get you in the spirit for Halloween, Thanksgiving, Christmas and a brand New Year!

1. Enchanting Eve

2. Love is at the Table

3. Mistletoe Madness

4. New Year in Paradise

Sugar Plum Romance Series

Christmas, cooking, and chefs falling in love!

1. Charlotte's Christmas Charade

2. Bella's Christmas Blunder

<u>Love & Marriage Series</u>

Steamy, emotional, relatable characters, these older woman, younger man love stories are both racy and romantic.

1. The Quiet of Spring

2. For Love & For Money

3. Stars in the Sand

About the Author

Darci Balogh is a writer and indie filmmaker originally from Colorado. For most of her life she lived in Denver where she raised her two glorious, intelligent daughters to functioning adulthood. This is, by far, one of her highest achievements.

Darci recently moved to the shores of Lake Huron in Michigan to get closer to nature, experience more cold weather, and be closer to her parents. Darci has a love-hate relationship with gardening, probably should dust more, adores dogs and is allergic to cats.

She has been a writer since she was a child and enjoys crafting stories into novels and screenplays. Big surprise, some of her favorite pastimes are reading and watching movies. Classic British TV is high on her 'Like' list, along with quietly depressing detective series and coffee with heavy cream.

For more books by Darci Balogh, click through to the Also by page or visit www.knowheremedia.com/books

www.ingramcontent.com/pod-product-compliance
Lightning Source LLC
Chambersburg PA
CBHW050754190726
48285CB00005B/1651